P9-DMI-380

Blanca & Roja

ALSO BY ANNA-MARIE McLEMORE

Wild Beauty

When the Moon Was Ours

The Weight of Feathers

Blanca & Roja

ANNA-MARIE McLEMORE

FEIWEL AND FRIENDS
NEW YORK

A Feiwel and Friends Book
An imprint of Macmillan Publishing Group, LLC
175 Fifth Avenue, New York, NY 10010

Blanca & Roja. Copyright © 2018 by Anna-Marie McLemore.
All rights reserved. Printed in the United States of America.

Our books may be purchased in bulk for promotional, educational, or business use.
Please contact your local bookseller or the Macmillan Corporate and
Premium Sales Department at (800) 221-7945 ext. 5442 or by e-mail at
MacmillanSpecialMarkets@macmillan.com.

Library of Congress Control Number: 2018936436

ISBN 978-1-250-16271-7 (hardcover) / ISBN 978-1-250-16270-0 (ebook)

Book design by Danielle Mazzella di Bosco

Feiwel and Friends logo designed by Filomena Tuosto

First edition, 2018

1 3 5 7 9 10 8 6 4 2

fiercereads.com

To Nancy Warner & Christine Reynolds

You probably don't remember me.

We only met for about ten minutes.
But that ten minutes changed my whole life.

You probably had no idea.
So I wanted to let you know.

Snow-White said, "We will never leave each other," Rose-Red answered, "Not as long as we live," and the mother added, "Whatever one has she must share with the other."

–The Brothers Grimm, "Snow-White & Rose-Red"

"Fly out into the world . . ." said the queen. "Fly like great birds who have no voice."

–Hans Christian Andersen, "The Wild Swans"

PART ONE

October Boys

ROJA

Everyone has their own way of telling our story.

Some say it began generations ago, with a girl lured by the white birds in the woods. The moment she reached out a small hand toward their wind-fluffed feathers, a swan bit her, poisoning her blood.

Others say it started with a flock of swans gliding over our great-great-great-grandmother's house. They flew overhead at just the right moment to hear her cursing her own family's blood. So the swans cursed her, and all the daughters after her.

Some insist it was two sisters, squabbling for years over who was more beautiful. A bevy of swans in a nearby pond grew so weary of all the noise, and struck them with a spell that would take one of each of their daughters.

The worst one tells it this way: Once, a del Cisne woman—probably one of our great-great-great-grandmothers—stole a groom from his bride on their wedding day. The bride's family hated our bisabuela and her name so deeply they cursed her brown skin and her dark hair to become white feathers, and for the same fate to befall a del Cisne daughter every generation after.

These are the stories they tell, tales of winter storms or spiteful witches. Because when there is a family in which one of every two daughters grows an ink-black bill and a pale-feathered neck and snow-bright wings, people like to think they know why.

Few think to ask us.

This is the story we believe to be true:

A mother once raised her daughter among swans, hoping they would teach her their grace and beauty. And this daughter, with the swans for her sisters, grew lovely in both appearance and manner. When she married, she bore only sons, three and then five and then ten sons. And though she loved her sons, she wanted a daughter, so that she, too, could raise a girl with the grace of swans.

So she went to the swans she had once called her sisters.

"Please," she told them. "All I want is one daughter."

"We will give you better than one. You will have two," they said, with a magnanimous bow of their necks. "There will always be two daughters. But we will always take one back."

"Which will you take?" the woman asked.

They lowered their wings. "That will be for us to decide."

There may be as many versions of the story as there are daughters our family has lost to it. But this is the one my sister and I know. A woman wanting something so badly she did not understand the weight of the swans' pronouncement.

There will always be two daughters. But we will always take one back. The swans would take not just one of the woman's daughters, but one of her daughter's daughters, and one of her daughters, and one of hers. There would always be one daughter taken, and one left watching the sky in winter, wondering if a far-off flick of white was a coming snow or her lost sister.

Even when there were sons, there were always daughters alongside them, two sisters, whether they had brothers or not. Always two, always enough that the swans could take one and leave behind the other. My bisabuela had already raised three sons, sure she was too old for more children, when her daughters arrived. My great-great-aunt, intent on having one child, delivered, to her surprise, twin daughters. My second cousin thought she had defied the swans by having a single son and a single daughter, until the child thought to be a boy declared herself as the girl she had always been.

The way our aunt and our great-aunts tell it, our family never knows which daughter the swans will take.

But I've always known it would be me.

If I wanted to, I could believe everything was decided when we were born.

But I've always known it was earlier than that. And not just because the colors of girls are decided before they're born, though that's something I know to be true.

What I believe instead is that, in the moments of my sister and me becoming our own little lives, it was already written into us.

In the wisp of blood and not-yet-breath that was Blanca before she was born, there were already the beginnings of how her hair would grow as gold as October leaves.

Her eyes would be brown, the same as the rest of us, and that was something our mother would consider a great misfortune. But they were a brown as light as acacia honey, like amber. A brown that could be forgiven.

A few months after Blanca was born, I was a new wisp of blood and not-yet-breath. My own colors were already waiting. By then, Blanca had grown a crown of hair as fine and blond as a duckling's down. Her tiny hands patted the growing round of my mother's belly, where I was, slowly, becoming.

While my sister had a face as fair as the almonds my mother blanched each fall, mine would turn out as brown as the almond's skin, dark and delicate, that my mother swept off the counters. I would have eyes and hair as dark as the coffee grounds my father spread over his roses in winter.

My hair grew not only dark as those coffee grounds, but red. Not the copper or strawberry of green-eyed girls, but deep red, a red so dark it looked wet. It was a red that wouldn't take dye, not even the black walnut the señoras gave my mother. "Blood-soaked hair," they called it, my mother shuddering at the words, my father saying them back with as much pride as if they were a new knife, fine and just sharpened.

My father counted it as such a point of pride that he named me for it, setting his hand on my small forehead and declaring me *Roja* while my mother slept off a birth fever. The kind of birth fever, the señoras reminded me on my birthday every year, that Blanca hadn't given her.

If I wanted to, I could believe it was our colors that decided Blanca would be the gentle sister, pure and obliging, and I would be the cruel one, wicked and difficult. She would be the blessed daughter, the one the swans would spare. And I would be the one the swans would take.

But my sister saw our story ending another way.

BLANCA

I was five, maybe six when I first saw the swans. I remember because Roja was still having her tantrums, so she couldn't have been older than four. Our parents were trying to train them out of her, our mother by clutching her arm when she wailed for more than a few minutes, our father by crouching to meet her eyes and talking in a voice that was low, and neither harsh nor gentle.

"You can scream and cry if you want," he said. "But what you have in you is power."

His words were so level and sure, they made Roja quiet. Her tears froze on her cheeks.

"You let it wring you and throw you around like you're a doll," Papá said. "And if that's all you let it do, you'll be a fool forever. Because that power, that anger in you, that is the best thing you have." He gave her a nod as proud as if she were a son. "So claim it. Pick yourself up and use it."

My mother pulled me into the kitchen. Not like I was seeing something I shouldn't. More like she wanted to guard me from my sister. As though Roja might throw off shards of glass that would catch me if I got too close.

The kitchen still smelled like pomegranates from when my mother and I had split open the rinds that afternoon, spilling the jewels inside. Mamá had seemed happy, the two of us sitting at the table, her legs crossed at the ankles, my bare feet swinging off the chair. She was patient when my pudgy fingers squished the pith into the fruit. She laughed, rubbing sprays of red juice off my forehead and showing me how cutting the fruit into quarters and then plunging them into water made them give up their seeds.

Now Mamá stopped a few steps from the back door.

"Do you want to see them?" she asked.

I didn't know what she meant. I nodded anyway, nervous but thrilled by the promise of a grown-up secret.

From the living room came the flat sound of my sister driving her fists into the carpet. She wasn't crying anymore. Her face was against the floor. She had worn herself out.

The sound of her fist on the braided rug was as familiar as my own voice. I could almost smell the salt of her tears. The warmth of the wool under her flailing body. The thick vanilla of the hierbas in my father's pipe, which he lit as though to say he had nothing but bored patience, that he'd wait all night for her to pick herself up off the floor.

All these things smothered the pomegranate smell like a blanket over a flame.

My mother took me outside with her. The night air was a little sweet from the Ashbys' flowering trees, waking up from winter and turning blush-pink.

My mother must have smelled the swans' feathers on the air, because we had just set our feet onto the chilled ground when their shapes crossed the moon. The flashes of their silhouettes flickered over the gleaming round, and then they were gone.

They did not fly lower. They did not sweep down into the trees and toward our corner of the woods.

That, according to our great-aunts, would not be until Roja turned fifteen.

Then the swans would come for us. Los cisnes, birds as beautiful as they were terrifying. Their arrival always marked the season when they would decide which daughter would remain a girl, and which they would take.

From where my mother and I stood, those swans looked as distant as if they lived on the moon. That was what Roja and I would be to each other one day, after los cisnes finished with us. One of us would stay rooted to the ground, the other bound to the sky.

The thought of it felt like my veins being ripped from my heart. Roja was not just my blood. She was the sister who chased garden lizards like they were kittens, but hid in her bed every time a cricket got into our room. She saw my fear during thunderstorms and told me lightning was nothing but ribbons, no different from the ones we set in our hair, just made of stars.

I could not let that kind of distance spread between me and the girl I'd mapped the woods with, both of us learning them as well as each other's faces.

The next morning was still pale silver when I got Roja up out of bed. I buttoned her into the berry-red coat our father had bought her for Christmas, and I put on the cream wool one my mother had picked out for me. I brought her outside, and from the garden we took everything I thought might save us. White roses and red ones. Sour berries and sweet. Herbs with every kind of leaf.

We started with the herbs. I gave Roja the ones with rounded leaves, to smooth her out. I ate the ones with prickly edges that looked like ripped paper, so I'd grow sharper edges, too. Then the berries; I gave my sister the ripest ones while I let the sourest pucker my tongue, to make her the sweeter one.

And last, the roses. We slipped the petals onto our tongues like the communion wafers at church. I swallowed the red ones, and Roja the white, each of us eating the opposite of our names.

"Why are we doing this?" my sister asked. Not impatient. Not whining. Just because Papá had taught her to ask questions.

"If the swans can't tell us apart," I said, "they can't decide which of us to take."

PAGE

I'd heard how everyone talked about the del Cisne girls. At best, they whispered about them with a storyteller's thrall, like they might have about a lake filled with vicious mermaids.

The feathers are in them already; they're born with them under their skin. That's why their mother took them out of school last year, so everyone wouldn't see their wings coming in.

I heard when the moon's full their father doesn't sleep. That's how he gets all his work done.

Don't ever go into their house. Angel's trumpet and bittersweet berries grow through their floorboards.

At worst, they blamed the del Cisnes. If lavender bushes didn't take, or jam didn't thicken, mothers threw their hands up, shrugging that it must be swan season. If blond, water-eyed girls' barrel ringlets fell out before dances or ballet recitals, they hissed the name *del Cisne.*

I saw one of the del Cisne girls out in the woods once, after they weren't going to our school anymore.

She had hair almost like mine, but the yellow of hers was so vivid and rich that I couldn't think of it as anything but gold. It had weight and warmth, like the last threads of sunlight before the sky deepened.

But it wasn't her hair that stopped me.

It was her eyes, a brown so shining and deep I found their glint from across the forest pond. They caught the light even in the trees' shadows. Like blueberry honey, or the topaz on my mother's favorite bracelet. A hundred facets, brown and glimmering.

I watched her through the aspen leaves, their flickering yellow hiding and unveiling her.

She was looking out over the pond. I couldn't tell why. I kept waiting for her to skip stones or throw pennies in for wishes.

It got cooler and darker, and she buttoned the extra buttons on her sweater. When she crossed her arms over her chest like she was still cold, I knew she was about to go inside. Her family didn't live far. I didn't know that from following her. Everyone knew that, how the del Cisne girls lived in a house deep in the trees.

I waited for her to turn away from the pond, her hair fanning out in a sweep of gold.

But then her gaze lifted off the water. Her eyes moved across the screen of trees.

They stopped where I stood.

That brown caught me. Against the aspen-yellow of her hair, the color was as startling as it was beautiful. This girl was her own woods, gold and brown.

She didn't flinch. She didn't glare at me.

Her gaze didn't break even as leaves fluttered between us. Heat spread over the back of my neck, and I wondered if she'd known I was here the whole time.

YEARLING

The first time I ever talked to Page Ashby was when he found me in back of the school and hit me in the jaw.

He did it fast, no warning, and he did it while saying words my brain was too rattled to register. Something about how my grandmother had besmirched the honor of his grandmother. I didn't catch everything he said but I caught that much. He really did say it like that, too. *Besmirched her honor.* I half expected Page to pull out a glove, slap me in the face with it, and challenge me to a duel.

What, exactly, could Grandma Tess have done to *besmirch* anyone? Let alone Lynn Ashby. The only thing I could think of was something about the fruit the Ashbys grew. The best apples for a hundred miles came from their trees, and everyone knew it. Any insult to them was grave as cursing their mothers.

But Grandma Tess liked them as much as anyone else, and if she ever didn't, she wouldn't have mentioned it. *Not worth it all around*, she would've said.

Page Ashby stood in front of me, waiting. He was small, even adjusting for how I had two years on him, fourteen to his twelve. Under his overalls, he wore a plain shirt—white, cotton, the kind my mother said should never be seen in public because they were underwear. It darkened at the sleeve hems, the tint of dust and dirt off his family's orchard. His hair was light as the unfinished wood of the apple crates. It looked like he'd cut it himself, a try at a nondescript boy's cut that didn't look half bad in the front but went uneven in the back.

He stood with his hands in the pockets of his overalls. Unafraid, like he either knew I wouldn't fight back or was ready for it.

"You call that a hit?" I asked.

Sure, it had hurt at first, but the pain landed shallow, and faded fast. It was all snap and first impact. There was no force behind it, no solid path.

I wondered if the insult would make him hit me again, but he just blinked at me.

"Come on." I stood next to him. "Let's teach you to do this right."

"You're going to show me how to hit you better?" he asked.

"I hope not," I said. "But I can't let you go around doing that again."

He looked too surprised to argue.

"Show me how you make a fist."

He did.

"Do you want to break your thumb?" I asked.

"No."

"Then don't put it inside your fist."

He slipped it out and set it alongside his curled fingers.

"Didn't your father teach you this?" I asked.

"He's not really the fighting kind."

"Lucky you." My laugh was supposed to sound thoughtless, like shrugging something off, but it came out bitter. "Okay, now imagine going past whatever you're trying to hit. If it's me, you're not aiming for me, you're aiming for the brick behind me."

That was a trick Liam had taught me. Good of him, too, since he was usually the one I was trying to punch through.

Page charged his fist into the air in front of him, slow, but I could see him imagining it.

"Throw from your shoulder, not your arm," I said. "If you think too much about your hand, you end up bending your wrist."

He squared up his stance, unrounding his shoulders.

I stood in front of him. "Feel like trying again?"

"You want me to hit you in the face again?" he asked.

"How about you go for my arm?"

"What if I hurt you?"

That was a nice change from two minutes earlier. If Liam and I could have shut down our fights this fast, we would've both had time to learn the violin.

I touched my sleeve halfway between my shoulder and elbow. "You won't."

He did it. It hurt, the pain spreading out through the muscle in my arm.

"Better," I said.

He heard it in my voice, that pain I held at the back of my throat and the pride of knowing I'd taught him to do that.

"The next guy you sucker punch doesn't stand a chance," I said.

His face brightened into a smile.

"I'm Barclay," I said.

Page set his mouth like this was some kind of test. "I know."

ROJA

I surfaced to the sound outside, gasping awake. "They're here."

In the space of those two words, Blanca was up and out of her bed. It made me wonder if she'd fallen asleep at all.

"They're not," she said.

I sat up, my hands propped behind me. "I heard them." I tried to tune in to the sound that had reached through my dreams, a clicking and stirring like wings. But now I couldn't find it. "Didn't you hear it?"

Blanca turned on the lamp and sat on the edge of my bed. "It's just the trees."

She picked up the cream ribbon that had fallen onto my pillow. We slept with each other's colors in our hair, a white ribbon tying off the end of my braid, a red one nestled into her blond hair like a headband. It was one more way we tried to make ourselves so much the same that los cisnes could never choose one of us. It was the same reason Blanca sprinkled gardenia perfume under my pillow and the lightest dusting of chili powder under hers.

That feathery sound kicked up again. I sat up straighter, listening.

"It's the wind." Blanca tied a bow in the ribbon like when we were little. "It's nothing."

At the sureness in her voice, my breath evened, my heart steadying.

The brush of her fingers in my hair was as warm and familiar as the smell of pan dulce or the feel of my father's books.

When the swans wedged their way into my nightmares, it was not the thought of losing my own body that pinched the breath out of me. It was not even how much I imagined it would hurt, my skin growing feathers, my neck thinning and stretching.

It was the loss of Blanca, of being her sister. I could count the ways I loved her like charms in a jewelry box, how they weighed against the reasons I might have hated her.

The way anything more than a thimbleful of Tía Verónica's xtabentún left her dream-eyed and stumbling made it impossible for me to begrudge how our mother looked at her and not at me.

How she'd taught me to loop twinned cherries over my ears in summer, our earrings before our parents let us get piercings, left me unable to envy the candle-gold of her skin.

Her certainty that, together, we would survive the swans made me forgive her for having had the luck to be born with yellow hair.

She slipped back to bed, clicking off the light.

"Blanca?" I asked through the dark.

"Yeah?"

"What if the swans still come?"

"They won't," she said.

"How do you know?"

"You've been fifteen for months," she said. That had always been the moment del Cisne girls dreaded, the day the youngest sister turned fifteen. The swans never waited long after that. "If they haven't come yet, they won't."

"But what if they do?" I set my fingertips against the cold glass, reaching toward the charge in the air, that bristling cold like before the first snow. "Something's happening out there."

"Not everything is about us, Roja." Only Blanca could say such words without any tint of meanness.

The soft certainty in her voice was so familiar to me that I knew its meaning on the first syllable, how she meant it as comfort, not reprimand.

Stop swatting at the air. The bee's not going to sting you unless you bother it, Roja.

Don't you think a ghost would have something better to do than move around the bowls in our cupboard?

The coyotes are more afraid of you than you are of them, Roja.

Blanca settled back onto her pillow, the red ribbon bright in her hair.

Just before she closed her eyes, she said, "Not everything that happens out there has to do with you and me."

PAGE

The day Barclay went into the woods, I saw him. He didn't know it, but I did.

Barclay stood at the edge of the orchard, holding one hand in the other, then switching.

Blood striped the left side of his face and covered his knuckles.

He took a step forward, then took it back. He shifted his weight between his feet.

Then his shoulders dropped, a giving-up look.

He turned, bloody and shaking, and went into the woods.

It'd been three years since that first punch, since the strange result of Barclay and me becoming friends, and I knew more than he liked to think I did. I knew he wore the bruises and split lips he got fighting Liam like things he'd won, but that they were leaving marks on him he couldn't see.

I knew his father and his uncle encouraged it. The way every fight turned out meant whoever won got a little more of his father's pride, and whoever didn't lost it.

I knew Barclay's and Liam's mothers never asked about the

bruises, the blood, the occasional ring finger taped to the third. That would've been something far too unpleasant for Liam's mother to consider. And Barclay's mother, famous around town for her twenty-two-inch waist and her eyes blue as alpine flowers, had better things to do.

And I knew about the time Tess Holt came over to yell at Barclay's father and uncle. *Don't you see what's happening here? They're your sons. They're good kids, and look what you're turning them into.* And Barclay's father saying that if she ever came into his house telling him how to raise his child again, it would be the last time she saw her grandsons.

Tess loved Barclay in a way that was both hard enough for Barclay to push back against and soft enough for the way he was breaking inside. But the Holts didn't let Tess see Barclay except to take him to church.

Barclay didn't know why.

I did.

I just never told him.

There was a lot I hadn't told Barclay that day I saw the woods take him. They folded him into their shadows and boughs like he had always been part of them. He walked into them willingly, like they were reaching out their branches for him. He slid into their whirl of leaves and their earth smell, and they made him theirs.

The thing that bothered me most, the thing I never figured out how to tell Barclay, is how grateful I was for the questions he didn't ask.

My mother and father loved me. I knew that. I felt it in the patient, slow way they showed me how to check the trees for blight or peel apples all in one spiral. I warmed with it when, in response to my cousin asking *But what is she?* my father told him to take a long walk, in far less polite words. I heard it in their whispers when they thought I was asleep, their careful conferring on whether I had mentioned interest in a girl or asked to borrow one of my father's ties, as though, given enough information, they could solve me.

But the ways in which they tried to understand me always reduced down too far, to them asking if I just liked wearing jeans and boys' shirts, or if I was a boy who wanted to be called *he*.

I tried saying *yes* and *no*, that it was both and neither one, and also more than these things. That I was a boy, but that it was not as simple as me wanting to be called *he*. That I liked being called *he* and *him*. But that I would've liked being called *she* and *her* sometimes, too, if it didn't let everyone settle into the assumption that I was a girl. I had never been a girl, would never be a girl whether I lived here or a hundred towns away, whether I spent my whole life in a town this small or a city so full I'd never see the same faces twice. But here, to me, *girl* would have meant not only accepting a word that did not match me, but all the requirements folded into that word. Skirts that were neither too short nor too long. Makeup in flushed pastels. Swearing enough to be thought interesting but not enough to be considered vulgar.

I didn't know how girls here mapped all those rules, especially the girls who could not fit them or did not want to. Girls who only ever wore pants, or who wore heavier eyeliner than the dress code allowed, or who wore no makeup at all.

Girls like the del Cisne sisters, who seemed to prefer each other's company to anyone else's, thereby offending the rest of the town. Who gathered the armfuls of purple sage that drooped onto the sidewalks before anyone could cut it back. Who lived in jeans and their mother's old sweaters, or dresses that everyone else dismissed as befitting Sunday school teachers more than teen girls.

As much as the adored girls called our town old-fashioned, no one made a move to change it. There was no room for me to ask to be called both *him* and *her.* There were already too many people who thought I was just a failure as a girl. They wouldn't listen long enough for me to say that I had never been one. I was a boy who had to bear the same assumption so many girls endured, that I was simply the wrong kind of girl.

All this, and my tries at explaining all this, made my parents nervous, and scared, like they didn't know how to love me anymore. They wanted a guide to understanding me, something that could be memorized and applied as crisply as which trees fruited in which month. They wanted me to call myself a boy or call myself a girl and have that tell them everything, and if I could have done either one of those things, they could've stopped being scared.

But I couldn't answer their *are-you-this-or-this* questions.

Barclay never asked those questions in the first place.

So I followed him into those woods, those rustling, whispering trees that all seemed to breathe together. Their yellow leaves fluttered like eyelashes. I felt the sap flowing through their trunks like blood through one body.

In the next moment of the wind turning, my own body became part of that. I couldn't tell my skin from bark or moss. When I tried to tune in to the rhythm of my pulse, I felt it not in my own blood but in sap or water. The sense of my own limbs sank beneath the feeling of being branches or a buck's antlers, and it was only in that last second that I understood.

The trees I'd loved my whole life, the woods I'd grown up at the edge of, they had a price for everything.

YEARLING

Probably, I went into the woods because I didn't know where else to go. Grandma Tess's was out; I didn't want her seeing me like this. So was Page's, same reason. And there was no going back to my family. So I let my steps pull me into the trees' shadows.

The pain in my temple and my jaw and my ribs dulled and faded, and with it the feeling that my body was mine. I drifted more than I walked. I felt less like myself and more like rain left in the ground. I was the last of a tree's warmth, held in its heartwood and the centers of acorns. I was a blackbird left by its flock for the winter, hungry and wondering which way they'd flown.

Maybe the woods took me because they felt sorry for me. But I don't think that was it. There wasn't anything like pity in the October air, chilled and smelling like wood and ash.

Maybe it was because of my name. If I believed the writing at the front of Grandma Tess's Bible, it meant *birch tree*, or *birch forest*. It was a name whose meaning held how our family had come from hills wooded with those straight-trunked, pale-barked trees.

When we were younger, Liam liked reminding me of that while

he jabbed me with the branches, needling me into starting a fight with him. He laughed while he did it, some kind of *stop-hitting-yourself* joke.

Whether the woods knew my name or not, they took me. So I became blackbirds, birch trees, water. I existed as whatever part of the woods would have me, rocks or crows or fallen leaves. I spent time in whatever creek or poison red-and-white mushrooms let me in.

I was all of these things and none of these things. I never became them. They were still themselves. They just let me live in them for as long as they could take the deadweight of my heart.

But eventually, I ended up in the body of a yearling bear. And even though I don't know why the woods took me, this part I'm pretty sure I do know: I ended up as that yearling bear because of a story Grandma Tess used to tell Liam and me when we were little. A story about two sisters, and a prince who got turned into a bear, and all the ways magic can save you but also fuck you up.

Grandma Tess told us a lot of stories. But for some reason that one stayed with me the longest. And I think the woods knew I had that story in me, enough that they made me into it.

BLANCA

The cygnet wandered into our back garden on a Thursday, under skies as pale gray as his fluff. With his beak, dark gray as washed stones, he pecked at the blackberries that hadn't yet fallen away from their vines. He floated on the stone birdbath, flicking his stubby wings. He shivered, and each soft wisp of down shivered with him.

Roja and I knew we shouldn't have taken him. We were old enough by then to know better. But he was all on his own. Roja couldn't find his mother or brothers and sisters around the garden or at the pond or the cranberry bog. And I had heard the story of the ugly duckling too many times not to think of cats and hens chasing him.

I held out my hands, wondering if he would come. He flapped off the water and his wet feet dampened my palms. He shook droplets from his gray down, and I took him inside and fed him oats, halved grapes, the soft hearts of walnuts. The fluff of his down and the shape of his wings were so pure gray he looked drawn in pencil.

Roja and I filled the bathtub, drawing the linen curtains to keep the heat in. The cygnet hopped off the edge of the tub, making little splashes as he flicked his wings.

My sister watched him, the settling water bobbing him up and down.

"Go on," I told her.

Roja reached out her hand to his gray down.

The cygnet shuddered away, flitting to the other end of the bathtub.

We were not small. I was sixteen, and Roja had just turned fifteen. But the way Roja's shoulders fell made her look as small as when I brought her outside in her red wool coat.

With our sweet and bitter berries and our red and white rose petals, we had held off los cisnes, even past Roja's birthday. The swans had not come.

But maybe they had sent this cygnet in their place, a way less showy than the flutter of white wings.

A way they thought we might never notice.

With a tiny one of them, they were trying to seed jealousy between us.

But Roja shook off that small look. She lifted herself, straightening.

"He likes you," my sister said. Nothing jealous or bitter in her voice. She said it as though it were her hands the cygnet swam toward.

That was when I knew we could win. We had already gotten past Roja's birthday, and no swans had appeared. We were becoming enough the same girl that they could never take one of us. It would be as hard as pulling apart two trees with their roots intertwined.

ROJA

I could pretend it had all worked, the white rose petals and the overripe blackberries Blanca meant to make me sweet. I could pretend that was the reason I looked after the yearling bear that wandered near our house one night.

But mostly, I wanted something soft to like me as much as the cygnet liked Blanca.

I knew his mother could have charged out of the trees' shadows and torn me to pieces. But he was rooting around like he was hungry and lost, and I knew bears his age were always hungry, so I gave him pieces of cooked pumpkin and potato my mother wouldn't notice missing from the cazuela.

At first he didn't do anything. He stayed still, the only movement his wind-ruffled fur.

I kept watch on his ears. My father had taught me that ears pricked back meant aggression, a warning sign. But the bear's ears stayed forward, so I kept on, pushing everything a little more into his field of vision.

The bear moved just enough so a crescent of white fur on his chest flashed into view.

The pale shape seared into me. Other forests may have held countless bears with ink-dark coats and white moons on their chests. But here, in these woods, where the bears were brown, not black, I'd never seen one with a moon.

It felt like the warning of something, the badge of the nahuales Blanca and I had been taught to fear. It would have been a small, bright way for a nahual to wear the moon on his coat, a piece of sky shown to anyone who dared look at him.

I edged back, ready to get to my feet and run if I needed to. He may have been young, but he still had teeth. The muscles in his shoulders and back showed through his fur when he moved.

He bit at a piece of pumpkin, nosing it first before taking it into his mouth. Then it was like that first bite reminded him he was hungry, and he ate the rest of what I'd brought him.

So I kept feeding him every day after that. Handfuls of blueberries. Sunflower seeds and pepitas. Pan dulce my mother assumed I'd taken from the kitchen and eaten myself.

Some nights I found him so still I could've mistaken him for rocks or fallen branches. Watergrass whipped at his fur and he didn't flinch. I found him by listening for his slow breathing.

I let the leaves crunch under my feet, so he'd know I was there. If I came up too quiet, he startled, tensing when my fingers brushed the tips of his fur.

What I brought him, on its own, was never enough to make him get up. I had to prod him. I stroked the fur on his back and talked to him in a voice lower than the wind. "You have to eat, osezno."

Then he would, the white patch on his chest showing when he lifted his head.

It got colder, red leaves twirling on half-bare branches and unveiling the sky. I brought him a blanket no one would miss. Not because it was not beautiful—Bisabuela Elena's ojo blankets always were—but because her hands were so quick she'd made ten of them.

I set the blanket over his back. He didn't flinch at the wool's weight.

Blanca found me like that, my hands in his fur as I talked to him.

"His mother won't like that," she said.

"I haven't seen his mother," I said.

But I knew it wasn't just about that.

Blanca had seen the moon on his chest, too. We were sisters enough to think of the same thing at the same time.

My mother used to tell Blanca and me stories about nahuales. She said they lived among humans but at night became wolves or owls, flying on the wind like la llorona. Sometimes they made children sick and sucked the blood of their parents. Sometimes they withered crops with the touch of their wasted fingers. They drew souls halfway from their sleeping bodies and then dropped them like handfuls of water.

Nahuales filled the ghost stories Blanca and I told each other on fall nights. I swore the man who gave us the eye at the hardware store was a nahual. Blanca and I kept our lamps on all night, dreaming of those feathers and fingers and silver claws. I told her tales of nahual owls hooting laughter when children shrieked at the sight of them. She made up stories of nahual turkeys chasing women who ran from the gleam of their eyes, and their beaks that curved into grins.

Those stories made me laugh the most, because I didn't believe a bird stupid enough to drown in the rain could hurt anyone. (I stopped laughing after our father calmly told us over breakfast one morning that the drowning-in-the-rain was a myth, and that turkeys—and nahual turkeys—were far smarter than they looked.)

Nahuales, to me and Blanca, had always been wrath and cruel mischief. They were stories of poor farmhands whose bodies crawled, still asleep, through grain fields in search of their pilfered souls. They never found them until morning, when the nahuales grew bored hiding them.

"Leave him alone," Blanca said, her eye still on the curve of white against his brown fur.

"I'm not hurting him," I said. "He likes me."

Blanca smiled. She didn't want to, but she did.

BLANCA

My mother took Roja and me to see the señoras every time we were sick, but I had never gotten used to the way they looked at us. Their gaze still left the back of my neck cold. They stared like they could see our souls through our skin.

The tall, thin one especially. Her sister, the short one, told us stories and gave us sprigs of hierbas to take with us. Her stout frame, as graceful as it was wide, moved through the shop with the sureness of a cat.

But the tall one, I never knew when she might take my chin in her hand and make me look at her.

Today they had summoned us. Just us, without our mother. Roja and I sat in the small room at the front of their shop, wondering why. Our fingers worried at the frayed chairs. We watched the closed door to the room where they gave remedios for susto or winter coughs that went down into the lungs.

Roja leaned into me. "Think they know about my ankle?" she whispered.

I pressed my lips together so I wouldn't smile. Maybe the señoras had seen Roja walking home, limping on the ankle she'd twisted climbing out our window. It had healed, but I didn't put it past them to make us tell our mother.

Or maybe they knew I still had a flush of acne between my shoulder blades, and wanted to lecture me about being lazy with the hamamelis. But I couldn't reach the spot myself, and there was something about asking Roja to spread the witch hazel on me that made things feel backward. She was my little sister. When she got poison oak, I was the one who splashed the señoras' jars of ocean water onto her back. And I was the one who boiled mejorana for her every month.

I nudged Roja's shoulder with mine. "Let's hope it's not the smoke cure."

Roja shuddered in a way I could almost feel, the way she did every time she remembered our mother guiding her head down onto the kitchen counter. "I'm never admitting to having an ear infection again."

"Oh, come on, that can't be worse than the salt water."

Roja leaned back, her braid brushing the wall. "I disagree."

Maybe the señoras had found a remedio for the pain that burrowed into her each month. Maybe they would press their hands into her belly and take it from her. My hope came so sharp that I didn't dare speak it.

"Think they're taking another try at my hair?" Roja asked.

"With what this time?" I asked. The señoras had tried everything from coffee and vinegar to manzanilla and walnut shells to darken my sister's hair. Deepening the red to black, they were certain, would better her temper. "Fountain-pen ink?"

The harder I tried to make her laugh, the more I could forget my worry that I already knew why we were here.

Roja had heard something on the wind the night two boys vanished. She had lain awake, listening to the woods' whispers, while outside, two boys disappeared so completely it was as though the air had spun them into clouds.

For the last few weeks, everyone had grasped at the small things they thought might tell the story. A shirt left out on a bedroom floor. Scribbles at the edges of lined paper. A book never returned to the library. But by now those scraps had been talked over so many times that they'd worn and frayed. There was nothing left to sift through and speculate on.

"If they ask you about that night, about Page and Barclay—"

Roja cut me off. "You think *that*'s why we're here?"

"Nobody knows anything," I said. "And if they think you do—" I lost the tail of the sentence.

"But I don't," Roja said. "I don't know what I heard. I thought it was . . ." Now it was Roja who held words on her tongue she could not say.

The swans. Los cisnes.

I scratched at the chair's worn upholstery, already working myself up to telling the señoras that Roja didn't know anything about those boys, that the night they vanished had given her nothing more than swirling, shapeless dreams. She'd heard the brushing breath of the wind, too low to be the wail of la llorona but too sharp to be leaves shearing off the trees. That was all. If they thought they were going to tear her open with questions she couldn't answer, I would shove my way into that room with her.

The door to the room opened.

I squeezed the inside of Roja's elbow, a years-old habit to tell her not to be afraid.

The tall one set her eyes not on Roja, but on me.

I looked at Roja.

My sister shook her head, her way of telling me she didn't understand any better than I did.

Maybe I would leave with an order to eat more squash blossoms, or put almond oil on the stretch marks that showed where my hips had come in.

The tall señora took me into the dim room, the walls smelling of sage and soaked wood.

She stared into my eyes longer than usual.

The brown of her eyes gathered what little light the room held, glinting almost yellow. I wondered if maybe she had found, just by looking at me, the only secret I'd ever kept from my sister. That one vanished boy meant more to me than the other.

Not the one everyone talked about.

The one everyone forgot.

I pretended not to listen to the whispers those first weeks, the speculations that these boys had not been taken, had not gotten lost, but that they wanted to be gone from us. They had had a choice, and their choice had been to leave.

I didn't have a right to let that wound me. I doubted this boy even knew my name.

Now I was sure the señora could see all of this in me.

The silence left my mouth dry. I wished I had something to hold in my hands, to remind me I would not turn to ash or dust under this woman's stare. Maybe one of the ribbons Roja and I tied to our bedposts when we weren't wearing them. Or a sweater we shared that smelled like both of us at once. Or my cygnet, his rubbery feet on my palms while his fluffy down brushed my fingers. But I kept losing track of him lately. I would look away, and he would be gone. He would only show up again in our flower border when I gave up hope of finding him.

"You're growing up to be very beautiful, aren't you?" the señora asked. She sounded like she had just realized, like she had never quite looked at me.

I caught the twist in her voice, as though growing up beautiful was something I could choose if I wanted it.

If I could have chosen, I would have grown up to look like my mother, like most women in my family. I would have wanted skin the same as hers, the brown of the inside of a walnut shell. I would have wanted her hair that was black by moonlight and brown-gold in the sun.

I stared back at the tall señora, her face as tough as ground masa, her hair streaked with silver.

"You're going to be a good girl," she said, "because if you're a good girl, you can get a blue-eyed boy."

I tensed to hide my shudder. I didn't want her to see how the words *blue-eyed* struck me, the distance they stood from the grayish-brown eyes of a boy I missed.

A sound rose in the room. At first I felt it was coming off the walls, then lifting off the floor. I couldn't find the source. I couldn't pin it down.

"And if you can get a blue-eyed boy," the señora said, "then you will save yourself."

It sounded like wings.

"No," I said, backing from both her and the sound. "No. I won't do it."

The tall señora did not startle. She only watched me, with a slight lift of her chin.

Her silence pressed more words out of me.

"I won't do anything that helps me but not my sister."

The sound lifted from the crisp flapping of a butterfly's wings. It grew into the hum of dragonflies or hummingbirds, close and loud.

"If there's a way I can save myself, then she can save herself the same way," I said, my words higher, more frantic than I planned, so that a choked "Can't she?" slipped out after.

The señora kept her stare on me for a few more seconds and then turned to the door. She nodded to the short señora, who lifted a ribbon of Roja's hair and clipped it halfway down.

Roja gave me an eye roll so carefully timed that neither señora noticed. That eye roll spoke of all the rosemary and common nettle and sage they'd tried on that red.

The way Roja could slide a joke between us undetected—a feigned yawn during a boring Sunday school lesson, a perfect impression of how our aunt's tongue stuck out as she folded letters in thirds—was its own art form. More than once, I'd sat in a church pew biting back a laugh.

But now I couldn't even offer her a smile.

The tall señora took the lock of hair and shut us both inside the room again, the door closing between me and my sister.

I was still watching the door when I heard the rasping whine of scissors next to my ear.

A length of my own hair fell into the tall señora's hand. She held both locks, one ribbon of blond and another of red. She brought them over to the blue candle, the one she said had the most pure and blessed flame, and let them catch.

The locks of hair went up, tingeing the air with the bitter smell of used-up matches. I drew back, worried she'd singe her fingers. But she let the candle flame swallow each of them, flaring to blue.

I waited for ash to fall to the wooden table.

The sound rose to the sharp cut of great birds crossing the sky.

Like swans.

The sound of their wings, the whisper of feathers. The noise Roja and I thought we would never hear.

When the twin flames flickered out, they didn't leave ash.

What fell first was the wisp and vein of a swan's feather.

Then came the pale lock of my hair.

The flame had burned it up and then turned it back. It had given us this searing proof that the tall señora's words had landed on me.

I couldn't give them to the sister I promised I'd save.

ROJA

On the way home, Blanca did not look at me. She folded her arms, hands on her elbows, like ice crystals were frosting the air around her.

"Blanca?" I asked.

She held her arms tighter, and I knew she hadn't heard me.

I wondered so hard what the tall señora had told her that my brain hummed.

"Did she measure you again?" I asked. Blanca had three and a half inches on me, and the tall señora insisted that if Blanca only held herself straight and drank the right hierbas at bedtime, she could grow another two.

Without looking at me, Blanca shook her head and gave a weak smile. I could see her forcing it, the tension held in her jaw.

"Then what?" I asked. Sometimes the short señora held her responsible for me biting my nails or scratching at the little scars on my knees, as though her good influence should calm my hands. Maybe the clipped lock of my hair was meant as a prop to lecture her, ask why she hadn't made sure I combed in caléndula every night.

She didn't answer.

"Blanca," I said again, when we got closer to the house.

My sister stilled. But not at my voice. She lifted her face toward the sky, like she was watching for a storm.

Then I heard it, the distant flutter of wings.

I shuddered toward the trees, as if those wings might brush my skin and turn me right now.

This was how it happened every time, del Cisne girls hearing the warning in the air, their humming sense of how the swans would soon claim their next daughter.

Swaths of white flashed between the trees.

There, in the deepening blue that comes before every fall evening, I found them. They glided down toward the pond near our house. Their pale bodies stirred the gray-blue mirror of the water. They settled onto the surface, their wings like a snowfall landing all at once.

The light drone of their feathers trembled through my body.

Blanca thought we could keep them away. She thought the small magic of rose petals and our refusal to turn on each other would save us. Once my fifteenth birthday passed with no sign of white wings, she was sure.

But the swans had come.

For a while, they would stay close enough to consider us. They would decide. Then they would take one of us.

And it would be me. My body would turn to feathers and down. And worse than losing myself, I would lose Blanca, the sister who watched birds' nests for months to figure out if they'd been abandoned. The sister who left bits of ribbons and thread for birds to make new ones. The sister who made me the remedio that got me through the worst night of every month.

As soon as we were upstairs in our room, Blanca shut the door. She set her back against it, palms pressed flat to the wood.

"Roja," she said.

I opened my mouth to thank her, for trying as hard as she had. For being so certain I could be saved.

She cut me off.

"Roja"—now she took me by the shoulders, so I had to look at her—"this is not over."

BLANCA

I had done this. In the morning the swans were still there, the bright white of them sickening in the daylight.

In the moment of the señora telling me those words, in the beating of wings, I had doubted. I had feared los cisnes for that one minute, and that was enough for them to find their way between me and my sister.

It had been enough to seal the tall señora's words, for her to give me proof in flame and feather and pieces of our hair. I would survive los cisnes. Roja would not.

I sat on my bed, my temple against the wall. The light from the window touched my lips, and everything in me rang with the understanding that I had brought the swans here. We had gotten past Roja's birthday; with most del Cisne girls, the swans came days after the youngest sister turned fifteen. But a few words, a chilled gaze from the tall señora, that far-off sound, and I had flinched.

Roja was downstairs, in the small warped-wood-floor room my father had lined with his books and turned into a study. I couldn't make out their words, but I could hear my father's low voice, his tone of reassurance that she could survive the swans.

I wondered if he thought of how one sister surviving always meant the other losing herself.

My mother came in and patted my hair like it was a cat's fur.

"Tan linda," she said. But her usual way of calling me pretty now held a catch of worry. She had seen the swans, too. She could use words that insisted this was any other fall day, but her voice gave up the fear she'd folded inside her.

I couldn't look at her. Because I had shown the swans my fear, they would now take either me or my sister. One of us would be lost to our mother and father, and we would both be lost to each other.

"Mija?" my mother said.

I wanted to lock the secret under my tongue. To confess the words would introduce their poison into the air. It was a violet spell, laced with venom and the lie that Roja was the lesser daughter, undeserving of the señoras' blessings. I didn't want my mother to breathe that poison any more than I wanted Roja to believe those lies.

But my mother saw the truth stirring and roiling in me. And the words grew so heavy, I couldn't carry them on my own.

I told her. I admitted that I had heard the swans before they'd arrived. I confessed the words that had brought the brushing noise of feathers. *If you're a good girl, you can get a blue-eyed boy.*

My mother drew back. Her hand stayed on my hair.

Her eyes opened wider at me. Not like I had done something terrible. More like she'd put her hand to my forehead and found a high fever.

Her lips parted.

She had words to tell me. I rose to them like surfacing toward light. Maybe she could help me pick apart the señora's words like tangles of thread, until we knew why they had brought the sound of swans' wings. *If you can get a blue-eyed boy, then you will save yourself.*

But saving myself meant my sister losing, and me losing her.

The door opened, cutting off my mother's effort at words.

My second cousins, some younger than my mother and others older than my grandmother, stood in the hall. Footsteps downstairs echoed theirs.

They had all come. The del Cisne women who had survived the swans. The ones who had not been turned into swans themselves.

The ones whose sisters had.

"Es hora de irse," the older ones said.

"It's time," the younger ones repeated.

"No," my mother said, without any cut of fear in her voice.

But they took hold of her like she was no bigger than a child. Their hands—some weathered and wrinkled, some younger and smelling of the perfume on their wrists—drew her toward the stairs like they were a front of wind.

"They're my daughters." Mamá looked back at me.

"And you have to let them alone," Mercedes said.

I followed them down the stairs, pulling at Mercedes's and Luisa's sleeves like I was a little girl trying to get their attention. They ignored me the same as they would a moth.

Downstairs, more of them were shooing my father out of his study.

"You can't keep us from our own children," he protested, more offended than afraid.

"You love them too much," Sofía said. "You'll never let the swans look at them."

"You have to let the swans see them without you watching," Julieta said.

"If you don't let them," Beatriz warned, "they'll take them both."

The truth of their words drifted down over all of us, the stories of how, when mothers and fathers interfered—trying to scare off the swans, or whispering advice to one daughter or another—the swans sometimes took both daughters out of spite.

Del Cisne women refused to lose more daughters than they had to. They would drive mothers and fathers out of their own houses if that was what it took.

Roja grabbed at our cousins' and second cousins' shoulders, the ones shoving Papá toward the door.

I couldn't hear her words. All I could make out was the ripping-cloth sound of fear and grief in her voice.

She was calling after Papá.

She was calling after the father she thought she'd never see again.

Our father, a del Cisne son, who had carried the swans' wrath in his blood, cursed to lose a sister and then a daughter.

"Let us say good-bye," I shouted at our cousins.

At least her, I almost added, but stopped myself. I heard it how my sister might hear it.

I didn't want Roja thinking the swans would take her any more than she already did.

Isabel snapped her head toward the sound of my voice. "Haven't you both done enough?"

My feet stopped on the floorboards.

The first flash of her eyes was anger; Roja and I were the wicked girls who swallowed rose petals and thought we were above the swans' reign.

But behind that anger, I caught her fear. She worried over what we had done, holding off the swans until now, months after Roja's fifteenth birthday. And now I felt the swans' coming wrath, loud as a bird's cackle. The truth rattled through me, how we had tried to outsmart them, how they would break our hearts into pieces.

Our mother and father looked back, but their words got lost in the rush of leaves and stones under their feet, and the voices of the women the swans hadn't taken.

I grabbed Roja. I held her. Half because I thought she might rush outside and hit at our cousins to get Papá back. Half because I thought if I held on to her tight enough, the swans could never take her. I would hold her in her own body, her brown skin and red-black hair, and she would not lose it.

ROJA

Blanca held me back from clawing my own primas' eyes out. She held on to me like I was a cat she would lose if her grasp fell. And there, with her keeping me still, with our bodies holding the same broken heart, I understood everything I'd tried to forget.

My sister and I had been born fair and dark, her looking like a girl in a fairy tale who would grow up sweet, a princess, and me like one who would grow into a cruel witch. I had seen the pictures in storybooks. I knew what I was, with my bloodstained hair. Girls like me were marked for the swans. How could they ever take a girl like Blanca?

Blanca had tried to save me. She had tried to make us the same, so the swans could never choose. And her belief that she could was as sweet and young as the certainty she once had that fireflies were fairies. It made me feel like I was the older sister instead of her.

She had been so sure that if we loved each other, if I didn't let a cygnet sow jealousy in me, if we did not let fear of the swans wedge its way between us, their power would wither.

But she had been wrong. Soon I would become one of those

awful, pale birds, and I would never be my father's daughter again. I would never again get to show him a polished stone I found by the pond, or a leaf with a few perfect jewels of rain, or the thin ribbon of a green snake. We would never again go outside to see the early December constellations, the almost-winter smell coming on clean and sharp.

The next time he saw me, he wouldn't recognize me under my coat of feathers.

I let my body slacken, so Blanca would think I'd given up fighting.

She let me go, and I slipped toward the pond so quietly she probably thought I'd gone inside.

Maybe Blanca wouldn't let me get my fingernails into my cousins.

But I could make sure the swans saw me, that they knew what they had taken from me.

"Hey," I called out as I neared the edge of the pond.

I stood at the waterline. Those white birds stared at me with their ink-smooth eyes, and the only thought I had was that they had no right. We were our own girls. We weren't offerings for them to choose from.

"Hey," I yelled again, louder now.

They slowly turned their heads, lifting their slender necks, considering me.

I threw everything I could touch. Pinecones that broke the water and startled them back. Smooth stones that cut through the air when I hurled them; the swans flitted away from the rings in the water. Branches they had to dodge unless they wanted the wood to ruffle their down. Handfuls of wet leaves that floated on the pond or stuck to them; they fluttered their wings to shake them off. I warmed with the satisfaction of seeing dirt dull their perfect white feathers.

I got to them. They rose off the water, like swaths of snow retreating back into the clouds.

Then they swept down again.

They filled the air around me.

Their feathers sliced at my skin. Their dark gray bills nipped at my neck and wrists. Their wings struck my hair. The force of them knocked me to my hands and knees.

My body trembled too much for me to stand, so I crawled. The rocky soil tore at my knees and palms.

The swans beat their wings down on me, keeping me on the forest floor.

That was where I saw him, the yearling bear, between flashes of white. But he wasn't rooting for hazelnuts I'd left for him in the watergrass.

He was clicking his jaw, showing his teeth.

The whole time I'd been bringing him blueberries or pumpkin seeds, I had forgotten he was bigger than I was.

I edged away from the swans and away from him.

The more I watched him, the more I caught the look of a nahual, all those stories Blanca and I had gasped or giggled over but that I could not laugh at now. That moon on his chest. The aggression that didn't match his youth. That stare, the way he came toward me, how the flickering of my pulse seemed to draw him.

I didn't care if he was young or soft-coated. In my mother's stories, the most harmless-looking nahuales—doves, rabbits, deer—were the ones to fear most.

The swans would weaken me, and then leave me to him. He

would draw my soul from my body and spill it out over the forest like glitter from a cascarón.

The bear kept a straight line through the trees. I crawled, dodging the papery bark of yellow and white birches.

The swans followed. Their feathers, soft when still, became the thinnest knives as they sliced through the air. Thread-thin cuts stung my skin.

The yearling bear came after me. He crossed the underbrush and the bright yellow of fallen birch leaves. He wove through the beating of wings. Wild thorn-apple spines combed his fur, and feathers ruffled his coat.

I knew better than to run. My father had told Blanca and me that when the coyotes came down from the hills, the only thing to do was stay away from them. If you saw one, turned, and ran, they switched from stalking you to hunting you at the sight of your back.

But my body acted before I could calm it with my father's sense and logic. I scrambled away from the nahual bear, and now both he and the swans were coming for me.

His jaw let out those clicking sounds. The crescent of white on his chest flashed like a thumbnail moon. Low, gruff noises came from his throat.

The nahual's fur brushed my skin, his coat smelling of wet bark and the must of dry leaves. I clenched my molars to stop my breath from wavering. I felt his nose through my shirt as he took my back collar in his teeth.

He seemed so much bigger now, feral in a way I'd seen in cats. The first time I fed him sunflower seeds, I thought of him as no more frightening than one of Blanca's stuffed animals.

I grabbed at the ruff of fur on the back of his neck. I made my hands sure enough to show him I wasn't afraid of him. I felt it like a spark through my palms, how, for just a second, I was a girl who feared neither swans nor nahuales.

Good, my father would have said. *Make sure he knows he can't push you around.*

My hand stopped on a hot, damp patch. The nahual let out a short groan from the back of his throat. My fingers came away shining and wet.

New blood dampened his fur, and old had dried and hardened, matting his coat.

In the next flash of white wings, I didn't feel the yearling bear's fur under my hands.

I felt skin.

YEARLING

I kept all the broken things that were mine. I didn't want to leave them in the woods, not after the woods had given me somewhere to go.

When I lived in the ground, and the wind and rain weathered it, the deepest part of me got weathered, too. When I was in trees that caught fire blight, I took the blight with me when I left. I carried it in me so long that my own heart was turning and falling away like leaves.

And when I was a yearling bear, and a grown bear saw me as enough of a threat to leave warning gashes on my back, I made them mine.

They were what I felt first, those deep cuts in my back.

My back. Not a yearling bear's. Mine.

I came back because she needed me, this girl who fed me when I was hungry and when I couldn't get near other bears without them swiping their claws at me.

I had gone into the woods already broken, and now I had collected so many other ways of being broken, I could barely carry them.

But this girl hadn't let me starve, so I couldn't just leave her. The swans were going after her like they wanted to tear the flesh from her body. They threw their wings at her, hard enough to leave cuts on her.

So I came back. She had her own pull to her, a way that stirred the air around us, and I gave in to it.

The sight of the swans through my eyes—not the yearling bear's, but mine—came brighter and more glaring than I'd braced for. Their wings looked so bleached, the color pierced into my forehead. That white was so stark against the trees' shadows that I squinted against it. It stung worse than the sun through the branches.

I thought maybe my eyes couldn't focus, that I was seeing more of them than there were.

But they were here, the truth of it beating down on us, this many white wings.

My vision didn't clear. I kept blinking, like trying to shake off the fluffy, not-quite-defined look things have before you're completely awake.

It didn't work.

I shut my eyes tight, still trying to shield this girl from these awful birds even when my vision couldn't pin them down, and then opened them.

Then I realized. The truth that this was not going away pressed its fingers into me.

My eyes didn't see quite like they had when I'd gone into the woods. I hadn't known when I'd been a bear, or the leafed skeleton of birch branches, or anything else in the weeks I'd been something other than myself. But now it came on strong. Not just the throbbing on my left side that Liam had given me. It was more than that.

It was the feeling of my left eye having a filter on it, dimming and fuzzing everything. It clouded the swans and the boughs overhead, like seeing them underwater, like everything out of my left eye had distilled down into its rawest forms, into blurs of light and shadow. It made all those birds whiter, painfully white, and made the woods recede and darken like they were pulling back. Moving my head, letting my right eye catch as much as it could, was the only way I could make sense of all these terrifying white wings.

I would've had a hard time coming up with a worse moment to have to relearn how to see.

The girl's hands froze on me, my fur gone, my skin in its place. I couldn't figure out if her wide-open eyes were about the swans, or about me.

The swans pulled back. They kept wary gazes on me as they flew off, like they didn't trust a bear who'd turned into a boy.

The girl didn't watch them.

She watched me.

She knew who I was. I was close enough to see the black centers of her eyes flashing in the deep brown, and that told me she knew everything.

The sound of the swans' wings faded.

My eyes adjusted. They made sense of the light and the shadows, the brighter colors from the paler ones, until it was just the left side of my vision that stayed cloudy and dark.

The girl was still looking at me.

I had the vague memory that we'd been in school together once and then she hadn't been there anymore, something about her parents teaching her and her sister at home. That was as far as we knew each other.

But there was some flicker of recognition in her face, enough that I knew she was going to say my name.

I was already a boy again, but if she said my name, then there'd be no getting away from how I'd once been Barclay Holt. Worse, she'd probably say it like a question. *Barclay Holt?* That was all I'd be to this girl, a name. Some guy who'd gone missing at the start of this fall. Sometimes, when I had been trees or rain, I'd caught this town's whispers. I knew what I was to this place.

"Don't," I said the second I saw the girl's lips part.

It was the first word I said. I landed on it hard.

She flinched, closing her mouth.

She could not say my real name. If she named me, I'd get pinned to everything I'd been trying to get away from. I'd lose the feeling of being a bear who had no name.

I remembered Grandma Tess's story, the one that had been in me when the woods made me into a bear.

"Call me Yearling," I said, because I had to give her something else.

BLANCA

I turned my back and Roja got away from me.

The swans had come, and the touch of their feathers was like a spell driving away all that I loved. First the cygnet. Then Mamá and Papá. Then Roja.

I found my sister out in the trees.

She wasn't alone.

She was with a boy, one who wore the same kind of thin cuts on his arms as Roja had on her cheeks.

I grabbed a branch and wielded it at the boy. "Get away from her."

His panic rustled the leaves around us. It wasn't the guilt of someone who'd been caught. It was fear, clear and so animal that for a minute the way he moved seemed less like a boy and more like a startled raccoon.

He dropped his hands from Roja's arms. It wasn't until he widened the distance between them that I registered how he'd held her. It wasn't him grabbing her or making her stay still. It had been the loose hold of guarding her, his body a shell around hers.

"Blanca," Roja said, her voice out of breath but level enough that I could hear her talking me down.

I lowered the branch, but didn't drop it.

Something about this boy made me turn back through things I knew but hadn't thought of in weeks. A newsprint picture. School photos in old passed-around yearbooks. A boy I'd known from school before our father started teaching us at home.

A misplaced boy, now squinting up at the white sky of the morning.

I caught a flash of paler skin on his chest, an almost-moon shape. It echoed a shape I'd seen before, white fur set within brown.

Understanding rushed into me so fast, my forehead ached.

The yearling bear.

Barclay Holt? Roja's bear was Barclay Holt?

I skimmed back over the way he'd tolerated Roja petting him, his patience like an old cat's. How he flicked his ears in a way that seemed like he was trying to make conversation. How he'd eaten pepitas out of her hand. None of that matched up against what I knew of the Holts. Their brick houses, so big they cast shadows onto the road. Barclay's mother, who looked at other wives in town like she was some proud queen and they might dirty the hem of her dress. Barclay's father and uncle, embarrassed by how their own mother wore her flannel and hunting jacket to church.

A tiny white feather fell from Roja's shoulder.

The color slid into me like the shock of a winter morning.

The swans.

They had come after her, and he'd shielded her from them. The fine cuts on them both were from the sharp edges of their wings.

I found his gaze, to tell him thank you.

But the color of it quieted me.

It was the last proof I needed that this was Barclay Holt. That color was the same as his mother's. Roja and I had watched her in town as little girls, her winter coat and her gloves deepened and lightened shades of that same blue.

His eyes were the blue of the filled cranberry bog. They were coins made of sky. They were a color the señoras had fastened to me as though it were a blessing.

And it was the worst news I'd gotten since the swans arrived.

ROJA

I had considered that the yearling bear might have been a nahual, a wrathful spirit living in an animal's body. That white moon on his chest had warned me.

But Barclay Holt? The bear—my bear, that soft, patient osezno—was Barclay Holt?

Somehow, that was so much worse.

Barclay Holt, a boy who'd gone missing, probably after some argument with his father over whatever rich boys argued about with their fathers. Or just because he was bored. Barclay Holt, who'd taken his best friend with him, because it's not enough for rich boys to wreck their own families, they have to wreck everyone else's.

But I did what he asked. I called him Yearling. I wasn't giving any reverence to his last name. It brought with it thoughts of the Holts' great brick houses, Barclay's mother and aunt in the kinds of shoes and scalloped-hem dresses you couldn't even buy in this town.

I brought him inside. It was less kindness and more my fear that someone might see us and wonder what a wicked del Cisne girl had done to this misplaced boy.

I threw at Yearling whatever clothes I could find. If it was too big, it was his problem. I pulled out a set of Abuelito's jeans and a flannel shirt, ones he wore to work at the cranberry farm.

"Thanks," Yearling said, lowering his head as he buttoned the jeans and shirt onto himself, slipped the belt through the loops.

The shirt gave off an iron-and-salt smell. A wet bloom showed on the plaid flannel.

Barclay Holt was bleeding.

A patch of his shirt was stained red, washed out to rust in the yellow of the lamps. The staining was off-center, the same as the wound on the yearling bear's back.

"What happened?" I asked.

He slid his shirt up, examining gashes that were thin, but deep. Wounds, not the thin slits from the swans' wings.

"Older bear didn't like the look of me," he said.

They ran alongside each other, evenly spaced, the other bear's claw marks. Reddened, raised skin surrounded them.

"Stay there," I said.

"Where do you think I'm going to go?"

I found gauze, tape, and a bottle of peroxide in the upstairs cabinet.

"What happened to you?" I asked when I came back, hands full.

"I just told you."

"I meant where have you been."

He shrugged. "Just around."

Yes. Barclay Holt was going to be exactly as big a pain in the ass as I first thought.

I streaked the peroxide onto his back, like he was anyone else. A relative. A classmate. A stranger.

Putting hands on him when he was a boy and not a bear carried the strangeness of who he was and who he was not. He was Barclay. Yearling. He was not a nahual I should be afraid to invite into our house. He would not draw a dozen more slouching nahuales from the forest.

The gashes turned pale and bubbled white. He set his teeth.

"You're getting off easy," I said. "Blanca uses rubbing alcohol."

I taped gauze over the gashes.

He looked at me through the hair that got in his face. "Thank you."

He was shorter than Abuelito had been. When he wore my grandfather's jeans, the hems trailed on the floor. He was different from the pictures they'd run of him, like the woods had carved him, and put him back not quite like he'd been before. I wondered if his bear's body had been like this under all the fur. The muscle and sense of being almost grown but still growing.

He smoothed his shirt down over his back. "Are your parents here?"

"No."

He looked around. "When are they coming back?"

"They're not."

He stared at me, the light catching first his right eye, then his left.

"I mean they're gone for a while," I said.

I tried not to stare at the brown in his left eye. The mixing of brown and blue had the swirling look of pictures in my father's astronomy book, one cloud of cosmic dust colliding with another.

In Blanca's storybooks, princesses and heroes had two-color eyes to mark them as special, and they were always described like jewels.

A girl with one eye like an emerald and the other like an amethyst. A boy with one eye like a cut sapphire and the other glowing like poured gold.

But Yearling's eyes were not polished jewels, each shining and distinct from the other. It was just that blush of brown that made the left different from the right. Both were a blue that was dark but not bright, a river-in-winter color, and that blurred sliver of brown at the lower, outer edge of his left eye looked like the sudden intrusion of summer or fall. Against the blue, the brown looked so warm it made him seem fevered. This wasn't the deep, clear browns of my family's eyes. It was a thin crescent, clouded at the edges, like silt gathering in water. Muddy but with a kind of light behind it.

I wanted to keep looking, not because he was pretty. Because there was something desperate and flickering in his eyes that had nothing to do with the color. I wanted to stay close to it in the same way I liked staring down lightning even when I knew to run from it.

"Do you want to call your family?" I asked.

"Not really."

"They probably want to know you're okay."

"I'm sure they're busy," he said. "Booked solid. You gotta get yourself an appointment months in advance."

I didn't want to laugh, but I did.

The thin slashes on my skin prickled, both from the swans' feathers and from the sting of a debt unpaid. Barclay Holt had helped me. I didn't want to owe him anything. If I had anything to say about it, we were settling up now.

"Do you need somewhere to stay?" I asked.

"I'll figure it out."

"Want to stay here?"

"Why?" he asked.

"Good point. We're the del Cisne girls." I gave him the widened eyes of a vengeful witch. "Who knows what we might turn you into?"

"I meant why would you let me."

"I won't unless Blanca says yes." He had to know this. The swans had to know this. There was no putting distance between Blanca and me. Not with the force of all those wings. Not with a bear who became a boy. This once, I could be fearless and sure for her the way she'd always been for me. "If she wants you gone, you're gone, okay?"

I turned toward the kitchen, looking for where I'd seen Blanca's shadow a few minutes ago.

The kitchen stood empty and dim.

I checked out the window. My sister stress-gardened, the same way I ate twenty pieces of hard candy before every time we saw the señoras. Maybe Blanca was in the back, tugging out foxglove and bluebell that sprung up where she didn't want them. When it came to our garden, no one knew better than Blanca that beautiful things so often choked things trying to grow.

I set my fingers against the chilled glass.

"Blanca?" I said through the window. But I couldn't find her.

Who I saw, instead, coming through the leaves' shadows, was my father.

BLANCA

I waited for them at the pond. When they came they landed like snowdrifts bringing winter with them. They came with the flicking sound of their wings and the wax-and-earth smell of their feathers.

Some landed and bent their necks to me. Others flitted away, as though I wasn't worth the attention.

I winced at the sight of their wings, remembering the fine cuts on Roja's cheeks and Barclay Holt's back.

They wanted me to look away. They wanted me to understand the threat in those cuts. First, with a thousand rose petals and jagged-edged leaves, I had tried to deny los cisnes their claim on either one of us. So the swans had turned all of this into a game that started with a few words from a señora's lips. A game I'd refused.

So they'd gone after the sister I loved.

"I understand," I told them, chin lifted. "If you want to hurt me, you'll hurt her. If I defy you, you'll hurt her."

Their marble-black gazes bore out from their pale bodies. It took all the stillness in me not to rip the finest feathers from the tips of their wings, the ones that had landed sharp on my sister's skin.

But I held myself back, fingers interlaced. They knew my heart lived deep in my sister's rib cage. They could always hurt her to hurt me. They had that on me, like the point of a jewel-hilted knife held between my shoulder blades, perfect and deadly, the pressure slight but never giving.

I didn't break my stare away from them. I stayed, feet planted into the ground. I needed them to know I wasn't afraid. I needed them to think I was worth granting a favor.

However much I had failed Roja so far, I could still bargain for her life.

I could not let her smile become a sharp beak, her eyes become swans' eyes, small and shining. I could not let the brown of her skin be bleached to pale down and her hair turned to feathers.

I had promised Roja we could fight back, that we would be sisters so much like each other that the swans could never choose.

It wasn't a promise I could keep anymore. The swans were here. They never left without taking a daughter with them.

But I had one more way to save her.

"I know what you want," I told the swans.

Piecing the words together still left me cold. *If you're a good girl, you can get a blue-eyed boy.*

A blue-eyed boy who had appeared the morning after the swans arrived.

They wanted me to play their game, to give in to the blessing they had probably whispered to the señoras with the brush of their wings.

"This is how it's going to go," I said. "I'll do what I'm supposed to do. I'll get him."

Now they bent their necks to me. They were listening.

"And when I do," I said, reveling in how closely they paid attention, "you'll take me instead of her."

I knew the rest of the tall señora's words. *If you can get a blue-eyed boy, you will save yourself.*

But if I saved myself without saving Roja, I would be a girl hollowed out, a tree withering from its heartwood. When we were small, there were times when our classmates' mothers could not tell us apart in shadow. Without the difference of color in our hair and skin, we blurred to them. We moved and laughed and reached for sorrel blossoms or books in ways so alike that our silhouettes could have been one girl. Sometimes our mother's friends would call one of our names across a road at dusk, or whisper it through the low-lit stacks at the library, drawing back when the other turned around in response. It happened so often that until I got taller, my sister and I were used to answering to each other's names.

Roja and I had woven the roots of ourselves together so well that if she was ripped from the ground, I would be wrecked.

Maybe I was born yellow-haired. Maybe Roja was born with skin as brown as our mother's, and red-stained hair no one else in our family had. Maybe everyone thought they knew us just by looking. To them, Roja's hair was a sign of her wickedness. To them, I was weak, a girl born without fingernails or teeth sharp enough to get into anything. The swans probably thought they could soak me in water like cotton candy and I would fall apart.

But I would not let the swans write our story for us.

A shared gleam passed across the swans' eyes. They lowered their graceful heads, slowly, but it still was enough to be a nod.

PAGE

She still saw me.

If I thought about it too much, I started to wonder. Because how could she have seen me when I was aspen trees, or water, or wind-weathered stones, or the night air itself? How could she have seen me through bright leaves and frost and the earth freezing at night and coming alive again each morning?

How could she have seen me when I wasn't there to see? When the woods took me, I was not Page anymore, not in a way anyone would have recognized. I did not wear the body that had been mine when we saw each other across the pond.

But I swear she still saw me.

She stood outside every evening as the sun was falling, arms wrapped around herself against the cold. Her wrists and elbows pinned her sweater to her body. Her hair flew against her cheeks and up off her shoulders like a spray of yellow leaves.

She shut her eyes and she breathed in, so deeply that when I was the night air itself she breathed me in. She took me into her and she held me there until she had to let me go. When I was rain, she stood out in the downpour with her face upturned, lips parted, hands open. So I filled her palms. I slid onto her tongue and into her mouth.

By now, I had already lost track of Barclay. At first I kept the sense of him being close. Sometimes I felt us both living in the same tangle of birch roots or the same leash of foxes. But then I lost him. So Blanca del Cisne became the star that drew me closer, whether I was a wolf cub or a clearing of blue chicory or whatever part of the forest would have me.

There's a lot of stories around town about the del Cisnes. Some of the whispers say their mother took them out of school to study witchcraft instead of geometry. Others swear their father can grow roses so red because whenever a much-loved family member dies, he plants their still-warm heart in the earth. Others insist that Blanca and Roja eat handfuls of hemlock and moonflower each night at bedtime, the poison as harmless to them as milk.

But the one story everyone believes is about swans. How every generation one del Cisne girl's arms turn to wings and her skin to feathers, and no one ever sees her again except in flashes of moon-white over the cranberry bog.

I guess that was why the woods gave me to Blanca as something she would understand, something written as deeply into her body as the possibility of feathers. The kind of young gray bird that grows into a swan.

But now the grown swans were here. And with each flutter of their wings, I felt the gray edges of my cygnet's down vibrating like winter stars. They wouldn't let me pretend to be one of them, not for long.

They knew I was on her side, not theirs.

ROJA

If I'd been a good sister, my first thought would've been to go look for Blanca.

It wasn't.

The shame of how much it wasn't drew over me like fog. But this moment of my father reappearing wasn't something I wanted to share. Not right away, not even with Blanca. And definitely not with the boy I'd just brought into our house.

I threw my arms around my father, tamping down my voice so I wouldn't exclaim *Papá!* too loud. "You came back."

His hug back was so stiff it felt formal, like I was the daughter of one of the businessmen he kept books for.

"I don't have long," he said, holding me tighter for a second before letting me go. "They don't know I left."

I stepped back, but held on to the edges of his coat. "Where are they keeping you?"

"Your great-aunt's house." He gave me a weary smile. "Don't worry, we're fine. The worst thing is I can't get a moment's quiet for my work. And I have to sneak my mezcal when no one's looking."

He tried hard with that joke, so I gave him a laugh. All the humor and will in him seemed dimmed by worry and lack of sleep. The brown of his face looked a little grayer, like dust-frosted wood.

"How can they do that to you?" I asked. "You're not their children."

He took my hands and drew them off his elbows. He checked over his shoulder, as though watching for what might come through the trees.

"I need to tell you something," he said.

His next words billowed around me until I was veiled in them.

If you can get a blue-eyed boy, you will save yourself.

The tall señora had told Blanca something she had not told me. These were the words she had said just before the swans came.

"Your mother doesn't know I know," he said.

"How do you know, then?" I asked.

"I heard her talking with your primas," he said.

"But why wouldn't Blanca tell me?" I asked the ground underneath me more than I asked my father.

But my father answered.

"It's all superstition." He waved a hand. "They're all so scared of those birds, they're so afraid of breaking the rules."

There was something in how my father held his head, or in the way he didn't quite keep his eyes on me, when he usually had a stare so unyielding I couldn't meet it.

I didn't know if my father never lied to me, or if he was just good enough at it for me not to know. But I knew now. And where my father did not tell me the truth, I could fill it in.

It wasn't superstition. It wasn't even the swans.

My mother did not want me to know, because she wanted Blanca to win. Blanca was her favorite, as much as I was Papá's. She didn't want to give her up to the swans when she might have a chance of keeping her.

My father probably thought this would hurt me. He probably thought I hadn't already noticed.

"Blanca wouldn't keep something like that from me," I said. "Not if she thought it was important." Blanca wouldn't even let me hold books far away from my face, warning me it would make my reading headaches worse, or let me suck on lemon wedges on hot days, insisting it would wreck my teeth. If there was anything Blanca thought might hurt me, I heard about it.

Maybe the tall señora had meant for Blanca to take her words as counsel about los cisnes, but Blanca hadn't realized it. If she had, she would have said something. I knew it with the same depth and certainty with which I knew my own body. We had always fought the swans together, one overripe or sour blackberry at a time.

"Look out for yourself anyway," he said.

He rubbed one hand with the other. The small motion drew my eye.

A reddened bruise crossed his fingers. Even broken from one knuckle to the next, I could make out the mark's shape.

A swan's beak.

Swans didn't have the sharp teeth of a wolf or the pointed beak of a hawk. To make that kind of bruise, one must have bitten as hard as its jaws could clamp.

"Papá," I said.

He bristled. "It's nothing."

"They hurt you," I said. "For coming back?"

The warmth in me that he would do this, risk returning under the watch of the swans, was weighted with the understanding that they had hurt him for it.

With los cisnes, nothing was free.

"You worry about yourself." He hid his hand in his coat pocket. "None of this is fair, remember that."

"You think I ever forget?" I asked. "All this because one poor woman a hundred years ago wanted a daughter?"

"No," he said. "I mean this time. This is a test. And if I hadn't come back, you wouldn't know the terms. Only your sister would."

"There's no test," I said. "They'll just choose one of us."

"They might have. But they're angry with you."

"Me?"

"Not just you. You and your sister."

"What did we do?"

"You thought you could stop them from coming."

My lungs took in the smell of the sharpest herbs in my mother's garden.

My father knew about that? Had he seen me swallowing the sweetest leaves and Blanca the bitterest? Had he noticed me trying to quiet the jealous part of me that hated how the cygnet liked Blanca better?

"That was your sister's decision as much as yours, if not more," my father said. "She should pay for it, too. She shouldn't leave you alone in this."

"She's not."

"I hope you're right." He watched the windows. "But the swans have a way of coming between sisters."

"Blanca loves me."

"And do you think you'd be the first sisters who loved each other before los cisnes made them enemies?" he asked. "What do you think happens when only one girl can be saved and they both know it?"

The smell of the bitter greens took on a harder edge.

We'd been brave and arrogant and sure in a way only young sisters could be.

"I have to get back," my father said. "I never thought I'd be this old and sneaking out like I'm your age."

"I've never snuck out," I said.

My deadpan made him laugh, just like I'd hoped.

I kept that laugh. I kept it as my worry mixed with my certainty that Blanca would never keep secrets from me. They swirled together, oil and water that stayed and would not mix.

I tried to put my arms around my father again. I tried to remember the way we'd talked about me visiting him when he was old. How we'd trade favorite books. How he'd let me take as many blooms from his rosebushes as I wanted so I could fill my apartment with their perfume.

None of that would happen if the swans took me.

My father stopped me. He held me away from him.

"No," he said. "You're not going to act like this is the last time. Because it's not. You're going to live."

He checked the trees at his back again. He was leaving me now.

But I need you here, I wanted to tell him. The words echoed, small and too young. I caught them behind my teeth and kept them quiet.

"I don't care what those old women told your sister," he said. "You can survive this."

"How?" I asked. Blanca's conviction that she could save us both had turned to ash in our hands. The swans had come. They wouldn't leave without one of us, and it would never be Blanca. Perfect, beautiful Blanca, with hair a gold that showed up in our family as rarely as black moonflower bloomed in our gardens.

The moment the swans came, I had already lost.

"Let them see you," my father said. "Let the swans see you're a girl who deserves to live."

Papá set his hand on my shoulder, and I felt like a son taking a father's benediction. I always thought men would prefer sons if given the choice, that my father just made the best of having daughters. But when he placed the full weight of his hand on my shoulder like that, I believed he wouldn't have chosen a son in the world over me.

These were words from a man who'd lost a sister he never spoke of. As a child, he had witnessed the swans' wrath.

"Los cisnes will lay you bare," he said. "They have a way of doing that. Once the swans see you, they'll decide. So make them recognize you, and respect you."

"But how do I do that?"

"Remember what I always told you."

I let my eyes fall shut. "I have teeth."

I opened my eyes in time to catch his nod.

"So use them," he said.

BLANCA

I could do this for Roja. I could hold to my bargain with los cisnes. Reminding myself of these things had a rhythm, an off-and-on like the steady background noise of my heartbeat. If I had to win Barclay Holt's heart to keep the swans from taking my sister, I could do it.

And if one of us had to kiss a boy we didn't want to be kissing, at least it was me.

So the next time Barclay and I passed each other in the hall downstairs, I did.

I pretended he was the same as the few boys I'd kissed behind the school after our parents pulled us out. I thought about what to do with my face. I tried to take his lead.

Except Barclay Holt wasn't leading. He didn't move his lips. He didn't move at all, like I was a wasp that had landed and might sting him if he flinched.

When I pulled away, his eyes were already open.

"What was that for?" he asked.

Embarrassment flushed up my neck, made worse by knowing I

had messed this up. An awful first kiss. Now I'd have to try even harder.

I grabbed for the first lie in reach.

"They—" I tried to make myself say the words, *the swans, los cisnes*, but I couldn't. "They were going after my sister. You scared them off. I don't know how, but you did. So, thank you."

"Oh." His shoulders relaxed. He now probably thought this was how we greeted each other in my family. "Don't mention it."

I should have eased my fingers up his arm. I should have drawn him close enough to feel my breath on his neck. But the veil of air between us felt hard as the floorboards. All I wanted to do was ask him things. *Where's Page? What happened to Page? Why didn't Page come back with you?*

The memory of the swans bowing their heads, the small mercy of them granting me what I asked, quieted me. The thin feather-slashes on Roja's skin kept me silent.

"Hey," Barclay said, "do you think maybe you could do me a favor?"

"What?" I asked.

"Do you think you could call someone for me?"

"You don't want to do it yourself?" I asked.

"I can't."

It sounded like half a sentence. I waited for the rest.

He looked at the wall instead of me. "It's a long story."

My impatience chilled what little warmth I had for this boy. But the way he hesitated, hands in his pockets, the pained way he held his shoulders, left me curious.

"Page Ashby," he said.

The name tore through me, fast and hard as hail.

"Can you just tell him I'm okay?" Barclay asked.

Any hope that Barclay had the answers I wanted dulled and flickered out. The story of their vanishing, some hint of how Page might come back to us, I thought he carried all of that with him.

"No," I managed. "I can't."

"Look," Barclay said. "I know none of this is your problem, just—" His eyes flashed like he was shuffling through a deck of possible things to say, but all he added was "please."

"No," I said. "I mean I can't call him."

In the slight widening and closing of his eyes, I caught that same hail-streaking feeling. The sense of something breaking through you, leaving a hollow space to mark its path.

"What?" he asked.

I resisted the feeling of thawing to Barclay Holt. Even as I tried to hate him for not bringing Page back with him, his concern, his panic, got into me.

"I thought it was both of you," I said.

Any speculation about what had happened always tied Barclay Holt and Page Ashby together. They had disappeared on the same day, so it had always followed that they must have made the same choice or met the same fate.

They're never coming back, Cara Miller had whispered, with the kind of finality no one wanted to ask after.

The river took them, Mr. Garcia had insisted, shaking his head. *It was never safe, I've been saying that for years.*

They ran away together, Emily Benson's mother said, smirking like she was impressed. *I bet you anything.*

If they ever came back, we'd thought it would be together. Or they'd be lost for good, together.

Now there was just this bewildered boy standing in our hallway. The other had fallen into the space between rumors and guesses.

Barclay stayed quiet, his mouth half-open like he was still waiting for words.

"I thought you'd know," I said.

He looked unanchored, like the floor was splintering under him. "What are you talking about?"

ROJA

I'd believed my sister. I had always believed her that if we held our hands tightly enough together, the swans could not tear one of us from the other. Maybe I was the dark and she was handfuls of stars, but we were still one night.

So I wouldn't have believed it if the cracked door hadn't shown my sister with Barclay Holt.

My sister kissing Barclay Holt.

If she'd wanted him, I would've shoved him her way. I would've left them alone in the kitchen together, or locked them both out in the back garden.

But Blanca held her body stiff, a way that got her close but still kept distance between them. Even with her lips against his, she kept her eyes open.

The truth sank into me like rain into our garden.

Blanca was kissing a boy she didn't want.

My father had been right.

But now I knew even more than he did.

Barclay Holt was the blue-eyed boy. Blanca would win him, just like the tall señora had told her to. She would save herself.

All the rose petals and blackberries we'd eaten at midnight, all the stories we'd made up when the wind shrieked on autumn nights, all of it fell away. It had all turned to ashes the minute the swans arrived.

YEARLING

He was gone.

He hadn't been in any of the places I'd imagined him. In his room, reading a book with ten paper clips in hand as book-marks, because there were always pages he wanted to come back to. Down in his family's kitchen, him and his father saving seeds, wondering what kind of apples they'd grow. Out among the trees whose blooming and grafting seasons Page knew better than I knew anything.

Everything I had done had so much weight, it had pulled Page off his family's orchard. The secrets I'd kept had sharp edges I didn't warn him about. The way I'd left had carved a space so deep he got drawn down into it, like the current of a whirlpool.

Where are you? I said to the whole world I'd lost him to.

However much the world off my left side had darkened and gone cloudy, however much I had trouble telling the shade of one tree's leaves from the next in low light, this made it worse. The loss of Page dimmed everything worse.

Where is he? I wanted to ask the ground, the air, the sky. I wanted to ask the moon because when Liam and I were little, Grandma Tess used to say the moon saw everything. I wanted to reach my hands into the wood of every tree and feel for the rhythm of Page's heart-beat. I wanted to break the rocks open like the ones in my cousin's geode set and see if, instead of amethyst crystals or jagged silica, they held the bright color of Page's heart.

I wanted to break open the moon itself, because if Grandma Tess was right, it held all the secrets in the world. Even how I could get someone back when it was my fault he was lost.

Dammit, Page, what happened to you? I couldn't tell if I was saying the words or if they were just getting ripped out of me, thinned into quiet once they hit the air.

Where is he? I asked again.

But the woods and the whole world didn't answer.

PART TWO

Rose & Snow

BLANCA

A knock shuddered the front door.

I answered expecting one of our cousins. But Tess Holt stood on our front steps.

I held back a gasp so hard I almost choked on it.

I couldn't pretend I didn't know her. Everybody around here knew the Holts.

If I could just forget she was a Holt, maybe my throat would ease up.

Barclay's grandmother was not the type of grandmother drawn in storybooks of *Little Red Riding Hood*. She wasn't like Lynn Ashby, with her whipped-cream hair and her smile like she'd be a grandmother to anyone who didn't have one.

Tess Holt had the solid look of a woman whose idea of a whim was hiking the edge of town in winter. She was taller than either of her grandsons. She wore a men's hunting jacket, and her hair, silver as iron shavings, was held back with a scarf that looked more for use than style.

"May I help you?" I cringed as soon as I said it. It was a carryover from one of the offices my father kept books for. I answered phones for the weeks Evie Tilton was out having her baby, and ever since, the words *May I help you?* formed on my tongue when I didn't know what else to say.

Tess slid a strap off her shoulder. She set a shotgun into my hands so quickly I didn't register that I was reaching out to accept it. It was the kind of reflex that came in response to certainty, a meeting of the other person's expectation that you will do what they want.

My hands found more wood than metal, blond with age and lacquered with oil. The word *ancient* came to mind, like this thing was from a time before there were any guns at all. I didn't even know how it was staying together.

"What's this for?" I asked.

"For however long you two are on your own," Tess said.

I chilled at the idea of how much Tess had seen, if she'd been passing close enough to our house to witness our primas taking our mother and father.

I angled my body so she couldn't see in the house. "We're not."

"Uh-huh," Tess said, her tone a warning, but still permissive, like she'd let my underestimation of her slide this once.

"I don't want this." I tried to hand back the old shotgun. Where was my sister right now? She'd know how to hold this thing, how to store it, and, most important of all, how to make sure Tess Holt left with it.

But I did not have the same conviction as Tess Holt. When I held it to her, she did not open her hands.

"I can't," I said.

"Sure you can," Tess said, already shifting her weight, halfway to leaving. "It's not my favorite. I won't miss it. You girls can borrow it until your mom and dad come back."

"But I don't know how," I said.

"I'm not telling you to take aim at anyone," Tess said. "So don't. Just use the look of it to scare off anyone trying to bother you."

I settled into the understanding that I might not win. I might have to bring a stranger's shotgun into my mother's house.

"It's not loaded, is it?" I asked.

"Birdshot." Tess crossed the flat stones set into the grass. "So don't fire at anyone, okay?"

I fumbled the thing in my hands, scrambling to keep the barrel down. "Why would you load it? I don't know what to do with this."

"All the coyotes and wolves that come down from the hills in the summer?" Tess said. "You're telling me your father never taught you how to scare them off? I've seen him driving crows out of your mother's vegetables."

When had my father done that? The last time I'd seen him with a shotgun in his hands had been one he borrowed from the cranberry farm. If he'd shown either of us how to shoot it would've been Roja, not me.

"Tess," I said, following her down the walk. "I've never held a gun before."

"You're doing just fine." She said this without looking back.

"Tess," I called after her.

Grandmother or no grandmother, she moved faster than I could think. Before I could come up with a good reason to go after her, before I could weigh the risks of being a del Cisne girl seen chasing a gringa grandmother with her own shotgun, Tess was gone.

ROJA

I saw the upstairs hallway window before I saw Yearling. An arc of five small circles dotted the cold-clouded pane, the five points where the pads of his fingers had been.

He was watching Tess Holt, his grandmother, cross under the trees that stood between us and the road.

The thin sun showed me his eyes were glassy. That film of water startled me. In some lights, I still thought of him as a nahual, more warning story than living boy. I thought all feeling in him had turned to instinct, like the nahuales with their animal bodies.

Yearling's hand fell to the sill. The heel of his palm pressed against the edge.

I said his name.

He jumped back from the window.

"Don't do that," he said, with the clipped sound of catching his breath.

"Do what?"

"That," he said.

"What?" I asked. Annoyance slid into my voice.

He sighed, like he was clearing the air between us. "I don't see so great off my left side. So if you come up on me like that, be noisy about it, okay?"

Yearling traced shapes on the cold glass, two panes over from where he had warmed it with his palm.

The oddness of him being in our house came back to me. A boy who'd been lost to all of us had washed up here. Brown hair, and boy-sweat, and secrets he wouldn't tell us any sooner than the trees would.

I drew a line through the fog on the window. "Do you miss her?"

He nodded without looking at me.

Something in me cracked, like ice thawing and splintering. He missed his grandmother in the same way I missed Papá. I still felt the pull of my father leaving, like a little of me had trailed after him. If that was Tess to him—and from the look on his face, she was—how could he let a set of stairs and a front door keep him from seeing her?

"Why don't you go talk to her?" I asked.

He dropped his hand from the window. "I just can't."

YEARLING

It wasn't like I hadn't thought of going to Grandma Tess's before I just let the woods take me. I had. I'd thought of coming in her kitchen door, the thyme-and-juniper smell of her house cutting through the smell of my own sweat.

But then I'd thought of her seeing all the blood on me. I'd thought of how she'd look at me, lips held thin and straight, eyes narrow but watching.

And I couldn't do it.

I couldn't do it now, either.

So I stumbled through this house I did not know, knocking my left shoulder on a doorframe, catching my left hip on the corner of a counter so hard I could feel it in the bone. I couldn't blame it on how many rooms and corners I had to map; the del Cisne house was a lot smaller than my father's house, which he'd built up an addition at a time in competition with my uncle (my mother and aunt eventually demanded they both stop before the houses became, in their shared word, *garish*).

But this house was unknown enough that it felt as wide and forbidding as a museum. I had never been in the del Cisne house, so I had no muscle memory for it. I reached for the narrow, worn-wood banister that ran alongside the stairs, and my fingers missed it. I rounded a corner I was sure I knew the shape of and hit it with half my body. I was no match for even the soft things in this house. I saw a cloth-covered chair from one angle, and then from another angle it would seem like it had moved on its own. I missed a woven rug and ended up stumbling on the edge.

When Blanca gave me a kindergarten-teacher-like tour of the house so I would know where everything was, I stayed back like a disinterested student, trying to hide when I rattled a potted plant I hadn't seen, or knocked a table hard enough for water to slosh up the side of a glass. Her tour didn't stop me from, an hour later, mistaking the stairwell for a hallway and tripping against it, my shins hitting the hard edges of the steps.

I got a look at myself in the del Cisnes' bathroom mirror and then wished I hadn't. I looked tired in a way that made me more tired. The tiny comet-trail scars were still there, pale and faint but there. And even though my eyes were mostly the muddy blue they'd always been, the left one had gone brown at the lower edge. Not the clear, strong-tea brown of Roja del Cisne's eyes, but reddened, like iron rusting over.

I couldn't let Tess see it. Because if she saw, I'd have to explain how it happened. And that meant telling her everything.

Thinking of the day the woods took me brought back the stinging pain in my lower eyelid and left temple, like I could still feel the blood getting caught.

I'd really thought I knew what I was doing. I thought I was doing the right thing, for once. But all it got me was the backs of my hands broken open and my ribs cracking like branches.

And it had gotten Page lost, too. The guilt of knowing what Blanca told me bit into me. It pulled me outside and got into me like the bite of winter air.

Somehow, I had dragged Page down with me. I didn't even know where to start looking. Page could've been anything. A stray fox. A handful of quartz gravel at the edge of the pond. A downpour through trees I'd never recognized. And that was if the woods had Page at all.

If there was any chance they did, I had to try.

"Page," I said to the light between the trees.

If I stood there long enough, I could pretend the wind was answering.

"Page," I said again, in case he could hear me. "You gotta come back."

I was talking to the air. I was actually talking to the air. It was the kind of thing that would have made sense for the del Cisnes, who got chased by swans and who could stir up the wind just by walking through the woods. But me? I could almost hear Grandma Tess's commentary. *Try all you want. Around here doesn't know you like they know those girls.*

But I still had to try.

"You can't get lost," I told the trees in front of me, hoping the air would carry the words to wherever Page was. If Page was here at all. "Come back."

BLANCA

The only time Page Ashby and I had ever touched was once when we collided on the sidewalk outside the florist. In my flustered apologies, my attempts to help gather up the notebooks and cereal box I'd knocked out of Page's arms, all I managed to do was ask insulting questions.

In the rustle of paper, I'd wanted to make Page laugh, to break the quiet between us, as badly as I wanted Mamá's sleeping cure on full-moon nights.

But the best joke I came up with was "I swear I didn't wake up this morning thinking, 'Why don't I throw myself at him today?' "

Page blinked at me, eyelashes so sun-bleached I had to stare to see them.

I felt around for my mistake.

" 'At *her* today?' " I tried again, cringing my apology.

As soon as the question was out of my mouth, I wanted to fold myself into my own book bag just so I'd stop talking. I braced for horror on Page's face, for Page to tell me to mind my own business. I would've deserved it.

"Help me out here," I'd said, biting my lip each time I paused to breathe. I should have bit it hard enough to keep myself from talking. I had to stop talking.

"Are you asking which one's right?" Page said, with just enough of a laugh under the words that I thought maybe I hadn't ruined everything.

I nodded, because God knew I wasn't about to try talking again.

"Both," Page said, and then, in a show of charm I never would have expected from this pale figure who always walked head-down, smiled at me.

Page took the notebooks, and the cereal probably just picked up from the store. Page walked away, but kept smiling at me over one shoulder for the length of three more sidewalk squares. Yes, I counted. And I swear to la Virgen, if Page had proposed right then I would've said yes.

I could almost feel the women in my family looking on. Over Page Ashby, they would have traded either smirks or confused glances. *Be a woman or be a man*, they would have said, a criticism applied to daughters they thought spent too much time climbing trees, sons they thought spent too much time in their mothers' kitchens, and children who played dress-up games in both their grandmothers' old gowns and grandfathers' slacks. They had little regard for women like Tess Holt in their duck-cloth jackets, or the young men in tight jeans who met at a bar just outside town. My second cousin had only understood her older daughter, the daughter she had once thought to be a son, because she was so much what we thought of as *girl*—flowered dresses, and white Mary Janes on her brown feet, and a laugh that was tinkling and demure instead of the loud cackle my sister and I shared when a joke surprised us.

But I kept my back to those voices. I looked for Page in town after that, in gray jeans and Mr. Ashby's hand-me-down high school sweatshirt, fraying at the cuffs, a hundred washes' worth of soft.

It had just been the one time. I knew I had no right to this sense that the inside of me was flickering out like live ash. I wasn't anyone close enough to Page to feel what I felt now, all of me breaking open like I was a pomegranate. All of me spilling everywhere like red-jewel seeds.

I'd always thought that if one of our town's lost sons appeared, they both would. Through all the whispers when I walked past the grocery store or the yarn shop, I believed that.

Now Barclay Holt had come back, and Page Ashby hadn't. Barclay had no idea how to get Page back, and I tried to quiet how much I held it against him, the blame roiling in me.

But I could still do this. I didn't have to love Barclay. I just had to get him to love me.

I went out. I couldn't breathe in that house. It held Roja and Barclay and a thousand echoes of the señora's words. The air thickened, like summer with no open windows.

There was no room for my heart, still full of a boy I'd seen through falling leaves.

My heart was so weighted with everything Page that it was becoming gold and gray and the deep reds of the Ashbys' apples. My heart wasn't a living thing anymore. It had turned hard and solid, a silvered box where I kept what little of Page Ashby I could call mine.

Maybe it was this, my jewel box of a heart and everything I set inside, that pulled Page back to me. Like in a storybook, a fairy deciding I was worthy of looking after an enchanted boy.

The woods made Page, out of the white-and-silver lichen

trailing off tree branches. They made Page from the sheet of wavering light on the surface of the pond, and the reflection of tall spruce branches with their violet cones. They made Page Ashby out of stars I could not see in the morning. From the wings of dragonflies, as delicate as tissue paper and glass.

A last flash of gray-fluffed cygnet, and then Page was there. Page's hands, callused from work on the Ashbys' orchard. Brushfield-blond hair, wind stirring the strands. Shale-colored eyes staring into me like I was the one the woods had just made.

Before I could think about it, I came close enough for my fingers to brush Page's shoulder, to see if this boy was here or if I had dreamed all of this.

Page let me, and stayed.

PAGE

If I thought about it too hard, I lost it. The Blanca del Cisne I knew turned thin and filmy. Barclay taught me that sometimes looking right at a star makes it harder to see. The light fuzzes out and blurs. But if you look just to the side of it, a little off, it sharpens, and brightens, like watching a firefly's light.

That's what it was like with Blanca. If I looked right at her, I lost her. I lost the feeling that she had never forgotten me. But if I caught just the flick of her hair, the lantern-brown of her eyes, the peach-red of her parted lips, I knew.

I could have hidden forever. I could have lived as a brush rabbit, or as streamers of lace lichen. If I stopped being a cygnet, there were other corners of the woods that might take me.

But now there were so many versions of me everyone had made up, before I went away and after. I felt the whispers carried in the air like the electricity before storms. They were static sparking at the edges of my gray down.

I had to be the one to say which Page was true.

I'd followed Barclay to make sure he wasn't alone. But now Barclay had come out of the woods, the fur of his bear-body falling away.

Now I felt the pull of them, and I rose to it, like surfacing to light from underwater. Blanca, the girl who seemed made out of aspen leaves and the outer bark of silver birches. Barclay, who'd been folded into the woods until there was no him anymore, but now was Barclay again.

And my own draw, the want for my own body, even with all the questions it brought with it. Not my questions; everyone else's.

But it was still my body.

I felt the woods letting go, the clouds murmuring that it was time to come back. Barclay had left his hiding places. Now I had to.

So I wove myself out of all the gray and silver in the woods. Lace lichen and cygnet's down. Wolf cubs and river-worn stones. Low pewter clouds and the faint tint of frost on wild grass. I spun back into what I was, like threads taken back from birds' nests. They came together.

I came together.

And I was Page again.

BLANCA

I brought Page in the back door with me, slipping us through a ribbon of quiet in the house that made me wonder where Roja and Barclay Holt were.

Abuelito's jeans would never fit Page's hips. Page was a kind of thin that, in my family, would have been counted as starving. My mother would have pinched Page's collarbone and asked, *Doesn't anyone feed you?* My grandmother would have shoved plates of chiles en nogada at Page, hoping the cream sauce would fatten this boy up. Page's chest—I tried not to look, but once we were upstairs, I did—was small handfuls of masa.

Page was a shape I'd only ever seen on gringos. Wider shoulders, but thin-framed, and almost flat-looking from the side, at least compared with me and Roja. When someone like that came into our house, the women in my family always worried.

I gave Page a pair of my jeans, straight-legged ones I got from the secondhand shop and that I was pretty sure were a boy's brand. I gave Page my plainest pair of underwear, white cotton ones I never used unless my blue and yellow ones were all in the wash. And I had to settle for one of Abuelito's shirts; it would be too big, but I knew the cut and scalloped collars of my shirts and Roja's would make Page cringe. I remembered Page in school, in town. On weekdays, sweaters and corduroy pants—the corduroy pants drew even more ridicule than Page's careful study of apples. On weekends, plain sweatshirts, jeans, dirt-scuffed sneakers with blossom petals or leaves caught under the laces.

I could almost hear the swans' laughter, haunting and musical. *Did you think this would be simple? Did you think we would let any bargain you made with us come easily?*

The boy I had wanted to come back to us had, at the worst time. Page was here, close enough that my heart felt spun into threads as fine as fairy floss.

And I had to make another boy fall in love with me.

I wanted to go outside and take the swans by their pale, graceful necks. *Page is not something for you to play with,* I wanted to yell into their pretty faces. *Page is a person, not a part of your game.*

But they would have thrown their honking cackles in my face. They would have laughed at how I thought I was a girl with any power at all.

When I came in, Page was sitting on the edge of the bathtub, rubbing one foot against the linoleum.

Every curve of Page's anklebone showed. It looked so sharp, and Page's skin was pale as peach tulips with the sun coming through them. I worried the bone might break through.

"Here." I handed over what I'd found.

"Thank you." Page looked at me with a hint of that smile I remembered, the kind of confidence that filled in all the places I was unsure, and hesitant.

Page had gotten me with that smile. I had never gotten free of it. And now, this close, my veins felt like the shimmering arms of some far galaxy. All stardust and swirling heat.

"Do you want me to . . ." I twirled my fingers at the door, feeling a kind of awkward so thick it was catching in my throat.

Page laughed. "Does it matter?"

"Good point." I dropped my hands.

I'd already seen Page naked. But watching someone put on clothes felt as intimate as watching them take them off. So I kept my eyes down.

That made Page laugh again. I liked this about Page Ashby, how even when Page was the one naked, I was the one blushing, and Page was the one laughing.

Page pulled on the jeans, turning away to put the shirt on.

In this light, I caught how there were strands of silver flashing in the blond of Page's hair. That was something they said about the Ashbys, how they went gray young. Mrs. Ashby's hair had already turned when she met Page's father, even though she'd been in her twenties. Instead of thinking she was odd for it, Mr. Ashby had told her she looked like a fairy, or a water sprite, her hair spun out of pond-silver.

"Are you going back home?" I asked.

"No," Page said.

"Why not?" I asked.

Page finger-combed that silvered blond, uneven from growing out. "Because it's too hard."

"For you?" I asked, bracing for the answer. I loved the Mr. and Mrs. Ashby I'd gotten to know through this town's whispers. The story about how he'd fallen in love with her gone-gray-early hair. The orchard where my mother and I bought apples; she let me pick out the prettiest ones even though she knew I wouldn't eat any.

The Ashby boy I'd been too shy to talk to when we were small, my mother prodding, "Say hi, Blanca," and me hiding in her shadow and the apple trees'.

I did not want Mr. and Mrs. Ashby to be the kind of mother and father who tried to make Page something different. I didn't want them to have tried shoving Sunday dresses at Page, or putting sewing scissors in Page's hands when what Page wanted was to tend the grafted trees alongside Mr. Ashby.

But if it was true, I had to hear it. It was Page's truth to tell.

"No," Page said, buttoning the last shirt button. "For them. It's too hard for them."

I nodded, as though I understood.

"Are you hungry?" I asked without thinking.

Page's response was a half shrug.

"Sorry," I said. "Habit."

"What do you mean?"

"In my family when we don't know what to do, we try to feed people."

Page looked down, laughing softly.

I shivered at the familiar sound of that particular laugh, how it mirrored that day on the sidewalk, when I said things that were stupid and wrong and somehow Page turned them into something worth laughing at. I didn't care if that smile was a little at my expense. I didn't mind amusing this boy.

"I'm sorry," I said.

"You've got to stop saying that." Page looked up. "What this time?"

"That I . . ." I stopped. I couldn't bring myself to use the word *naked*. "I'm sorry I saw you."

"Don't be."

"Why not?" I asked.

"Because you don't look at me like I'm something you're trying to figure out."

I watched Page Ashby button the cuffs of my grandfather's shirt.

"Page?" I asked.

"You're a boy, right?"

Page nodded. "Yeah."

"But *she* or *he*," I said, careful on each word, remembering that day in front of the flower shop, "both of those work?"

"Yeah," Page said, the same kind of level as the first *yeah*. "Just please don't call me a girl. Or *young lady*. They never really fit me."

"But doesn't *she* get you called *girl* and *young lady*?" I asked.

"Maybe," Page said. "It shouldn't, though. *Him* and *her*, I kinda like getting called both. It's like all of me gets seen then. Doesn't usually happen, though. Most people can't get their head around *boy* and *she* at the same time, I guess."

"Do you want me to?" I asked. "Call you *she*, I mean."

"If you want to, go ahead. It'd be kind of novel to be called *she* by someone who gets that I'm a boy."

The sense that Page Ashby was trusting me with this, something as small as a few letters but as bright as the whole sky, made my cheeks feel like matches flaring.

"It shouldn't be," I said.

"What shouldn't be what?" Page asked.

"It shouldn't be novel. I'm sorry it is."

Page tossed her head, flicking her hair off her face. "Thanks."

An unsettling warmth filled me. All the ways I'd gotten Page Ashby wrong trailed off me like the ribbons Roja and I tied onto trees, but at least this I had gotten right. I braided the words together, weaving them into what else I knew of Page Ashby. Brown-gray eyes. The sugar-and-leaf smell of apples. A science fair project about the effect of centripetal force on seedling growth. (Page had repurposed Lynn Ashby's barely working record turntable.)

"Blanca?" Page asked.

"Yes?"

"Thanks for asking."

"You didn't mind?" I asked.

"I don't mind questions," Page said. "Most people never bother asking."

ROJA

How completely Blanca had forgotten me, forgotten everything but keeping her own skin and teeth, needled into me. But she was my sister. After years of counting out lightning during storms, I had to give her one more chance to tell me the truth.

The next time I caught Blanca alone, I took hold of her elbow and pulled her toward our room. "What are we going to do?"

She breathed out. "I don't know yet."

I tried not to look toward the window. "But they're here," I whispered. "And he's here. And eventually someone's going to realize he's here and—"

She cut me off by lifting her hand. "Roja." I could see her taking a long breath to steady herself.

Like I was a child she had to deal with.

"I need you to trust me," she said. "Do you still trust me?"

"Of course I do." I felt the sharp edges of the trap I was setting. I didn't plan it. The lie just happened. "Is there any reason I shouldn't?"

It was fast, flashing over her face like the sun through leaves. But I caught her doubt, her hesitation.

Her guilt at everything she was hiding.

"I will figure this out," she said. "I promise you, I will."

I?

It had always been the two of us holding off the swans. Now it was *I*?

The word burrowed into me, sharp and barbed.

We were not Blanca and Roja anymore.

She was Blanca, the blessed del Cisne girl.

And I was the other one.

If you can get a blue-eyed boy, you will save yourself. When the prize was a heart, Blanca would never lose. Not with her lips, the color of tea roses. Not with the gold of her hair and the honey-amber of her eyes. Not with the demure way she looked down, her eyelashes casting feathery shadows on the apples of her cheeks.

I was alone now.

The floorboards shifted downstairs.

Blanca's eyes flashed in the direction of the noise. "There's something else I should probably explain."

I rushed down the stairs ahead of her.

"Roja," she called after me.

I might have thought the fair-haired shape in Yearling's arms was Blanca. I even recognized her least-worn pair of jeans.

But Blanca was behind me. And this was a boy in Yearling's arms, one who stood a little shorter than Blanca.

If I didn't register this fast enough, I registered it when I saw how they hugged each other. This was something passing between boys. They hugged each other like boys did, forearms across each other's upper backs in a way halfway between patting and hitting.

There was the rush of questions. There was the shaking of the blond boy's head so his hair got in his eyes. There was Yearling putting his hand on the pale boy's upper back and taking him aside as they kept talking.

"You came back," Yearling said. "You didn't . . ." He grasped for the next word, avoiding the fair-haired boy's eyes.

"I'm okay," the fair-haired boy said. "I'm all right."

"I'm so sorry, I never would've . . . I didn't know you were . . ." Again, Yearling struggled to finish a sentence.

"I'm fine," the fair-haired boy said. "Really."

"But you . . . what happened?"

The fair-haired boy's laugh was slight, but sad. "Same thing that happened to you."

This boy's features resolved into a name, lost but then picked up again like a found coin.

"Page?" I asked.

But they didn't hear me.

So I stood there, staring, caught in the wonder of how this town's second lost son had come back to us.

Blanca's stare struck my back so hard I could feel the heat of it.

But when I tried to meet her eyes, she wasn't looking at me.

She was staring at Page Ashby. Blanca looked like her body was untethered from the floor, floating underwater.

My sister—my sister, who the señoras had told to get a blue-eyed boy—wanted clay-eyed Page Ashby.

It was the first favor the swans had ever done me.

They had given me a chance.

If my sister could get a blue-eyed boy, so could I. If she thought she could save herself by going behind my back, I could go behind hers. Barclay Holt was nothing to me. He was some rich boy from a family who'd made their fortune buying and selling land hundreds of miles from here. If him falling in love with me could save me, I'd make him.

"Page," I said, my voice sweet as my mother's aguas frescas. "Why don't you stay with us for now?"

Page's eyes crawled over to Blanca.

"You two are friends, right?" I asked, looking between Page and Yearling. "You'll figure out what to do together."

A twist of malice grew in me. First I let one boy stay so I wouldn't owe him for the cuts on his back. Then a second boy whose presence would unsettle Blanca too much to let her win.

"You're okay with that?" Page asked. His eyes swept in both me and my sister.

The muscles in Blanca's neck tensed, her tell for when she was trying to stay still.

"Of course," she said.

"Good." I tried not to flash a smug grin as I pushed past Blanca on my way up the stairs.

Now the boy Blanca wanted instead of Yearling was in our house.

The chance the swans had given me was small. But I was taking it.

I shut the door to our room behind me, wondering what it was like to be her, torn into pieces. She was half the sweet, caring sister who tried to defy the swans, and half a ruthless girl who would do anything not to become one of them.

For a minute I sank into the perverse dream of her looking right at me and telling me, *I'm not going to be the swan, they're not going to take me.* And imagining that, I couldn't hate her. How could I blame her? She was perfect and beautiful, spun out of gold. Of course she wouldn't let herself be remade into feathers.

It was her lie that rose and spread in me. It bloomed like the poison bells of my mother's foxglove.

I stood in front of Blanca's dresser and mirror, spreading my hands over the wood. I brushed on the petal-pink shimmer of her blush. I ran my ring finger across her rose lipstick and rubbed it onto my lips. The glass ball of her perfume bottle weighed heavy in my hands as I sprayed the powdery scent onto my shoulders.

I patted my wrists together, the way Blanca had taught me to spread perfume (rubbing them together destroyed the fragrance molecules, she'd read in a magazine).

I could be her if I needed to be.

Maybe Blanca was the blessed sister. But she would make a better swan than I would anyway. Fairer. More beautiful. Even when dust swirled in the air, her feathers would stay clean as new snow. The other swans would adore her. Her bevy would make her its white-feathered queen.

But me? I had never come in shades of white and gold. I was brown. All of me, brown. My hair, my eyes, my skin, all different shades of brown, none of them swan-pale. I would be the swan whose feathers were always damp from the wet earth or stained purple-red from blackberry brambles. Where the other swans would find Blanca pristine, they would decide I was odd, a detriment to their flock of perfect white.

I could not be the one the swans took.

Maybe the rose-pinks of Blanca's makeup did not look the same on me. But I went to the pond smelling of her perfume and glinting with that same pink on my cheeks and lips. I would wear any colors I had to if it might make the swans reconsider me. Maybe the chance was as small and fragile as a blackbird's egg. Maybe the swans were already taking me under, sure as if I was caught in a tangle of pond-weed.

But I would not be my father's daughter if I didn't fight them pulling me down.

I took the kind of leveling breath I'd seen Blanca take. I drew back from the feeling that the swans might slice their feathers across my skin again.

I faced them, staring in their ink-drop eyes to show I wasn't afraid.

And I said, "Thank you."

PAGE

I'm sorry, Barclay said so many times I just wanted him to say anything else.

"I'm sorry," he said, this time adding, "I didn't know you were with me. I didn't know you were there. How did I not know that?"

I'm sorry, as though me going into the woods after him had been something that just happened to me. I couldn't figure out how to tell him *I chose this, I followed you, I knew you were hiding something, and I still know that,* without scaring him back out into the trees.

"Don't ever do that again, got it?" Barclay said the minute the del Cisne girls were out of the room.

"Do what?" I asked.

"Come after me like that." He sounded more shaken than angry.

"I was worried."

"Yeah, well, don't worry anymore." He kept checking the window like something might come out of the woods. Something other than us. "I don't want any of this touching you."

"Any of what?" I asked.

He shook his head, dragging his gaze off the glass. "Forget it."

"Barclay." I took a step closer to him. "Any of what?"

He slid his hands into his pockets. "I'm glad you're back."

The day I followed Barclay into the woods, I knew there was something he'd never told me. And he still wouldn't, even now. It didn't matter how many hours we'd spent by the river looking for marbled salamanders, their tails so thick they looked like tiny dinosaurs. It didn't matter how often we visited the rusted-out truck on the far side of the Lindley farm, the ridged steel bed filled with books Olive told us to read, or old radios we tried to fix.

"Look"—Barclay stood square in front of me—"stop trying to help me. All I do is drag you down."

He went for the door.

"So you're hiding out here forever?" I asked.

"No." He shook his head at the wall, breathing in. "Just until I figure out what to do."

I tried not to stare at his left iris, the edge darkened to red-brown. But he was my friend, and I had to ask.

"What happened there?" I lifted my hand toward his left temple.

I didn't know a shrug could look like a lie until the minute Barclay proved it.

"No idea," he said.

ROJA

It wasn't the first time I'd worn Blanca's clothes. I'd been borrowing her cotton dresses in summer and wool skirts in winter since our bodies settled out at almost the same size. One smile, and she could always get the men at the secondhand store to lower the paper-tagged prices.

But I'd never done it like this, slipping into a rose-printed dress so early in the morning that the sky outside the windows was blue-black. Dabbing her perfume behind my ears and sweeping her blush onto my cheeks. I imagined the fabric and the scent putting a little of her into my skin, like our sweaters picking up the smell of the lavender we tucked into our drawers.

It was one small way I could become her.

The other was waiting downstairs in the kitchen.

Maybe I hadn't learned to cook alongside my mother like Blanca had. But I could follow a recipe. I could be soft and nurturing, the kind of girl who smelled like vanilla and whose laugh made boys think of candle flames in December.

I yawned into my sleeve. If I wanted enough time for the dough to prove, I had to start now, hours before everyone else woke up.

I tipped each ingredient into the bowl, measuring and kneading the way my mother's handwritten, water-stained recipe said to. I added rosewater and berry color to the sugar shell, slashing a pattern that would open into petals as it baked.

Yearling wandered into the kitchen, rubbing the heel of his hand against one eye. "What are you doing?" he asked, his voice hoarse with sleep.

"Why are you up?" I asked, glad I'd already made myself pretty.

"Me?" he asked. "Why are *you* up?"

"I'm making breakfast."

"It's dark out."

"We have a small oven, I have to go in batches." I pulled the first sheet out of the oven, silently thanking the swans. Maybe they were helping me even more than I thought. Maybe they'd sent a little of their spell through the air and woken him up in time to see me with my first batch of pan dulce.

If I tried to defy them, they'd slash their feathers across my skin. But if I played their game, maybe they were with me more than Blanca and Mamá could ever guess.

I set the pan on an unlit burner. They were the perfect rounded shape, just like I'd seen my mother and Blanca make. The deep-red sugar shell on the tops of the pale rounds looked like crushed rose petals.

Yearling leaned against the counter. "Ever heard of cold cereal? It's great, done in thirty seconds."

"The perfect pan dulce may take time"—I slid one onto a plate—"but it's worth it." I handed it to him. "Careful, it's hot."

"They're pretty," he said. "You're really supposed to eat them?"

"I make them all the time," I lied. I set another one on another plate, ready to crush a piece of the soft dough between my fingers. "I could do it in my sleep."

Yearling crumbled a piece off, the red sugar shell turning to berry-colored dust, and set it on his tongue.

He winced, his jaw tightening.

I filled a water glass and handed it to him. "Too hot?"

"Yeah." He choked the bite down. "That's it."

I knew that look. It was the same look my father had when he was working late in his study, and I snuck into our kitchen to make him midnight molletes. It was a look of applauding the effort but tolerating the result.

"No, really," Yearling said. "It's great."

I broke off a piece and stuck it in my mouth.

It tasted like pure salt and syrup. Something had gone wrong with the yeast, or my measuring. They were beautiful, but awful.

I pressed my fingers into that pretty sugar top, the red breaking apart. The swans had given me a chance, and I had ruined it with the wrong measuring spoons.

"Please don't take this the wrong way," Yearling said.

"Shut up," I said before he could finish.

I felt the prickle of wondering if I should go back upstairs. I may have known the chairs in my father's study as well as my own bed, but here, at the stove and oven, I was an intruder. Sometimes, on holidays, I would stir the cajeta for my mother. Sometimes Blanca gave my father slow, gentle directions, as though he were an old man who'd never handled a carnival squash.

But mostly my father and I kept to washing and drying the dishes after dinner. That was when he answered all the questions that had gathered in my head that day. Over lemon-scented water, he told me how cranberries grew. What imaginary numbers were. How rhodopsin purple helped you see in the dark.

The range, the spice jars, the sauce-stained recipes, to me, they were books of spells only my mother and sister could read.

I threw the pan dulce into a pretty, terrible-tasting heap. "I'd like to see you try."

My mother hadn't taught me baking, and my father had thought I'd be fine not learning. *You can always buy bread, mija,* he told me. *But I will teach you courage, and that's how you'll make your way in the world.*

"You serious?" Yearling asked.

This wasn't how it was supposed to go. Yearling was supposed to wake up to me wearing Blanca's dress and perfume and holding conchas so perfect the taste would make him fall in love with me.

But now I was the kind of annoyed that slipped venom onto my tongue.

"Yeah." I crossed my arms. "I am."

Yearling looked around the kitchen. "Unless you want me ransacking this place looking for baking soda, you'll have to help me."

"Fine," I said. "What else do you need?"

"Milk, butter, eggs, you know."

I took it all from the fridge.

Yearling found the flour and salt before I could tell him where they were. I watched him take them down from the cabinets, his hand missing the salt jar on the first try, sliding over to find it.

He hit the side of his hand on the cabinet shelf.

"Dammit," he said, more shrugging than frustrated, a laugh at the edge of the word.

He reached for the flour with a kind of slow caution, like he couldn't be sure if it was closer or farther than it looked.

"What are you making?" If the answer was pan dulce, this gringo could leave my mother's kitchen the same way he came in.

"Basically a big pancake." Yearling broke a few eggs and fluffed a fork through. The fork chimed against the bowl. He gave me an apologetic look that told me he hadn't meant to be that noisy about it.

"A pancake's supposed to impress me?"

"I didn't say it'd be as pretty as all that," he said, gesturing at the pan dulce. "But it'll be edible."

I shoved his upper arm.

"Hey," he said, laughing and stepping back.

His hand knocked the milk carton over. I caught it before it hit the counter.

He grabbed a dishcloth and checked that none had spilled, swearing under his breath.

I handed him the carton. "It's closed."

"Sorry," he said. "I wasn't kidding. I don't see so good off my left side." He added milk to the eggs. "Got a really heavy skillet?"

I found it in one of the other cabinets. "What's wrong with it?"

He took the handle and turned it over. "Seems fine to me."

"I meant your eye. What happened to it?"

He handed me the batter to fold. "I don't know."

The lie was so flat I almost believed it.

"Can you see out of it?" I asked.

"Not much," he said, shrugging, but I heard the faint catch in his voice. "But the other one works, so I see fine."

I held my hand on his left side. "How many fingers am I holding up?"

He turned his head to look at my hand straight on. "Three."

"That's cheating."

He cut me a look laced with more anger than I'd seen in the short time he'd been in this house. "No." He moved the pan in front of me so I could pour the batter into it. "It's adapting."

I watched the batter spread over the pan, the back of my neck hot. I hadn't meant it that way. But now I could hear how it sounded. He was doing what he had to so he could make his way through the world with the eyes he had, and I'd called it cheating. My shoulder blades pinched as I realized there was little distance between this and the señoras wondering why I couldn't be as sweet as Blanca. The straw-gold of her hair and the lighter brown of her eyes cast a glow I couldn't match even if I went everywhere with a Bible in my hands and a sugar cube on my tongue. I did what I could with the colors I was, the same as Yearling did what he could with what he saw.

I grasped at a subject change, and came up with "You can't make one huge pancake." As though I knew anything about it. "It'll burn before it cooks."

"Don't let my grandmother hear you say that. She taught me this." He slid it in, the heat billowing out. "Can I ask you something?"

I picked up the box of baking powder. "If it's about my prowess in the kitchen, I'm throwing this at you."

"I wouldn't dare," he said. He looked right at me. "Why are you letting us stay here? You don't even know me."

"We went to the same school." The school our mother took us out of when she feared the swans were coming. "I've seen you around."

"Name one time we've ever spoken to each other."

"And that's *my* fault?" I asked. Barclay Holt had given off a don't-talk-to-me sense so strong, the air around him prickled. Teachers didn't even like having to tell him to tuck his shirt in. His cousin Liam had girls waiting to see who he'd ask to the spring dances, while Barclay rolled his eyes at the glitter-painted banners announcing each year's theme.

"I never said it was. I'm just saying you don't know anything about me."

If I knew nothing about Barclay Holt, that was his problem. He had always walked through the halls like he did not want to be known, and I believed him enough to avoid him.

"I know you were a lot cuter as a bear," I said.

If the swans broke through our kitchen window and started pecking at me to shut me up, I wouldn't have blamed them.

"Fair," he said. "And that made sense, you helping an animal. But you know better now. You know who I am. Why does any of this matter to you?"

"I can't just be nice?"

"Why? I'm not the kind of guy you should be nice to."

"Oh, are we answering questions now?" I asked. "Because I have one. Why aren't you at least telling your grandmother you're okay? Don't you think she'd want to know? This whole town thinks you took off because you don't care about anyone here. Is that what you want her to believe?"

This wasn't how I'd wanted to do it. I'd wanted to be Blanca, my words sliding into the air like honey into tea. But my words were not clean, squared-off sugar cubes. They were broken piloncillo, jagged and hard even when they were sweet.

The anger came back into his face, but it wasn't so undiluted this time. Fear ran underneath it.

"Just leave it," he said, tapping the back of his hand against the oven door. "I'll be back to take it out."

Perfect, Roja. My cringing understanding of my mistake took on its own voice, echoed by the swans' calls. *This boy is your one chance to stay a girl, and you just picked a fight with him.*

BLANCA

It wore at me, the secret I kept from my sister. It wore at me as Roja and I made our beds, and I remembered dreams of blue flames and locks of hair. As we put away the schoolwork we were supposed to be doing to keep up with the curriculum, but knew we would never finish as long as the swans were here. As Page and Yearling stood at the kitchen sink, washing and drying dishes like brothers who'd grown up doing this.

In the kitchen doorway, I passed within a few inches of Page. The fine hairs on the back of my wrist stirred. But I kept my eyes off this boy I'd once seen through falling aspen leaves. This boy who'd grown up surrounded by apple trees that wore pink blossoms in spring and jewel-heavy fruit in the fall.

I folded these details of Page Ashby into me like ribbons of sugar set on my tongue. I kept them there through that afternoon, when the trees shaded our garden so it looked like early twilight, and I picked the vegetables that would go into our dinner. Yellow carrots. Green-ribbed squash. A head of purple cauliflower. Late sun slipped its fingers through the trees, brushing gold onto the epazote leaves and orange nasturtium blossoms.

I knelt in the grass alongside the vegetable beds, choosing what Page would break into pieces. She could barely boil water, but the night before, I'd seen her chop vegetables and fruit like her fingers were knives. The blade flashed with the flick of her hands, oranges spiraling into lace-thin slices, white onions falling apart into translucent stars.

Every minute, every leaf and root I reached for, rang out with how much I was keeping from my sister. The potatoes cast their quiet judgment. The brush of silverbeet leaves whispered what a liar I was. The winter squash felt heavier in my hands.

But I had to guard her from this. If Roja knew what the señora had told me, only me, she would decide she'd been right all along, that she was the marked girl. She would lose what little faith she had left that we could survive this. And I couldn't chance that, not when my own faith slipping had let the swans in.

A stretch of shadow deepened. I flinched to see whether it was Roja or whether one of our October boys had dared leave the house in daylight. But the sense came closer, and I felt it, bigger than my sister or Page or Yearling.

I looked up, and found them, their good shoes treading down the filmy cups of my mother's Mexican poppies.

Boys we used to go to school with. The kind who were friends with Liam Holt. Boys with shirts that got sent out to be laundered and then were left on bedroom floors, picked up by someone else. Boys who, if they didn't care for what their mothers decided on for dinner, went out with friends after and bought dinner again.

I stood up. "This is private property."

One of them mimicked me, repeating the words in a high, mincing register I knew from how these boys imitated their own mothers.

The wind blew against my back, fluffing hair into my face. I let it hide me.

"Come on," another said. "I know you've got something for us."

The first time this happened, I crossed my arms over my chest, worrying about whether they wanted me to do things I wouldn't tell their girlfriends about. But then they'd pulled at the purple-edged white of the moonflowers, and the hanging bells of the angel's trumpet, tucked among papery green leaves. They thought our garden grew things stronger than what they found in their fathers' liquor cabinets.

"Get out of here," I said.

They picked at the heavy stalks of gladiolus, the wine-brown cosmos, the blush flowers crowning the wild marjoram, as though they'd never seen oregano growing before.

"Just tell us which ones," one boy said. "We'll even pick it ourselves."

"You got plenty," another said. "Look at all this."

Most of the time when this happened, I ran inside. I told my mother and father, who chased them off with the yelled threat that they knew their parents.

But neither of them was here.

If I wanted them gone, I had to do it.

Being a good girl did not mean letting the things we had grown be taken by anyone who wanted them.

One boy, the one coming farthest into the garden, trampled the thorn apples, splattering their spine-covered fruit.

"We're not asking for a botany lecture." He slouched to talk to me. "It'll just take you a minute."

I shoved him with the head of cauliflower. "I said go."

The second it struck his shirt, his face shifted.

He grabbed my wrists so fast, I dropped the leaf-covered cauliflower.

My arms stiffened, but my body went slack, until he was holding most of my weight by my wrists.

I couldn't look at him. I watched his hands tighten their grip.

With the pressure of his knuckles, large and pale, I understood that this was about more than me shoving him. In the slow second of my wrists throbbing, I studied his thin fingers, his trimmed cuticles, the ends of his nails smooth and squared-off, just long enough to dig into me.

To boys like this, the world was there to offer them things. But I had said this corner of the world was not his.

Girls like me were not allowed *no*, not by boys like this. Girls like me were allowed silence and *yes*, meant to be our whole language. But this was the garden Mamá and I had grown since I was five. Maybe los cisnes would take my body, but no one was taking this.

PAGE

We were boys hiding, Barclay and me. The world outside fogged the windows like cold, or brushed the walls like lemon leaves, and we pretended it wasn't there. The things Barclay wouldn't tell me. The family who wondered what happened to me or where I'd gone.

But when I saw Blanca through the kitchen window, I didn't think about any of that.

Roja came down the stairs in time to see me grabbing Tess Holt's shotgun. I didn't even pause long enough to ask how it had gotten here. I wasn't sure I wanted to know.

"What are you doing?" Roja asked, like she didn't like the look on my face, and liked how I had a hundred-year-old Winchester in my hands even less.

I held the shotgun's forearm and slipped out the back door.

"Page," Roja said.

By the time I got behind a tree, one of Liam's friends had Blanca by her wrists. Her body hung like a doll's, her eyes wide and made darker by her spreading pupils.

So I did it.

BLANCA

A shot sounded. The blunt noise of it broke and opened, vibrating through me like the buzz of a passing plane.

The boy jumped back and dropped my wrists. I fell, catching myself on my hands.

There was no blood, on them or me. The boys all scrambled away, crushing the lavender and marigolds.

I caught a wisp of yellow hair at the edge of my vision. A gray shirt. Jeans that once belonged to me but looked so different on a body that wasn't mine.

Page stood with her back against a birch tree, getting her breath, the shotgun butt against her hip.

She hadn't shot at anyone. She'd fired to scare them off.

The footsteps, crackling against the fallen leaves and the undergrowth, faded.

Page came out from behind the tree, the shotgun's barrel down.

"Are you okay?" She offered her hand, pulling me up so hard I fell against her.

She caught my waist, keeping my chest from meeting hers.

"Sorry," she said, the first time I'd ever seen her blush.

She felt bigger than I was, in a way I didn't understand except when I was this close. Most of the time, she reminded me of a sapling, a younger oak, and I wanted to feed her until she became some stronger tree. But like this, her frame felt solid, grown, like it had roots.

Roja ran out the back door and into the garden, Yearling showing up behind her.

Page's hands left my rib cage. The points where her fingers had touched me prickled, the loss of them so sudden it felt cold.

Roja's eyes wavered between Page and the shotgun. "What is wrong with you?"

She looked back at Yearling, sweeping him into her glare.

"What did *I* do?" he asked.

"I'm betting he learned that move from you." Roja tilted her head toward Page and then back at Yearling.

"Barclay didn't teach me to shoot." Page turned to my sister. "My grandma did."

The pride in Page's face came on like the flutter of swallows' wings, bright and alive.

Roja shook her head at all three of us and went back in the house.

On his way to following her, Yearling gave us a look both guilty and amused, like he knew he was about to get talked at by Roja, but also like he was looking forward to it.

I had to grit my back teeth together to keep from yelling after him, *You don't get to do that, you don't get to laugh at my sister getting riled up.*

Another thing that made it harder to pretend I liked him.

Page was almost to the door by the time I got her name out.

"Page?"

She turned back. "Yeah?"

I studied the oiled wood of the shotgun.

"Don't do that again," I said.

"I wasn't aiming at anything. I shot up."

"You still could've killed yourself."

"I was careful. I mean, I'm not saying it was the smartest move. But with a blank, I was willing to risk it."

"They're not blanks," I said.

"I'll bet you anything."

"Tess said it was loaded. With birdshot."

"She lied." Page propped it against the side of the house. "It's loaded with blanks."

I watched it with the same prickle down my back that I watched a snake at rest. It was just a matter of time before it moved.

"She told you that so you'd be careful with it," Page said. "Blanks are dangerous. People think they can't do anything, but even blanks have gunpowder. They have a wad. Close range, they can kill people. Same as anything else."

Page's voice was level, both assured and assuring, like she was leading me through a dark room. This was a different Page than the one I'd found under the trees, trembling with the shock of realizing she was herself again.

This was the Page who'd smiled at me over her shoulder. She was that boy again, with that charm that glinted over my skin.

"Tess didn't want you handling this like it couldn't hurt you," Page said. "All guns can hurt you. Or someone else."

"I didn't even want it in the house," I said. "How do you know they're blanks?"

"Never loaded anything but. Tess used it to scare crows off her property."

"But that was before you . . ." I stopped. I couldn't say it.

Vanished. Disappeared. Were gone from us. None of the words felt right in my mouth. It was cruel of me to point out that Page had missed enough of this fall that things might have changed when she wasn't looking.

"What if it's full of birdshot now?" I asked. "You could've gotten hurt when it came down on you."

"Birdshot BBs are really dangerous when they're fired, just like anything else," Page said. "But if they've lost all their initial speed and they're just falling, take in air resistance and spin, it'll probably feel more like bad hail. I mean, I don't recommend it. It's not harmless. Especially if someone doesn't know it's coming and they look up and take it in the eye, that's a big problem. But I thought I had a good chance with the blanks. Tess rarely loads anything but. And I had to do something."

"Oh," I said, quieted by the most I'd ever heard Page's voice.

She was talking to me. I had gotten this boy talking this much.

I stayed quiet, afraid that the wrong words might break whatever spell had fallen between us.

Page took up the shotgun. "Want to hold it?"

"It's not a puppy. No, I don't want to hold it."

"Come here." Page led me past the yard and into the woods near the pond. "You're right-handed, aren't you?"

I nodded.

"Same here. Barclay is a lefty. Teaching him was a bitch."

I laughed, more from surprise than from anything funny. It was the first time I'd heard Page swear.

Page wrapped my right palm against the wood. "Dominant hand on the grip." She set my left under the barrel. "Other one on the forearm."

"The what?"

"The part that moves." Page held her hands over mine. "Don't choke it, but you gotta hold it firmly or you could end up dropping it when you fire. What eye do you see better out of?"

"I don't know."

"We'll go with right," she said. "You close one eye when you shoot, and generally speaking, you want to leave your better eye open. Barclay always went off his left, but he'll go off his right now."

"What?" I asked. "Why?"

She shook her head, and I registered the expression, another Page-look I'd hold on to. A look of saying too much and then backing away, leaving it alone. "Forget it." She got behind me. "Pretend you're aiming at that tree."

"I don't want to aim at anything."

"You're not going to shoot. I'm just showing you how to hold it. And just so you know, a hundred-year-old shotgun isn't a whole lot worse than a pistol of the same era."

"But they're bigger," I said.

"Exactly. People wave old pistols around without thinking. That's how they accidentally shoot themselves and other people. People do stupid things with old shotguns, but it takes a lot more stupid—or drunk—to throw this long of a barrel around. It's easier to see where you're aiming." Page reached over my shoulder and pressed her fingers into the skin below my collarbone. "Feel this soft, squishy part?"

"Hey."

"I didn't mean it like that." She moved her hand and settled the bottom corner of the shotgun butt where her fingers had been. "This is where you'll plant."

My sleeve fell off my shoulder.

"Sorry." She slid it back over. "Never taught a girl to do this."

I straightened my spine so I wouldn't shiver at the brush of her fingers against my back.

"You need to be able to absorb the recoil," she said.

I looked back at her. "The what?"

"The recoil. The gun'll kick back when you fire. Newton's third law." She steadied my grip on the forearm. "You gotta plant before you fire. If you don't, it hits you. At best you'll get a bruise, worst you'll break your collarbone. You want it right there while you're aiming. And don't touch the trigger unless you plan on shooting."

Still, Page was talking. Still, with that steady charm I fell under like it was August rain.

This was what I had missed when I missed the boy I had only spoken to once. This was what I was afraid the tall señora could see when she looked into me.

"Okay." I pressed my lips together to try not to smile, and I glanced over my shoulder. "I'm holding it."

"You're still wrong." Page lowered the barrel. "Point at the ground for now. Pick a rock or something." She put her cheek close to mine, her hair brushing my temple. "You line up the bead at the front with the grooves at the back. Aim for the bottom of what you're shooting at."

"Why?" I turned my head, but stopped before my mouth met her skin. "Don't bullets fall?"

"Shotguns are slow-firing. When you shoot, they kick, and that lifts the top of the barrel." She put her hands on my waist. "Plant your weight into the ground. Bend your knees."

I dug my toes into the grass, a question blooming in me as I met Page's stare.

Why couldn't this boy have blue eyes? I wondered this even as I sank into the storm-brown of her gaze, the silt color of a river stirred by melting ice. Why couldn't Page Ashby match the color the señora had told me? Why couldn't this boy be the boy I was supposed to make love me? The question spun in my brain, growing louder the more I tried to quiet it. *Why can't you have blue eyes?*

As the words rang through me, they brought the echo of another question, nearly identical. It was one I had asked myself every time I looked into the mirror, staring at the reflected brown of my own eyes. I had wondered it watching the light-eyed girls at school. I had asked it, silently, as many times as there were blond strands on my head.

Why can't you have blue eyes?

As though having blue eyes was an act I could manage if I only willed myself hard enough. If I had been a blue-eyed girl, I would have passed so easily among the fair-headed girls at school. Put together, my blue eyes and blond hair would have made anyone who looked at me skim past the shape of my nose, the line of my brow bone, the set of my eyes, every small thing that gave me away as not quite gringa.

And now I had brought that same cold examining of features to looking at a boy I wanted.

I cut the question off, hard as snapping away a tree branch. I wasn't letting the ways I'd picked myself apart touch Page. I would not let swans or señoras put cracks in the ways I found Page beautiful, especially the slate-brown of her eyes.

Page gripped the front of my right thigh. "You gotta widen your stance."

I held my breath and moved my back leg until she dropped her hand.

She set her palms on my hips. "Hips ahead of your ankles. Shoulders ahead of your hips."

I held the gun steady and let my eyes close, tilting my head down and toward her.

"Always act like it's loaded." Her voice was lower, softer. I could hear her breathing. "Never aim at anything you don't want to shoot."

My top lip brushed her bottom lip, but neither of us put enough of our weight into it, and we pulled away.

Page took the gun out of my hands. She propped it against the back step and held my forearms to look at my wrists. "Let's get you cleaned up."

"I'm okay."

"You need ice or you'll bruise."

"I'm fine," I said.

Page set the shotgun back in my grip. "Then hold this like you're not afraid of it."

I could have pretended I didn't know what I would do until I did it. I could pretend it was instinct, or impulse. But I knew what I was doing when I kissed Page on the cheek, the blush of the apple against my lips.

For that second, I convinced myself that if I did this, it would be over. All I needed was this one touch of my mouth against her skin, and I could walk away. I could let this be enough.

Page shut her eyes, my eyelashes almost brushing hers.

I took a deep drag of Page's scent. The pond water smell that stayed on her even now that she wasn't a cygnet. Oiled wood. The wet starch of the purple potatoes she'd diced that morning. I took in as much of that smell as I could hold in me.

I imagined my mother standing in the garden we'd planted together, one curling squash vine and marigold at a time. I heard myself trying to explain why my lips were on Page Ashby's cheek instead of Barclay Holt's.

Then I pulled away.

Page opened her eyes. This close, I could see the full color of them, how they were both brown and silvered enough to look gray in some light. They reminded me of the shallows near a riverbank, where the water got warm all the way to the bottom. They were both the sheen of a pond's surface and the color underneath, muddied with earth that caught the sun.

"What was that for?" she asked.

"What you did," I said, that scent thinning with the distance between us.

Page bent her head and let her hair fall in her eyes. "Don't mention it."

ROJA

Even Blanca's clothes felt softer than mine, the patterned skirts and scarves like sweeps of warm water. I buttoned on her purple sage–patterned dress, her sweater the color of early lilacs.

I could be the gentle, caring girl with hands softened by flowerbed earth. All I had to do was stay out in the garden long enough for Yearling to see me among the yarrow and wild carrot seedlings.

I checked the bleeding hearts, cupping the delicate flowers in my hands and laughing in a high way that made even me shudder. But if that was who I needed to be, the soft princess in a fairy tale, I could do it.

At least until Liam Holt came up our front walk.

I froze next to the window boxes. Yearling's cousin was about to ruin my perfect tableau.

One more reason I hated Liam Holt. Not that I needed it. His rolling laugh when he told me how fat I looked in my Christmas pageant dress still rang through my brain.

He was nine. I was six, and already good at holding grudges. I still remembered all of it. The tear-salt rage of looking down at my own stomach and thighs in poinsettia-red velvet. The seething feeling of knowing I had to just stand there and not say anything, because I was younger, and smaller, and darker, wearing pretty clothes my mother would hate me for messing up.

It all came back so clear, like the tones of the handbells that night.

I greeted Liam with "What do you want?"

He gave the withdrawing lurch of being taken aback. But it came with half a smile. "Is that how your mother taught you to talk to guests?"

"Talk about your own mother, not mine." More than once, he and his friends had come around and bothered Blanca in the back garden, poking at the moonflowers and other plants they didn't recognize and asking which ones could get them high.

"Look, I need your help, okay?" he said.

I felt my attention turn toward him, like datura opening to the night sky.

Liam Holt wanted something from me?

And thought I'd give it to him?

"You have one minute," I said. And I was only giving him that much so I'd have the minute to think. This was my chance to order Liam Holt, and all his crisp angles and cologne, out of my front yard. However I told him off had to be as perfect as a flourish of my father's fountain pen.

His face both softened and opened, like he was trying to force words that weren't coming.

"I want you to get my cousin back," he said.

I had to press my feet to the stone path to remind myself not to look over my shoulder. My eyes wanted to flash back to the house so much they stung. I stalled, asking "What are you talking about?" as I tried to guess whether he knew Yearling was there.

But he wouldn't have said, *I want you to get my cousin back*. He would have said *I want my cousin back*. Or just *Where is he?*

"I want your help finding Barclay," Liam said.

At least now I could ask the right questions.

"And what makes you think I can help you?" I asked.

"Your family," he said. "You can do things."

His voice was so earnest—he and Barclay had never looked or sounded more alike than they did that second—and I had to try not to laugh. I'd heard the whispers about us, the del Cisne girls who didn't even go to school anymore. But did Liam think we could send out swans to find people, like they were hunting dogs? If so, he was as gullible as the boys who thought we could transform ourselves into birds and then back into girls, like slipping on different dresses.

"I don't know what you've heard," I said. "But I can't make people appear."

"I'm not asking you to make him appear," he said. "I'm asking you to find him."

"And how do you want me to do that?" I asked. "He could be anywhere."

"He's not," Liam said, with the sudden force of arguing.

His shoulders dropped, his tone coming back down. "I saw him." He looked toward the trees. "The other night. Around here. I saw him. One minute he was there, and the next he wasn't."

I wove my worry into pity. "Go home, Liam."

"I know what it sounds like," Liam said. "But I mean it. I saw him."

"Get some sleep," I said, with a shake of my head like he was all grief and illogic.

"I'm serious," he said. Not the kind of *Oh come on* I heard through the windows when boys wanted Blanca to sneak out at midnight, or when they asked us to turn into swans like it was a card trick. This was a kind of pleading I didn't think rich boys had in them. "Haven't you ever seen anything you knew was real even if you knew no one else would believe you?"

I felt it. His frustration pressing down the words.

"He took off because he thinks I hate him," Liam said. "But I don't."

"Why would he think that?"

Liam watched the ground between us. "We got into a fight before he left. A bad one. He messed me up enough that I was out of school for a while."

A memory slid over my skin, the gossip my mother brought home and told Blanca. Sometimes I caught scraps of their conversations as they sat in the dim kitchen drinking manzanilla.

After Barclay went missing, Liam stayed home from school for so long that everyone whispered their theories. Liam had gone looking for his cousin and now they were both lost. Or Liam had vanished at the same time as Barclay, and the Holts were trying to keep it quiet. Or Liam had transferred to a boarding school two hundred miles away because he couldn't stay somewhere that still held the echo of Barclay's laugh, the soft imprints of his footsteps on the damp mulch, the bricks where they'd marked their heights with an old wax pencil.

The best one—the one borne out when Liam showed up again, slump-shouldered and distracted—was that his cousin vanishing had broken him open. It had left him so hollow it was weeks before he looked anyone in the eye. We all believed it. I'd never thought there was more to it than that.

I had to force what Liam had just said into what I knew of Yearling. I had to weave it in among the soft fur of the young bear he had been, and the low laugh of the boy he was now.

But this was the truth about Yearling. And of course, it only made the possibility of him being with Blanca more perfect, more beautiful. Didn't a dozen fairy tales go that way, some brutal, angry boy transformed by the love of a gentle, golden-haired girl?

"I forgive him," Liam said. "And I need him to know that. We'll never be a family again if he doesn't know that. I know if we could see him it could be different. They think he's never coming back. But I think you know how to find him."

To him, I was the witch who could grant him whatever he wanted. And a stupid one. He thought I cared about putting his family back together? On parent-teacher days at school, I could have chilled a glass of agua de fresa with Mrs. Holt's stare. She lifted her chin at my mother as though not just the rusting lockers and worn linoleum but our whole family was beneath her.

I knew what Liam either wouldn't say or didn't understand: The Holts didn't want a runaway on their hands. Boys like Yearling were dangerous. They drew attention. They caused problems. They made people talk.

"Even if I could find him, why would I?" I asked. I didn't mean to say it. It came to my lips faster than I could bite it back. Rich boys thought the whole world was waiting around to do them favors.

No anger or offense showed in Liam's face.

He shrugged, the same shrug I'd seen on his cousin.

"I'm a good person to have owe you a favor," he said. "Trust me."

It was more offer than threat.

Then, like I'd dismissed him, he turned back toward the front gate.

Just before the last stone set in the grass, he looked over his shoulder.

"I'm sorry," he said.

"For what?" I asked.

"I don't know why you don't like me," Liam said. "But there's probably a reason, so whatever it is, I'm sorry."

I wanted him to say something about the Christmas pageant, about my red velvet dress, about the words I'd never forgotten. Proof that he remembered.

But rich gringos don't remember, as least not as well as brown girls in dresses their mothers picked out.

This was as good an apology as I'd get.

"School," I said.

He turned back. "What?"

"You were"—I reached for the right word, and it came breathless as snow—"awful to me in school."

The red Christmas dress had only been the first time.

The favorite prank of his friends was stealing dust-and-dirt-covered broom heads from the janitors' closets and cramming them into my locker, some joke about me and my mother being witches. When I opened the door, the bristles knocked into me. The worst part was me having to look for Martín's blue uniform and black-gray hair in the hall after school, so I could return it, both of us hanging our heads because we could do nothing about the pieces of ourselves we'd lost to laughing boys.

They never did any of this to Blanca. On a girl like her, rumors that she was a witch made her dreamy and alluring, like gray pumpkins and fairy lights and worn, white lace dresses.

"I believe it," Liam said. "I was a lot of things before . . ."

I wanted to hear the end of that sentence.

Before we lost Barclay.

Before Barclay disappeared.

Before. Just, *before.*

Liam was the kind of boy who looked the whole world in the eye, but his stare had fallen a little. Not much, just to the road in front of his feet instead of straight ahead. I wouldn't have noticed if I hadn't been looking so closely.

"Is that why you left school?" he asked.

"No," I said.

"Then why?"

"We needed more time to stir cauldrons and cast spells."

He laughed lightly. "I deserved that."

This time he did leave. I knew because I watched, and I didn't touch the front doorknob until I saw him reach the road.

When I came back inside, Yearling's eyes were on the thin lace of our curtain linings. He had his back to the far wall, out of view of the windows. He looked like he wanted to hide behind our sofa.

I could see him working to keep himself still.

"Thank you," he said, not quite meeting my eyes.

I didn't ask for what. I didn't need to.

But I could tell from how he held his shoulders, the way he forced himself not to fidget or pace, how much he wasn't telling.

Yearling had as many secrets as my sister and I did.

YEARLING

The first time they caught us, we were eight. Liam was shoving my head into a bookshelf. I was biting his upper arm. And when we saw my aunt and uncle standing in the doorway of Liam's room, we thought we'd be in trouble forever.

But Aunt Ava laughed it off. *You two have fun. No emergency room visits, okay?*

Grandma Tess always wanted to know if I ever felt scared of my cousin, since I was smaller than he was. I didn't.

At least not then.

It was just something we did.

Liam won every time. He was always bigger, and he was as mean with me in a fight as he was protective of me at school. When a boy two years older threw my biology book under the locker room shower, Liam hit him in the stomach so hard he didn't look at either of us for the rest of the year.

But I got stronger, and faster, until we started taking turns losing, no hard feelings. Sometimes, after, we ended up on the floor, sprawled out next to each other, laughing and swearing under our breath because we were already sore. That kind of fight was worth a couple four-letter words and a moment of recognition.

It took a while, but I got big enough to look out for Liam at school the way he'd always looked out for me, the way I'd learned to look out for Page Ashby. The time Liam misspelled *February* in front of his whole class, and some guy made fun of him for the rest of the damn day, I slammed him into the lockers. He went into them at an angle, messing up his shoulder enough that he was out of team practices for the rest of the season. My father could've killed me. He said Holt sons did not act like that.

I guess my father had already forgotten the fights he and my uncle used to get in. The teachers still told the stories. Once a blond boy from a visiting baseball team called Grandma Tess white trash. That fight ended with a broken trophy case.

But now that they had money, they pretended they always had.

My father's form of punishment was leaving me off at the Lindley cranberry farm, where Olive needed extra hands for the wet harvest. It killed him that I liked it, that Olive liked me, that I stayed on. The day the cranberries got knocked off their vines became my favorite day of the year.

That was before I knew everything I knew now.

"Barclay?" Page stopped at the same floorboard I couldn't move from. He came up on my right side, already adjusting, without comment, to how my vision had changed.

I felt pinned there, stuck in this one spot in the del Cisne house where I'd seen Liam out the window.

"Hey, Barclay." Page set his hand on my back. "Stay with me, okay?"

I flinched knowing how much he saw. I never wanted to get rattled in front of Page. He didn't need it, not after everything I'd already done to him.

"I'm fine," I said, shaking my head at the floor. "Really. I'm good."

PART THREE

Woods, Feathers, Frost

BLANCA

Roja held an apple in my face. "Just a bite, my pretty," she said in her best evil-queen voice.

I shrugged her away. But the hope that maybe things with us were ordinary and good filled me. She shoved apples at me each fall. I did the same thing to her during chayote season, holding the green rind out to her.

Under the distant sound of the swans' wings, this glimmer of us felt so bright I wanted to string it on a cord and fasten it around Roja's neck. We were the sisters who looked for the late-autumn icicles we could crack between our teeth. We were the ones who agreed that white cats, not black, brought bad luck when they crossed your path. We were the girls who went out with wet hair in winter, snapping off frozen pieces. That was the Blanca and Roja I wanted to remember, the version of us I wanted to take with me when I grew wings.

Later, when the kitchen emptied out, Page asked me, "What was that about?"

"Nothing." I set the tejolote back in its molcajete. The basalt of the pestle scraped lightly against the mortar. "I just don't eat apples."

"Allergic?" Page asked.

"No," I said, careful. I'd hated apples since I first bit into the red skin and pale flesh when I was five. But to say it like that, hard and blunt, felt like an insult to the Ashbys. "I just don't eat them."

"Why not?"

"I tried one once and I didn't like it, so I told my mother and she never made me eat one again."

"What didn't you like about it?"

"It tasted"—I winced at the memory of that first bite, flat and bitter on my tongue. It gave me the same shiver as having chalk dust under my fingernails—"grainy. And too sweet. And the skin seemed rubbery to me."

"Maybe we just haven't found you the right one."

"An apple's an apple, isn't it?"

"No, not really." Page's laugh was kind, allowing, like I'd stumbled trying to say something in another language. "A baking apple's not the same as a cider apple. And an apple you eat right away is different from one you store through the winter."

"What kind does your family grow?" I asked.

"All kinds," Page said. "Autumn Berry. Snow. Scarlet. Moonglow. Apricot Apple. Maiden Blush. Blue Pearmain."

They sounded like the names of jewels or the colors of paints. Apples were as unknown to me as the bluebead lily our abuela told us not to touch, its berries as deep as midnight marbles.

"Those are all apples?" I asked.

"Best for a hundred miles around." The pride in her face and voice reminded me of how Roja talked about our father. At school she'd thrown the facts of him at our classmates like spitting orange seeds, telling them he owned three hundred books and had read them all twice, that he could hold a thousand numbers in his head at the same time.

"I've never heard of those," I said.

Page cocked her head, considering me. I felt the blush of wondering what she saw.

"I bet I could find you an apple you'd like," Page said.

"Then you don't know how much I hate apples," I said.

Yearling stopped in the doorway. "You know any Ashby will take that as a challenge, right?"

Page's smile broadened. "He's right."

I wavered with the unease of feeling caught. I needed to stay away from the boy I wanted if I was ever going to get the boy I had to win.

But if I said no to something as simple as apples, and I did it in front of Yearling, all Yearling would see was me brushing away his friend.

Either answer trapped me.

"So what do you say?" Page asked.

YEARLING

Ever since that day in the hall, the first and only punch I ever saw Page throw, I could always tell when he'd decided on something. He got that same look, the air coming off him a little charged.

I saw it now, in the del Cisnes' house. I knew by the set to Page's shoulders that he was going out. Not to pull carrots Blanca wanted from the back garden. Not even for air. Page was going out, past the line of the del Cisnes' stained-wood fence.

"Should I even ask?" I said as Page reached for the door.

Page turned his head.

"If someone sees you, it'll get back to your parents," I said.

The Ashbys didn't know how to just let him be Page. They approached with a caution that came off both respectful and distant, like Page wasn't their son but a handful of metal pins or a static-shocked doorknob.

I didn't want them in his head. I didn't want him remembering that look they gave him, the awful, frightened, evaluating look like they'd never seen anything quite like a Page Ashby before. It was the world's job to take Page as he was. Forget anyone who couldn't.

"No one's going to see us," Page said.

"Us?" I asked, in time to hear the creak of the stairs, and see the flash of Blanca's blond hair. She had a gray coat draped over her arm.

"Oh," I said.

Good for Page. I thought he was just going out to sneak apples from the Ashby orchard, but he'd managed to turn it into a date.

"Don't worry," Page told me as Blanca put on her coat. "We're sticking to my grandmother's side. You know her hours. Up with the sun."

"And asleep with it, too," I finished. "Yeah, I know."

Blanca handed Page a worn duck cloth jacket, something that was probably her grandfather's.

"Page?" I said.

"Yeah?" Page slipped into the sleeves.

The words were on my tongue. All I had to do was say them.

Good-bye.

Don't worry about me.

I love you.

Any of those would've worked. I could've given Page something to hold in his hands when he came back and I was gone again.

But it all caught in my throat, and Page was still waiting. So I gave him the only words I had.

"Be careful, okay?"

ROJA

My mother's stories of nahuales made a bear turning into a boy no more astonishing than the first kaleidoscope of butterflies in spring. But a sudden sweep of brown coming into a blue eye? That didn't just happen. Nothing remarkable ever just happened. There were reasons girls became swans. There were explanations for brown appearing out of blue.

I sifted through every article I could find from earlier that fall. The pictures of the missing boy showed a sameness to his eyes, clear even in the black-and-white of yearbook photos.

The grainy reproductions stood in for memories I didn't have. Even in a town this small, you still had people you never talked to, and Barclay Holt was one of mine. Even before he was a yearling bear, fur matted with tree sap, Barclay Holt and I had never said enough words to each other for me to look right at him.

I went to my father's books, the ones about anatomy and medicine that he pulled down when I wanted to know why my bisabuela had died, or how twins happened. I paged through for why a sliver of brown might show up in a blue eye, sudden as the first flowers after a wildfire.

The best answer I landed on was a word I didn't quite know how to pronounce, an explanation of how a blue iris could deepen to brown.

I wasn't getting anywhere being sweet. Maybe I'd get somewhere if Yearling knew I was smart enough to ask questions.

Yearling must have felt me wondering about him. He stood near the door of my father's study, where I sat in one of the worn chairs, book in my lap.

"You really don't know what happened to your eye?" I asked, looking up from the pages.

"No idea," he said.

I closed the book. "Siderosis."

"Sorry?"

"The brown showing up," I said. "The only answer that makes sense is siderosis."

"What's that?"

"Iron getting in your eye."

His smile was sad but proud, like he was enjoying how wrong I was. "That wasn't it. I promise."

I'd already gotten that far. A shard of iron catching in his eye, slowly shifting the color of the outer edge, could have happened. It wasn't impossible. But it was less likely than me pulling up a cabbage from our back garden and finding a vein of polished rose quartz underneath.

I thought of my mother reading newspaper statistics at the breakfast table, my favorite part of the morning when Blanca and I were little.

Even when they had no relevance to us: *It's safer to travel by air than by car.* (Blanca and I had never been on a plane.)

Even ones that made me a little sad: *The odds of any single clover being four-leafed are one in ten thousand.* (My sister and I had borne this one out with a hundred afternoons spent looking.)

Even ones that left my fingertips feeling cold as on December mornings: *You're twice as likely to be killed by someone you know than a stranger.*

I got up from the chair, my sweater sleeves catching static.

"But there's another kind," I told Yearling. "Hemosiderosis. That's the iron in your own body doing the same thing. That can happen. Getting hit really hard in the right place, then all the iron in your blood builds up and that's how the brown gets in."

He still didn't say anything. But I could see him tensing.

The muscles just below my stomach ached, but I ignored it.

"So what happened?" I asked.

"I told you," he said. "I don't know."

The ache grew. "How'd you get hit that hard?"

"I said I don't know."

The ache bloomed into pain.

I tried to get out of the room before I doubled over.

"You okay?" Yearling called after me.

I stumbled to the kitchen window.

A thick slice of moon hung in the sky, the outer edge hard and solid, the inner light translucent, like an orange segment. Halfway between last quarter and crescent.

Es la luna, mija, my grandmother said every month when this happened. *It pulls at you.*

"What's wrong?" Yearling asked.

"Nothing." I kept my back to him. "Where's my sister?"

"She went out with Page."

"They went out?" I clutched at my stomach. "And you let them?"

He shrugged.

I wanted to pull back the words. Any worry over Blanca belonged in a time before the swans came. Now I should have celebrated her going out into the dark with Page Ashby. She probably thought she could have both, the boy she wanted and the boy she needed to want her.

She thought of me as so little of a threat that she'd leave me alone with Yearling. She didn't know I would grab at every chance I got.

Or I would've, if my body had let me. But now I gripped the win dowsill to keep myself up straight.

"Really," he said. "What's wrong?"

"Nothing."

"That's not nothing."

"It's my period, okay?" The words came before I could stop them. But I needed him not to see me like this, the way I'd be for the next few hours, and if that didn't scare him off, nothing would.

He stood there, blinking at me.

My next wince was for both pain and my own bad luck. Yearling had to be the one boy who didn't run at the mention of blood between a girl's legs. I bit back the way Blanca's absence had left me like a feral cat, injured and wanting to hiss at strangers who got too close.

"Do you mind?" I said, trying to get him to leave.

But I didn't wait to see if he would. I gritted my teeth and slid my hand along the walls. I followed the doorframes and banisters up to my room. With each step, each clenching between my hips, my guide was the bright memory of the sister I wished I still had. How she stayed upright and gliding even through headaches or fevers or ankle sprains, her own will spun into grace. And I hoped I looked more like her, more like a girl touching the grain of the wall paint than one barely holding herself up.

YEARLING

I shut my eyes to everything around me. I let there be nothing but the shadows cast by the trees, and the memory of giving up my body to these woods, and the hope that maybe they would take me again.

I thought of how it felt, the woods making me into something other than what I was, that sense that my heart was unraveling out of my body.

They could do whatever they wanted with me.

Before I could fall deeper into that feeling of losing myself, the smell of the birch trees got into me. It was as familiar as Grandma Tess's hands on my shoulders, her sure voice, her laugh that never took on a mean edge even when it was a little at your expense.

The trees' scent came on like vanilla or cinnamon, a sugary smell Grandma Tess said was from the sun heating a chemical in the sap.

But something else cut through it, harsh and bitter, like metal, or road-salt runoff after a storm.

I opened my eyes and caught the shine of sap. It ran down the bark in drops, like the amber of the only earrings my grandmother ever wore.

I took a step toward one of the trees, not realizing I was pulling closer until the light shifted.

The sap's color darkened. The metal smell hardened. The bitter salt scent grew so thick in the air I choked on it.

It was just that second, long enough to let me believe that the sap was blood and the birch trees were a body I shared a name with. Enough that I lost the solid, leaf-bristling feeling of the ground under me. That flash of remembering my own blood, the smell of it on my skin, dragged me back into that day, the hours before the trees took me, everything I did.

Everything I thought I could get away with.

I always put my father and uncle's offices back the way I found them. If my mother noticed anything, she took it as my interest in our family's business.

Every time I had the chance, I scrambled to get the file cabinets open, take what I needed, make it all look like it had before. But rushing means mistakes. It means I must have disturbed other files or left the pages in the wrong order, or put the keys back under my father's stapler when they should have gone under his glass paperweight.

When Liam threw open the door I saw the look that said he knew.

He hit me. His right fist, my left temple.

This wasn't the kind we swapped during our usual fights. It held a blunt edge that even our worst rounds didn't carry. The pain felt hard enough to crack my skull open. This was his rage, the force and rush of it.

He held the collar of my undershirt so I couldn't go with the impact. "What did you do?"

Liam wasn't even supposed to be around that weekend. He had a paper due Tuesday. Hadn't even started it. Aunt Ava had sworn if she saw Liam out anywhere except the library, she'd cut the fuel lines in his car.

That meant I had my guard down until my father came home. He worked every weekend now. He didn't even keep up the front of going to church anymore; Grandma Tess took me instead. And my mother was at one of her afternoons out with her friends, some kind of planning event for some kind of fund-raiser I'd be expected to put on a suit and tie for, but honestly, I couldn't tell one from the next. They were always more about who fit into what size dress, whose necklace had bigger stones in it, than they were about whatever they were raising funds for. My mother's friends shamed women out of hotel ballrooms by calling their dresses *interesting*, or their houses *quaint*.

I hadn't heard the low engine of Liam's car—fuel lines intact.

Now, with him on me like this, I held my forearm in front of me, trying to throw off his next hit.

"I didn't do anything," I said.

He got me in the stomach while I was trying to block his next try for my face.

"You think I don't know you?" He gripped my shirt so my body couldn't double over.

I wasn't fighting back. Not now.

"How many copies did you make?" Liam held on to my hair.

I tried to shake my head, but my cheek just fell to my shoulder.

Liam grabbed so much of my shirt the bottom hem rode up my stomach. "What did you do with them?"

I pressed my hands to the wall to try to get my footing. He hit me in the jaw, and I stumbled.

"Where are they?" he asked.

Blood filled the left side of my mouth. I coughed to keep from choking on the salt. "Top right drawer. On the track."

He pulled the drawer out of my dresser and threw it across the floor. It hit the opposite wall, spilling socks onto the baseboard.

"That's it." I tried to stand. "I swear."

He let go of my shirt. "If you're lying—"

I fell to my hands and knees. "I know."

A hard, clattering noise from the del Cisnes' house broke me out of remembering. It pulled me back. It was the first thing I registered about that sound, how it made the weeks from then until tonight spin down until I was back here.

The second thing about that noise was that it sounded like someone falling.

BLANCA

"Where are we going?" I asked.

"You'll see." Page held a canning jar by its rusted wire handle, one of my grandfather's old ones he'd used to hold nails and wood screws. A tea light burned at the bottom, the jar letting out a faint glow the glass tinted blue.

We were far enough into the trees that I couldn't see the road.

I breathed into the bark-and-rain smell. If this was about apples, all I had to do was go with Page, try whatever kind of wild apple she thought I'd like better than the ones at the store, hate it as much as I'd hated that first one, let Page declare me a lost cause, and go home.

"Almost there," Page said.

The lantern lit nothing but the ground cover of pine needles and leaves.

Page set her hand on the small of my back. She did it like it was only to guide me around rocks or fallen pinecones. But when she did it, I was that glass jar with a candle set inside. The heart of me was as soft as the wax of the tea light.

I dug my finger between the back edge of my shoe and my heel, and fished out a pond-smooth pebble. "Does my sister know where we are?"

"I told Barclay. If she asks, he'll tell her."

The tea light burned itself out. Page blew in the jar to cool it and reached a hand in to pick it out. Her fingers glowed in the quarter moonlight.

I was light for my family. I knew what it was to be stared at, to be the girl from the brown-skinned family but who had yellow hair, sticking out as much but in the opposite way from my sister, with her crushed-blackberry hair. A güera, my grandmother had called me. Lucky, my mother called me.

But I was not pale like this, colorless as uncooked masa. It almost made me worry for Page, the way my tía worried after anyone who walked in her door. I wanted to share the color of my family with Page the same way my tía fed all visitors, worried each was too thin. It made me look for what little color Page had of her own, to be sure she was really here—the gold of her hair, the gray-brown of her eyes, her lips vivid as carved coral. Page's paleness made her strange to me, like the cream-white buck Roja and I had spotted in the woods last November.

Page's thumb crimped the metal edges over the film of wax the wick couldn't burn. She blew on it again before she tucked it into the right front pocket of her jeans. She took another tea light from the left, but didn't light it.

My eyes tried to adjust to the dark, but I could only see her hands.

She slid her palm onto my back again, her hand catching in the space between my coat and my body. My shirt rode up from the waist of my skirt.

At finding my bare skin, she pulled her hand away.

I should have chosen right then. I should have let the tall señora's words be the light that led me.

But I guided Page's hand to where it had been. Because I was stupid enough to tell myself that this wasn't too far. I was arrogant enough to believe I could pull myself back.

I would give myself up to the swans. But before I did, I wanted this one night to know Page Ashby.

Page stayed, but fidgeted. Her fingers tangled in the eyelet fabric of my shirt. The dark glass jar swung from her other hand.

She stopped me as the woods thinned, and lit the new candle. The flame took, and I made out the trees before us.

Not wild apples. An orchard's rows, stretching out into the dark.

Page took a deep draw of the air, all leaf- and fruit sugar-scented. "These are my family's trees."

The canning jar's light reached the apples on the closest boughs, as dark and heavy as garnet. They were rounder and stouter than the long ones the grocery store carried. Bursts of violet broke up the deep red.

"They're beautiful." I admired the fruit even if I didn't want to eat it, the way Roja loved the pink-red of pitahaya but hated all the seeds.

Page cupped a piece of fruit on the highest branch she could reach, twisting her hand just before she pulled it away. "You said you didn't like apples."

"I don't."

"You don't know that." She took out a small, wooden-handled kitchen knife. She'd tucked it blade-down into the back pocket of her jeans before we'd left the house, and now she set it against the apple. Her thumb held it in place as the blade glided through. She peeled the round slice away, showing a full moon of yellow fruit.

She cut another slice just below the first and offered it to me, a circle of gold ringed with violet. "Try it."

"When I said I didn't like apples, I meant I hate apples."

"If you hate this one, we can go back to your house." Page turned the fruit in her hand, showing a patch where the violet turned almost to blue. Pale dots clustered like stars over the indigo skin. The harvest-moon slice reappeared with another half turn of Page's wrist.

I bit the smallest piece I could off the edge, deciding whether I should swallow it fast or hold it under my tongue until the taste faded.

It caught between my back teeth. The juice spread through my mouth. The fruit was coarse and crisp, not soft and mealy. It broke apart on my tongue, more like a cookie, the crumbling of a polvorón, than what I thought of as *apple.* The sugar was soft, blooming from the tart flavor, like a plum the day before it turns ripe.

It almost dissolved before I swallowed it.

"This is an apple?" I asked.

"Blue Pearmain." Page took the glass jar's light deeper into the rows of trees.

"Okay. You said if I tried it we'd go home."

"I said if you didn't like it we'd go home. Did you like it?"

"Yes," I said.

Page set the blue apple in my palm. "Then we're not going home."

ROJA

I pulled myself upstairs, setting my weight against the old wood of the banister. I curled onto my bed, in the now empty room I shared with my sister.

My grandmother had given me her remedio for cramps every month. Then, before she died, she'd taught Blanca, and asked her to make it from the garden every month. And Blanca always did. It didn't matter if we weren't talking to each other, if we were arguing over who'd ripped one of our mother's old party dresses, if we each blamed the other for scaring the wrens from the nest outside the kitchen window.

Blanca had done it each month, when that slice of moon pulled at me.

Now, I tried to sleep, wondering where Blanca had gone with Page Ashby, worrying that the wringing and twisting inside me was so loud Yearling could hear it.

The pain found me. It woke me. The moon reached its fingers through the window and squeezed the pear of my womb so hard the rest of my body went numb. Through the window, the green, almost sweet scent of the woods and the cranberry bogs slanted bitter.

The orange-slice moon tightened its grip, taking my breath with it.

I got out of bed, and fell to the floor. I reached for the doorknob and tried to pull myself up along the frame. But that pear inside me grew heavy as solid glass. It dragged me down.

I crawled along the dark hallway, through squares of moonlight.

Blanca wasn't here. I would have to wait out that orange-slice moon.

My hand reached for the next plank on the dark floor, but there was only empty space. My palm hit the first stair, and my body curled into itself as I fell down the rest.

The edges scraped my limbs. The splintered corners pulled at my hair. But the moon wouldn't let me feel it. All the pain I had was in that glass pear, heating to molten.

My back hit the floor. The air went out of me.

Blanca wasn't here. Blanca would never be here again. I had lost her the day the swans came.

And before the next time this happened, they would take one of us.

Yearling said my name and slid his hand under my neck. "Don't try to move."

No. He would never fall in love with me like this, with pain pressing into me so hard I couldn't remember how to be a different girl than I was.

He'd been sleeping. I could tell from how he was dressed, or not dressed. He wore his jeans but no shirt. He'd been sleeping that way each night, that strange contradiction. The jeans and belt still on, as though he wanted to be ready for night storms or wildfires. The lack of shirt seemed like a concession, a forced effort to look like he'd just fallen asleep in his jeans.

"I'm calling someone, okay?" he said.

"Don't," I said when I could breathe enough to talk. But that pear still tensed, choking my words. "Please, don't."

"Is it this bad every time?"

"Es la luna," I said, the memory of my grandmother's voice brushing under the words. I looked for the window, but my eyes opened so little that my eyelashes blurred my vision. "It's pulling at me."

Yearling put his hand on the side of my face. "Is it always this bad?"

I fell beneath one thought, then another, then another, like layers of snow. He was Barclay. Then he was Yearling. Then he was nothing but the bear-boy, the nahual. He would hold me down and drain my blood with his fingers, or put his hand between my hip bones until the pain killed me or he was bored. He'd leave my body for the leaves to bury. He'd go after my sister next.

I opened my eyes and thought I saw the crescent moon of white on his chest, like he'd had on his fur as a yearling bear. His nahual mark. It was almost the shape of the orange-slice moon, but it lay on its side like a bowl.

This moon was closer. It could pull on me harder than the one in the sky.

The faint glow of it sent a cold heat through my body, like touching dry ice. But I couldn't stop looking at it. In the dark, his body looked almost brown, and the moon stood pale against his skin.

That moon on his chest was my warning that we would not survive each other.

He lifted my arm over his head and set it against his shoulder. He picked me up, the pear inside me wrenching at the movement. I didn't have enough feeling left in my body to fight him. It had all gathered at one point, and left the rest of me empty.

"It's okay." He held me tighter, and my cheek fell against his chest.

It's not okay, I said. But the words caught in my throat.

It was Blanca who was there when I bled for the first time. She didn't say anything about the splattered red on the bathroom tile. She didn't say anything about how I bled so much more than she did, more in one day than she bled in a whole month. And when our grandmother was gone, it was Blanca who made me her remedio.

But Blanca wasn't here. She would never be here again. And I held my throat tight against sobbing for this, because I did not want the nahual to see how weak and easily broken I was.

The bear-boy put me in the downstairs bathtub and turned on the faucet. The water went hot, reddening his fingers.

Heat and water soaked the back of my shirt. The bear-boy set his palm between my hip bones. I braced for the pain to grow until it pulled the rest of my body in.

The moon gripped me tighter whenever I tried to speak, and no sound came. So I gave in, letting my fingers uncurl from their weak fist. I let my head fall to one side. I couldn't think past tonight, or remember how the pain usually eased by morning. When the moon wrung me out like this, there was no morning.

I just wanted it all to stop. The pain, the fear of the swans, the knowledge that no matter who the swans took, I would lose my sister. I had already lost her.

The heat of the bear-boy's hand and the water turned me from glass to blood again. The moon in the sky drew back its fingers, and couldn't reach me.

He took the back of my neck in his other hand and lifted my head out of the water. "You gotta breathe, okay?" He peeled pieces of wet hair from my face.

The moon on his chest was as faint as the off-color of a scar. And the moon in the sky was waiting to pull on me again. But it had loosened its hold.

ROJA

I did the best I could, everything I could remember from watching my grandmother and then Blanca.

I knelt in the backyard, the grass prickling my ankles. I filled my hands—lemongrass, parsley, and marjoram in my right, oregano in my left, on its own, so it wouldn't bruise. It was the thing that would start me bleeding. Everything else would spur the slow unclenching of my womb.

"You're gardening?" Yearling asked. "Now?"

"I'm trying to make what my sister always makes for me." I brushed my wet hair off my shoulders. It dampened the back of the shirt I'd changed into after Yearling pulled me out of the water.

The pain had dimmed enough to let me breathe. Yearling—his heat and his hands—had driven it out. But it was waiting.

Every time Yearling spoke, asking "Can I help you?" or "Do you need me to do something?" I shushed him, fearing that one more break into my memory would make me forget something. Guelder rose. The feathery tufts of lilac chaste tree. The champagne-bubble fluff of fairy candle.

But he kept asking, so I told him, "Can you boil some water?"

He nodded once and went back into the house.

A blunted sound came from the kitchen. Probably Yearling bumping into the counter on his left side. I knew exactly where he was, that edge that stuck out a little farther than it seemed like it should. I saw the same out of both eyes, and I'd hit that counter enough times that I could still feel the bruising.

I filled my palms with the blush cups and sun-yellow centers of evening primrose. And when I saw Yearling at the stove, his careful hands adjusting the gas flame, I stared without meaning to.

He looked up. "What?"

"Nothing," I said. "It's just usually my sister doing this with me."

"My grandmother says real men know their way around a kitchen."

I spilled the leaves and blossoms onto the counter. "I'm sorry. For what I said about you and Tess."

"It's okay," he said.

"It's just"—I grasped for the next words, but the only way I knew how to close the sentence was—"my father."

"What about him?" Yearling asked.

"If I were you, and Tess was him, nothing could stop me from seeing him." I threw leaves into the almost-boiling pot. "Blanca's the same way about our mother."

Standing at the stove, I remembered the last time I'd been in this kitchen with Yearling.

I swirled a wood spoon through the water, stirring up the green leaves. "And I'm sorry I said that other thing."

"What thing?" he asked.

"When I said you turning your head was cheating. I didn't mean it. I don't know what I'm talking about. Don't listen to me."

He laughed. "Don't worry about it."

I liked his laugh. It wasn't loud, but not quiet like he was just letting air through his teeth either.

"I'm sorry I didn't notice," I said, "you know, that you couldn't see out of that side."

"It's not like I expected you to just guess. I'm glad you know now, though."

"I'm still sorry." The steam off the water heated the wooden handle. "I don't know anything about what it's like to be you."

"And I don't know what it's like to be you," Yearling said.

The way he said it was so plain, so unguarded, that the spoon slipped from my fingers. The bite of lemongrass and passion flower sharpened the air between us.

"I don't understand you," I said, my breath pressing up under the words, giving away my wonder.

"There's not much to understand."

"That's not true," I said. "Your family"—I thought of overhearing the Holts at a back-to-school night, how they'd said there were some people whose names just weren't worth learning, and how I was pretty sure they meant people like my mother and father—"you could be like them. And you're . . . this, instead."

"Thanks?"

"I mean that as a good thing," I said. Every time I talked to Yearling I felt like I was reaching into some smoke-glass jar, grabbing at words I couldn't see and hoping they were the right ones. "You're not what I expected a Holt to be."

"That I'll take as a compliment." He took the spoon from me and drew it through the water. "You should eat something. All this won't get into you unless you eat."

I shuddered. This was the only time each month I didn't want to eat. Food reminded me of the dreams I had when I had cramps, fever dreams where my body was made of the things in my mother's kitchen. Soft apples were my heart, pomegranate seeds the tender alveoli in my lungs. Queso fresco was the marbled fat padding my hips and breasts, Oaxacan string cheese my ligaments. The fibers of squash and eggplant were my veins. A pear soaked in red wine held the cup of my uterus. When I woke up I couldn't eat, and ever since, whenever the pain came, I didn't want anything that looked like anything else. Even cooked corn tortillas were the paler skin on my stomach.

But there was something I ate sometimes, under the last quarter moon, that looked like no part of my body.

"Are you in the mood for ice cream?" I asked.

"That's what you'll eat?"

"Yeah, but it has to be the blue kind."

"That really fake-looking turquoise stuff? Don't tell me that's your favorite."

"Just this time of month." I pushed myself off the counter, the space between my hips pinching. "What kind do you want me to get you?"

"What?" he asked. "You're not going by yourself."

"Hey, you want to be older brother to someone, go find Page."

"You sure you want to go out?" he asked. "You don't look so good."

"Thanks," I said.

"I didn't mean . . ." I couldn't tell if he was blushing or if it was the bloom of heat off the stove. "I meant I can make you something. I promise I can do more than cast-iron pancakes."

"Trust me," I said. "There's nothing you can make me I can eat right now."

"You're still not going alone."

"You're just planning on taking a stroll with me?" I asked. "Someone will see you."

"No," he said, the word so sure I believed it, "they won't."

BLANCA

"You gotta bite into this." Page picked another apple, striped with light green and red like amaranth.

I swallowed to clear the taste of the other apples from my mouth.

First, I lost the mild sugar of the Sweet Sixteen, mixed with the faint acid Page said helped protect it from fire blight. Then the Apricot Apple faded, a taste like the white wine my mother let me and Roja try.

Now the strawberry apple, peridot-green with a cloud of pink-red, flooded me with the scent of dark garden roses. Page picked it gently, like she was cradling a bird.

"The skin bruises easy," she said. "Usually we need gloves for this one." Her fingers pulled the knife through, handling this apple even more lightly than the others.

She set a wafer of fruit on my tongue.

"It's like roses," I said, the taste bright in my mouth.

"Apples are related to roses," she said. "Pears, too. My grandma used to put bowls of these in the house instead of flowers. They make a room smell nice just as well."

Its aftertaste stayed. My mouth was full of rose petals.

Page crouched to the stream at the edge of the orchard and dipped another apple into the moving water.

"Here." She held the fruit, beaded with cold drops, to my lips.

I set my hand over hers. My teeth broke the skin, releasing the scent of gardenias and citrus trees. The spray of juice, still chilled from the river, bloomed into the taste of grapefruit and raw sugar.

I swallowed and opened my eyes to Page's shy smile. My gaze crawled along hers to the apple. My bite had exposed a circle of fruit, bright and pink as French tulips.

"It's not your lipstick." Page's mouth fit into the space mine had made. She bit it in almost the same place. The fruit stayed just as pink.

"See?" She took my hand and cupped my palm around the apple again.

"It's beautiful."

"They call it Pink Pearl," she said. "We used to make applesauce with it because of how pretty it'd come out."

I held it near my nose so I could memorize its scent, like candied violets and sugared lemon peel.

Page interlaced her fingers with mine. Both our palms were sticky with the apples' sugar. "I got a couple more, if they're ready. I'd have to check."

"Page."

She pulled me through the trees, bending the boughs out of the way so they didn't catch my hair. "You'll like them."

She hung the glass jar's rusted handle on a low branch.

"This one's called Maiden Blush, or Lady Blush, depending on who you ask." She reached up through the branches, her sleeve rustling the dense leaves. "It catches fire blight easy, but if it doesn't, it keeps its color, even when you dry it."

A few feet away, a shotgun round clicked into position.

Page froze, her arm still in the tree.

The sound repeated in my head a half dozen times. My body wouldn't move. My veins were growing through the soles of my feet and into the ground, tangling together with the tree roots.

"You kids think you can just run through here whenever you want?" A woman's steady steps crushed the fallen leaves.

Page grabbed me and got me in back of her, her body blocking mine. "Don't."

An old woman stepped into the ring of the candle's light. "Page?"

Page's breath wavered. "Grandma?"

ROJA

I slid into it like a too-hot bath, ignoring the prickling of the water. But now that I was in, the understanding felt like flinching awake.

Barclay Holt and I were stealing a car.

I voiced this objection as he opened the passenger side of the old four-door and waited for me to get in.

"Not stealing," he said. "We're just taking it out for a few minutes."

"This isn't your car," I said. In the dark distance, I could make out the cranberry bog. The dulled mint green on the car's finish told me the rest. "This is Olive Lindley's, isn't it?"

He reached under the driver's seat and found the keys.

"You've done this before," I said.

"She used to let me borrow it."

"Without asking?"

"Well, no, not if you want to get technical."

When my grandfather was still alive and working on her farm, there wasn't a week I didn't hear Olive's laugh, rough and generous. Now I only saw her around town, the red-blond of her hair bright against her sun-toughened skin. She dressed the same as her husband and the other men who worked the farm, the same as Abuelito had. Plaid shirts, jeans, work boots.

But at this moment, all I could think of was the look on her face when she got mad. She had a stare that could frost over a crop of tomatoes, one that kept boys from school off her land.

"Do you even know how to drive?" I asked.

"I got my license. And before that I drove the tractor-harvester."

The diesel engine gave a damp purr, gravel crackling under the tires.

I took what little money I had on me and wouldn't need for ice cream, and tucked it into the visor.

"What are you doing?" he asked.

"If I have to be a thief, I'm at least going to be a considerate one. She'll see the gas gauge is down."

"For five miles there and five back? No, she won't. Nice thought, though."

"If you put so much as a scratch on this car," I said, "I will tell her exactly who did it."

"She'll never even know," he said.

I curled into myself. The pain was waiting, but I could still feel the heat of his hand on me, keeping it back.

Yearling turned his shoulder to back out, and eyed the space between my hip bones. "Does this happen a lot?"

"Every month."

He whistled softly.

We left the Lindley farm behind us.

I looked back at the bog. "So tell me something."

"You want to be more specific?"

"What was a Holt doing working on a cranberry farm?"

"That was my dad trying to teach me a lesson," he said. "I got into a fight with this guy at school. And I got caught."

I gripped the edge of the seat as Yearling pulled onto the road.

He moved his head even more than the driving handbooks said to. He checked over his shoulder even when he wasn't changing lanes. As his gaze moved between mirrors, his eyelashes flickered like Blanca's when she was dreaming.

"What are you looking for?" I asked.

"Nothing," he said, his voice flat. "It's what I have to do to see everything."

I sank down in the front seat, wondering how many stupid things I'd have to say before I stopped forgetting how this boy worked, the adjustments he had to make to catch the light and edges of the world around him.

After a few miles, he pulled off the road again.

The front left wheel bumped the curb.

He cringed. "Sorry."

A neon sign flickered in the shop's window, letting off the only light in the parking lot.

I unbuckled my seat belt. "What do you want?"

"I don't care."

"You can't not care. It's ice cream. Everyone cares."

"I'll eat anything that's not pink."

I rolled my eyes. "Because real men don't eat pink ice cream?"

"Because pink ice cream tastes like cough syrup."

"Tell that to my sister. Her and her strawberry milkshakes." Of course Blanca, with her hair like lemon cotton candy, would love something that sweet, that pastel.

"Strawberry's the worst."

"Unless it's the kind with strawberry pieces in it."

"Exactly."

I opened the door. "I'll be fast."

"You sure you can walk?"

"Better than you drive."

"Hey." He put a hand to his chest like I'd wounded him, but a laugh broke up the word. "I'd like to see you try Olive's water reel sometime."

He slumped down far enough in the driver's seat that anyone watching would think I'd come here alone.

The bell on the shop door rattled when I went in. The lights were on, the freezer case unlocked. But no one was behind the counter.

"Hello?" I said.

The bell on the door sounded again.

"Guess they went out to milk the cows," said a boy who came in behind me.

I turned around and matched the voice to Liam Holt's face.

"Are you following me?" I asked.

A girl my age came out from the back. She straightened her necklace. "Hi, Liam."

"Hi," he said, the kind of halting "hi" people gave when they didn't remember someone's name. The "hi" Mimi Craft's mother always gave my mother because she thought my mother and Mrs. Becerra-Vasquez looked alike, and she could never remember who was who.

I sorted through pints in the freezer case, wanting Liam to order and leave first.

I found my blue ice cream—it was either "blue moon," "angel

blue," or "engelblau" depending on who'd packed and scrawled on the carton—and looked through the other kinds.

The girl watched me deliberating. "Our cotton candy flavor's pretty good."

"No," I said. "It's pink."

"What?" Liam asked.

"Nothing." I grabbed four different pints and set them on the counter, taking a guess at what my sister wanted and what Page liked.

"Are you eating all of that yourself?" Liam asked.

"Mind your own business."

I went back to browsing the freezer case until Liam left.

"How much is that?" I asked the girl, watching Liam get in his car.

The girl stacked the pints in a paper bag. "He took care of it."

"He did?" I looked out into the parking lot.

"He's just like that." There was no jealousy in her voice, just pride, like Liam was something to put in a town brochure. A three-hundred-year-old tree. A train car made into a house. A swing set that had withstood gale-force storms and termites.

I held the bag away from my body so it wouldn't take the heat from between my hips. "He's just like something."

Liam waited outside, the engine of his shined-up car humming. Its sound was a dull whirr, not the loud, throaty rhythm I loved hearing every time Olive Lindley drove by.

"Do you need a ride?" Liam asked.

"No," I said. "Thanks for the ice cream."

"Are you ever going to stop hating me?"

I thought of his friends, of brooms shoved into lockers. "Didn't you ever hear that absence makes the heart grow fonder?"

"Then I'd better start now." He shifted into gear. "This could take a lot of absence."

I laughed before I could help it.

He pulled onto the road.

I waited for his taillights to fade, then looked for Yearling slouched down in Olive Lindley's driver's seat.

He wasn't there.

Or in the backseat.

Or anywhere near the car.

I scanned the neon-lighted front of the ice cream place, the closed hardware store, the pharmacy my father did the books for that had moved to the center of town. "Barclay?"

YEARLING

I'd shaken myself out of it the last time I'd seen Liam. Page had said my name, and I'd come back.

But now, hiding in the front seat of Olive's car, seeing my cousin across the dark parking lot, I couldn't do it.

Especially not after Roja asked how I started working the cranberry harvests. I'd told her I'd gotten into a fight, but not why.

When Liam found out, he had yelled at me for three solid minutes. *How stupid can you be? Right there in the middle of school?* But when he was done yelling at me he nodded once, the closest he ever got to saying *thank you*. I nodded back, because for once I had gotten to take someone down for Liam instead of him always doing it for me.

Now it was a memory that bit into me. It felt as ancient as a fossil, something from another time, when Liam didn't see me as something he had to destroy.

Remembering it made the memory of everything else spin forward. I lost the hundred times we'd thrown punches for each other. I lost the sound of Liam's laugh, so loud I could hear it through walls. I lost how I was the only one he ever told the truth about navel oranges; Aunt Ava thought he didn't like them when really he was afraid of the little node of the twin fruit.

Everything I loved about Liam vanished into the thickening dark of what I'd done. Before I could pull myself back, the ache came on in my left temple, and I was slipping into the day the woods took me.

I remembered Liam's grip crumpling the papers I'd been hiding, him asking, "What were you doing with this?"

Instead of in the parking lot, I was on the floor of my room, saying, "I just wanted to know what happened."

"It's none of your business," Liam said.

"Yes, it is." And I remembered how much, at that moment, I needed to shut up. Even as I said the words, I had known I needed to shut up. "It's yours, too. It's our whole family's business. Don't you at least want to know?"

"It's not yours to know." His fingernails dug into the skin above my collar. "You're leaving this alone. Tell me you're leaving this alone."

I hated myself for it, how I buckled, how I let the fear put cracks in my voice. But I said it. "I'm leaving this alone."

I guess I didn't sell it enough for him to believe me.

Again, I tried to shrug out of the memory. I slouched down deeper into the driver's seat so I couldn't see Liam anymore.

But the memory kept going. It played, and it trapped me inside me.

I grabbed at it, trying to shove it back into the dark. But it clung to me. It dragged me down.

It wasn't that I hadn't thought of it since the day I went into the woods. But then, I was part of the woods. I was birch trees. I was a yearling bear. I did not have to remember this in my own body. And when I was something other than what I was, the memory didn't have to be mine. It could belong to anyone.

Now I was me again. The memory wove through the body I'd been in when it happened, and I couldn't get away from it.

It made me understand how much it was mine. It forced me back into the feeling of Liam's rage swirling around me. It made the air so thick it seemed like it was turning to water.

I didn't fight back. Not that day.

"Come on." Liam had pulled me up by the back of my shirt collar and grabbed my neck like a cat's scruff. "Let's go."

Then I was caught in the part where he dragged me outside. He took me past where my mother's carefully chosen landscaping ended, and into the trees.

The sight of Roja talking to Liam brought me back.

This was not the front of the del Cisnes' house. This was not broad daylight. This was my cousin in a dark parking lot with a girl who liked asking questions. And if she asked ones he didn't like, he'd be out of his car before I could get to her.

When I'd asked questions he didn't like, Liam became someone I didn't recognize.

I got out on the far side of Olive's car and went around in back of the storefronts. Even with the spill of neon light, the shadows were thick enough to hide me. I could do this.

But the memory still followed me. It put me in the moment when the light from our parents' houses faded behind us.

I'd tried to shrug Liam off. But he had a few inches and a lot of muscle on me. My body went where he wanted it to.

He stopped. I kept moving forward for a second, and his fingers twisted against my skin. He balled his other hand into a fist and hit me in the stomach.

"You're telling me the truth this time." He let go of my neck, and I fell. Pine needles pricked my back. Dead leaves cracked under my weight. The pain opened out through my ribs.

"How many copies did you make?" He stood over me and grabbed my collar, lifting my back off the ground.

I held my throat tight. Had he gone through Grandma Tess's house when she was at church or the store? I pictured him turning up the envelope I hadn't even told her I'd hidden in her house.

When Liam slammed me down again, one of my shoulder blades hit before the other. My arm caught under my back, wrenching my shoulder and elbow.

I caught my cheek between my teeth just before he kicked my side. My ribs let out a cracking sound like tree branches about to fall. The way it hurt was so sharp and sudden it felt like going into an iced-over pond.

Liam stumbled at the noise and stepped back. I held my rib cage with my free hand. Blood warmed the inside of my mouth. My breathing shortened to gasps because full breaths spread the pain through my chest.

Then he'd started hitting me again. And I prayed to God to help me stay still and hold my breath and not flinch at the bleeding from my mouth and temple. I prayed for my muscles to stop bucking against the pain and just let it weigh me down.

I let my eyes close. My body went slack. Blood from my nose stung my upper lip.

Liam stopped. I didn't move.

"Barclay?"

I clenched my stomach to keep from coughing. Coughing would spray blood on him and let him know I was awake. He'd think I had spat at him. He'd pull my hand from my chest and crack the rest of my ribs. This wasn't the cousin I'd fought with my whole life.

This was the cousin who saw me as a traitor.

"Barclay?" He backhanded me, lighter than usual.

I tried to pull myself back to now, to where I was standing at the edge of the parking lot. I tried to anchor myself in the cold shapes of the trees above me, the feeling of the asphalt under my feet, how it cracked and got rough-edged where it gave way to dirt. Anything I could grab on to that would keep me in tonight and not in that day. If I could just stop myself from remembering the rest, it could be almost like it didn't happen. If the memory just stopped, Liam could leave me there, and that would be it.

But I couldn't stop it, even weeks later, even after losing my own body and getting it back. That day had the kind of dragging weight I couldn't fight.

It wrenched me back into it, making me remember in a way so bright and sharp it was like I was on the ground again, trying to stay still. It was the same as a dream, things happening that I couldn't stop.

In that moment of Liam shaking me, I let my head fall to one side like it would if I was dead.

But I wasn't dying on his terms.

He grabbed me by my shirt again. "Barclay." He clutched the side of my neck and felt for my pulse. His hand bore into my stomach to see if I was breathing.

The pain in my ribs tried to make me open my mouth for air.

But I held my breath so my body wouldn't move. I didn't shudder at the blood from my mouth dripping onto my jaw.

Then I came back to life, my body deciding for me.

I went for him. I got him down on the ground before he understood. And I started hitting him, driving my fists into his jaw until I couldn't tell how much of the blood on my knuckles was his and how much was mine.

In that minute, he wasn't just Liam, the cousin who'd turned on me when all I did was try to find out what our fathers didn't want us to know. He was my uncle, Liam's father, who'd buried everything so deep, even I had a hard time getting at it. Liam was himself and our fathers, and he was this family, all of us, all the things we'd ever done.

I didn't stop. I hit him again, fists into his jaw over and over, until he grabbed a rock and drove it toward my temple.

It shook me out of it, the pain cracking down my cheek. It wasn't a right-on hit, but it got me at an angle hard enough that I felt my skin break.

The force knocked me back.

Liam sat up, jaw looking knocked loose, blood from his nose soaking his lips and chin. His eyelids were already swelling. Those eyes looked at me not with rage or even pain but with disbelief, as though I was some unfamiliar copy of myself.

Then I left him. I left my cousin there, him watching me with this shock, this lack of recognition, like I had become something else right in front of him.

I had hidden from all this for half of fall, in branches or storm-charged nights or the body of a yearling bear.

But now that I was back in my own body, I would never get away from this. The ways I'd turned on my own family. The places I'd bruised and how my skin still remembered. What I'd done to my own cousin, and what he would've done to me if I hadn't.

This was the body I now couldn't keep still. It wouldn't take the even breaths I wanted it to. Its heart wouldn't steady.

I crouched down in the dark, trying to get back the feeling of being a bear, closer to the ground. I raked my hands into my hair, trying to pretend it was fur. I bent my head, but that made breathing harder. It just deepened the pain in my forehead.

I couldn't breathe enough to keep everything still. It darkened and shifted in that nightmare way, like light was water that could all drain away at once.

"Barclay."

The sound of my name startled me. It came with her hands on me.

She cleared my hair out of my eyes. "Can you look at me?"

I tried to come back to her, but I couldn't. I was too deep in that day, the smell of my own bruises, the feeling of cuts on the backs of my hands.

"I can't," I said.

"Can you talk to me?" she asked.

I tried to level my breath out enough to say more than two words, but my lungs went tight, like muscles knotting. "I don't know."

Now I heard her breathing, slower and off-rhythm from mine.

"Tell me something about Tess," she said.

I shut my eyes, because I thought that maybe if I forgot that heavy, dulled feeling in my left temple, I would forget what had happened to my left eye, how it had happened, the force Liam brought down on me like he never had in our old fights. But closing my eyes just made me go back there, with Liam holding my shirt collar.

"Like what?" I asked.

"I don't know, I don't know her," Roja said. "You tell me."

She put her hands on the side of my face and made me tilt my head up.

It let me breathe a little deeper. But my breathing didn't slow. My lungs felt as small and useless as worn-out party balloons.

"Tell me something about her from when you were a kid," she said.

I braced my hands harder against my knees. "Like what?"

"Anything you remember."

"I don't know," I said. "She used to tell me and my cousin these stories."

"What kind of stories?"

Grandma Tess had never seen the point of softening fairy tales. She told me and Liam and our second cousins about doves who pecked out eyes, millstones that fell from the sky, swans that saved their sisters from being burned as witches.

"They were just stories she heard growing up, I guess," I said.

"Tell me one."

"Now?" I had to breathe deeper to get the word out.

"Yes," she said, and right then the lack of pity or sympathy in her voice felt like the best thing anyone had ever done for me. "Now."

"Are you trying to distract me?" I asked.

"Yes."

"It's not working."

"Well, maybe if you tried telling me one of the stories it would."

I narrowed my eyes at her without lifting my head. But in that second of glaring at her, my annoyance became something I could hold on to. It was a way out. It broke me out of being frozen. It let me leave this place I was stuck in, afraid to move because I still hadn't gotten used to how the world looked.

"Fine," I said.

I followed my memory of those stories, looking for "The Water Nixie" or "The Almond Tree." I tried to remember how "The Griffin" or "The Star Money" or "The Crystal Ball" went.

But the only one I could grab hold of was the one that had held on to me, the one that had been written so deep into me that the woods turned me into part of it.

"Snow-White and Rose-Red." The story of two sisters who were as different as their names. Even as a kid I could tell Grandma Tess was using it as a less-than-subtle way to remind Liam and me to get along.

The day I went into the woods, it was the story that chose me.

I took in the fullest breath I could get. "There're these two sisters, Snow-White and Rose-Red, and they have pretty much nothing in common but they love each other anyway. And one day they get to know this bear. And they let the bear into their house, and they use hazel rods to knock the snow out of the bear's fur. But they get kinda rough, and they keep beating him with them, and they're not trying to hurt him, they just don't know when to stop until he tells them."

"Why?" Roja asked.

"I don't know." I took a slower breath. "I guess the point is everything good can turn into something else."

"*That's* the kind of moral your grandmother wanted you to get out of her stories?"

"I didn't make it up, okay?"

What I didn't say was that it was true. Everything you mean well can twist and become something else when you're not looking. Everything has an edge if you know to watch for it.

"What happens after that?" Roja asked.

"The bear goes away, and then there's this goblin or wizard or something, I don't remember what he was."

The story wasn't holding together. I had crushed it in my careless hands and all I had were pieces that didn't fit.

But Roja just held on to me and asked, "What happens next?"

"The bear's really a prince who got turned into a bear, and he doesn't turn back into a prince until he and Snow-White and Rose-Red defeat the wizard, but then he does." I settled into the unexpected rhythm of my heart rate slowing. "I know, it doesn't make any sense."

"These kinds of stories *never* make any sense," she said. "Take the Little Mermaid story. She dies and turns to seafood . . ."

"Sea-*foam* not seafood."

"Fine, she turns to sea-*foam*, because she can't bring herself to kill the prince, but what's simpler than that? He forgot her. He didn't even remember the girl who rescued him. And now she has the enchanted dagger. If it was me, I would've just stabbed the bastard."

I almost choked on my next laugh. "Why am I not surprised?" I got it all out at once, not gasping between words this time.

The pressure lifted off my collarbone.

"You're okay." Roja held my hands. "You're okay."

ROJA

I pulled the car back to where the Lindleys kept it, slowing over the gravel.

When I set it in park, Yearling still wouldn't look at me. But he turned his head just enough to leave the sheen on his eyes visible. A film of water caught what little light there was.

He was coming down. But seeing Liam tonight had left him rattled in a way it hadn't in daylight.

"Thanks," he said.

"For listening to the strangest fairy tale I've ever heard?" I asked.

"I told you," he said. "Sorry for getting like that."

"Can we call tonight even?"

"I'd like that."

I looked at him, finding where the two colors met. Blue like Abuelito's jeans. Brown like the star anise my mother added to her mole rojo.

This was my chance. I knew it with the same certainty I knew the swans were somewhere in the dark.

I put my hand to his shirt where I thought the moon was. I traced its outline.

Even through his shirt, I could feel it, smooth like scar tissue, warmer at the edges and cooler in the center. The one mark the woods had left on him.

I brushed my thumb over his lower lip and felt a tiny patch of smoother skin, a scar. Then I stayed still. He had to be the one to come closer.

He did. It was slow, but he did.

My eyelashes grazed his cheek, and his brushed my temple.

I waited for one of us to move so I could put my mouth on his. I thought of my tongue finding that scar on his lip.

A rough sound startled us both away from each other, the hard break of a throat being cleared.

We looked up.

Olive Lindley stood in front of the car, arms crossed. The moon bleached the edges of her hair. She set her stance, the heels of her boots stirring the gravel.

For a minute I wished it was Blanca and me in the car. When one of us was covering for the other, we could almost get our stories straight without talking.

Yearling got out of the car, slowly. He hung his head, pieces of his hair shielding his eyes.

I followed.

I held out a pint carton. "Ice cream?"

"No," Olive said. "How about you introduce your friend?"

Yearling tossed his head to get his hair out of his face, taking a slow breath to keep himself from looking down again.

Olive studied him. I could hear from how her tongue clicked that she was holding it against her cheek.

"Huh," she said, the sound like a conclusion. No further questions needed. I wondered if she'd felt him this whole time, a nahual stalking the woods and the cranberry bogs.

She held up her hand.

Yearling threw the keys. He was three feet off, but Olive stepped to the side and grabbed them out of the air.

"You need these again, you come to me, you understand?" Olive said.

Yearling nodded.

She gave back one curt nod. I'd seen that nod on him. And I'd seen it before on Olive. I just hadn't registered how similar they were, how Yearling must have picked it up from her. That flash of similarity made me count everyone who'd been family to Yearling when his own hadn't bothered. Page. Tess. Olive. He'd had to go looking for what Blanca and I had always gotten from Mamá and Papá, that sense that we were as rare and valuable as star sapphires. They'd given us that with every careful examination of our kindergarten artwork, with every patient explaining of a recipe (Mamá to Blanca) or page in an astronomy book (Papá to me).

"You ever want your job back, you say the word." Olive looked toward the bog. "I've never seen anyone take to corralling berries as fast as you."

"Thanks," Yearling said.

Olive let out a slow breath. It sounded like an understanding that Yearling would never come back.

"You look good, kid," she said.

Yearling's nod this time was ducking, embarrassed.

We were slipping into tree cover deep enough to keep out the moon, when I heard Olive call my name.

I turned back.

"Take care of him, okay?" she said.

I couldn't say no to Olive's face. This was the woman who'd given my grandfather good work, work that didn't mean extra hours unpaid, or crop dustings that made his coughing come up with pin-prick sprays of blood.

I did what I would've done no matter what Olive Lindley asked of me.

I said, "I will."

I looked for that panic in Yearling again, the hard, uneven breathing, him bracing his hands on his knees.

But seeing Olive didn't leave him like that. He came inside with me, and for the few minutes of eating from ice cream cartons together, I could pretend things that seemed unlikely as fairy tales. I could pretend he and Page had never gone missing. That the swans in the woods were just birds, that Blanca and I didn't matter to them.

That the señoras had never made us rivals, and my sister had never let them.

I knew I needed to draw him closer to me. But I couldn't break this, the stillness of right now. Not when I could feel pain waiting at the center of me. Not when I'd just gotten him breathing again.

Yearling let his head fall against the back of the sofa, studying me.

"What?" I asked.

"Your tongue's blue."

"It's the ice cream." I held out the carton to him.

"No, thanks."

"Fine." I tapped the edge of the carton he was holding. "Enjoy your boring ice cream."

"I like boring ice cream. Food's not supposed to be blue."

"Blueberries are blue."

"Have you ever actually looked at a blueberry? They're kind of purple."

"You sit around looking at blueberries?" I asked. "Hard to believe you weren't more popular."

"Ouch," he said, the word cut through with laughing.

For that minute, the most remarkable thing about him was not that the forest had taken him in like a stray fox. It wasn't even how much he was like the nahuales in my mother's stories, a wrathful soul in the body of an animal.

The marvel of him was that he was here, with me and not with Blanca.

The phone rang.

I grabbed it before it finished its first ring.

"Get your ass over here," the voice on the other end said.

I sat up. "Who is this?"

"Tess Holt."

My throat felt stripped of water and sound.

"Both of you," she said, "over here, now."

"What?" I asked.

"You heard me. Lynn Ashby's house. Now."

"My sister's not home." I leveled my voice. "But when she gets back—"

"Not her and you 'both of you,'" Tess cut me off. "You and my grandson 'both of you.'"

She hung up.

"What's wrong?" Yearling asked.

"You want the good news or the bad news first?" I asked.

"Bad first," he said. "Always."

"Great." I threw a jacket at him. "Because right now that's the only kind I've got."

BLANCA

Yearling stopped just short of Lynn Ashby's threshold.

"Don't be mad at her," he said, as though Roja needed to be shielded from two grandmothers. "I asked her not to tell anybody."

"Get in here." Tess grabbed his upper arm and pulled him past the doorway. The force of her words made him wince, so that when she pulled him into the kind of hard hug I'd seen fathers give sons, he startled.

Tess didn't cry. She didn't seem like the kind of woman who ever did. Lynn Ashby did it for her, tears holding to the corners of her eyes like drops of opal, the way they had when she recognized Page.

Lynn Ashby, the woman whose house Tess Holt now lived in. When Page and I had first followed Lynn into the house, I'd passed wooden frames showing Lynn and Tess, sometimes together, sometimes on their own. They stood among the apple trees in sepia. Tess climbed an orchard ladder in black-and-white, her fingers inches from an apple that looked as dark as onyx on film. In an old one, Lynn sat on the edge of a swimming pool in a bathing cap and one-piece, the colors in the photograph faded so the water had become light as a robin's egg. Only the red of her lipstick had stayed bright.

Another, more recent, showed Lynn resting her cheek in the hollow of Tess's shoulder, her meringue-white hair brushing Tess's turtleneck. The sky behind them was gray, their eyes lightly shut. I could almost see the wind fluttering their eyelashes and hair. There was no mistaking their soft, eyes-closed smiles. It wasn't a look shared by sisters or cousins.

Page toed the floor as she whispered to Yearling, "I didn't tell them about you."

"You didn't have to," Yearling said when Tess let him go. "She just knows."

"Damn right, I do." Tess shooed him toward the kitchen, eyeing Page to go with them.

Page ducked her head further and followed.

"You two make yourselves at home," Lynn said.

I gave her a thank-you smile as she guided the kitchen door shut behind her.

As the door met the frame, I let the smile fall.

Roja sank onto a sofa the color of mustard seeds. "I hope it was a really good apple."

I sat down next to her, fluffing up the sofa cushion as I landed. "Not helping."

"Oh yeah?" Roja looked through a stack of old magazines. "What *would* help right now? We're done, you know that, right?"

"What are you talking about?" I asked.

"We're the del Cisne girls"—she tipped the magazine toward the kitchen door—"and we've been keeping them in our house. Think their grandmothers will get a crowd together to drive us out of town, or will they just do it themselves?"

"Stop it," I whispered.

"Who better to blame for the two of them vanishing into the woods than the creepy family who lives at the edge of it?"

"Hey." I lifted a hand in the space between us. "We are not creepy."

"Not my word. But it'll be everyone else's once we get blamed for this. They'll all say we've been keeping them in our attic."

"We don't have an attic."

"You really think anyone will bother to check?"

She flipped to a yellowed-page spread about how to speckle Easter eggs.

I resisted the idea that she might be right. But it swept over me, and I fell under.

If women here were so afraid of us that they didn't even wear white to their own weddings, how far was it to blaming us for this? What would I tell Lynn, soft, opal-eyed Lynn, about why I'd kept her own grandson from her?

My sigh fell heavy on the square of sofa cushion between us. "You're right."

"I know I am," Roja said.

Tess burst out of the kitchen door. "Where are your parents?" she asked us both.

"Business," I said, standing up at the same moment Roja said, "Family funeral."

We snapped our heads toward each other.

When it came to shared lies, we were out of practice.

Lynn gave the lightest shake of her head, a you-poor-girls look.

Roja elbowed me so slowly no one else would notice, a prodding for me to welcome Lynn's pity. This was how we would get out of this. If we didn't gratefully accept pity, scorn would take its place.

"Well, now that we've covered that." Tess looked back at Page and Yearling. "You two care to share anything about where you've been?"

I tried to catch Page's eye. But I couldn't. She and Yearling were swapping looks, the same unspoken language my sister and I had shared our whole lives.

I half turned my head toward Roja, trying to ask her a question without saying it. What had the four of them been talking about in the kitchen a minute ago if not where Page and Barclay had been?

Then the answer came, cut so clearly I wondered if maybe I still knew how to hear Roja without her talking.

Maybe Roja had been right. Tess and Lynn must have wanted to know if my sister and I had been hurting their grandsons, if we'd been keeping them when they did not want to be kept.

We were the del Cisne girls, the swan daughters. I understood it as a fair question, even as I took the sting of it.

Tess watched Yearling, still waiting for an answer. Lynn gave Page an encouraging nod, like she could begin whenever she was ready. But Tess didn't lift her stare off Yearling. He was older, so he took the brunt of explaining.

"It's a long story," he said.

Tess sat down on the other sofa. "Then start talking."

YEARLING

I'd been in Lynn Ashby's house with Page as often as I'd been in his parents' house. But now it seemed like a landscape that had shifted when I had my back turned.

There were still fixed points. The walls, with their patches of sun-faded wallpaper. The stairs that I could mark without looking. The sink that dripped so persistently Lynn had given up trying to fix it and just put a watering can under it. But there were other things that seemed like they'd just turned up here, like a magician had made them vanish from my grandmother's house and reappear in Lynn Ashby's. Stacks of books leaned against either side of the full bookshelf, one of which I almost toppled. The dresser that used to be in my grandmother's room was now a side table in the front hall; I bumped into it in a way that was both startling and familiar, like running into someone I knew on the street. An enormous vase Grandma Tess had bought from a yard sale now sat at the base of the stairs; I skidded to a stop just short of crashing into it.

But there were things my hands remembered. Even with my grandmother's life moved into Lynn Ashby's house, they remembered. I found the box of old clothes my grandmother never opened. The plain linen dress she'd married my grandfather in, the wool skirts she'd worn at the all-girls college, the first woman in our family to get past high school.

I wondered if Lynn Ashby and my grandmother being together was new, or if I'd been that slow to notice. A small, dust-frosted room at the back of the house held stacked cartons and old citrus crates. It all sat quiet, the only noise coming off the kitchen where Lynn and my grandmother asked the del Cisne girls a hundred questions.

Mostly, they were asking Blanca. Roja had gotten distracted with one of my grandmother's books of fairy tales and was flipping through for "Snow-White and Rose-Red." Not that I blamed her. My pieced-together version probably left her wondering how much I'd just made up.

My fingers found the envelope at the bottom of a box. When I pulled it out, the smell of my grandmother's perfumes—the powdery, flowery one she'd worn in college, the ambery one her mother gave her when she got married—drifted out.

The floorboards in the doorway creaked.

Page took another step into the room, hands in his pockets. "What's that?"

I tucked the flaps of cardboard under each other to close the box. "Nothing."

"Don't lie to me when you know I won't believe it."

If I told Page this, I'd have to tell him everything. How I'd almost killed Liam. How Liam had probably been ready to kill me.

"I don't want you to worry about it," I said.

"I'm already worried about it. And about you. You've been hiding something since you left, and I keep waiting for you to tell me whenever you're ready but I'm starting to think that's never going to happen."

"Page," I said. It sounded more like a warning than I meant it to. "You don't need to know. I don't want you to know. It's better that way."

"Better for who?" Page asked. "Your family? Because it's not you and it's not me."

"It's about my family." I slid the box back toward the wall. "I want you as far from them as you can get. Better yet, as far from me as you can get. I've never done you any favors."

"Are you serious?" Page asked. "It was being around you that stopped everyone at school from giving me hell. You really don't know that?"

The words stung more than they should have. Knowing what little I had done right for Page threw into sharper contrast all the ways I had failed him.

"I would have been there," Page said. "Whatever it was, I would have been there."

"I didn't want you involved, okay?"

"Barclay." Page laughed. "I went into the woods with you. How much more involved can I get?"

I lowered my voice. "You had enough going on. I didn't want to put this on you. Not with everything going on with your family."

"What was going on with my family is they were nervous around me. I could handle it. I didn't need you to do it for me. Your family, though . . ."

Page went quiet, like he didn't want to say it any more than I wanted to hear it.

"Yeah, well, how about your family?" I asked. "Your mom and

dad? They should've just taken you as you are. Everyone should. Screw anyone who can't."

This time Page's laugh was gentle, tolerating. "You don't get it." He shook his head. "You never have. You think you can just cut a path for me in the world and nothing will ever get in the way. But when you're like me, when you're anything other than what everyone thinks you should be, you don't always get to make those kinds of demands. I don't get to say 'screw it' to anyone who doesn't just accept me, not in a town this small. Maybe I should, but I don't think I'll get anywhere that way. You know how I get somewhere? Finding people who do. My grandmother. Your grandmother. You. Blanca."

"And Roja," I said.

Page hesitated. "I don't know about her."

"Why not?"

"I just don't trust her."

"Why?" The word came out bitter and sharp. "Because she's not Blanca?"

I could see Page holding his tongue against his teeth. "That's not what I meant."

"Then what did you mean?" I asked.

"I trust *her* fine," Page said. "I don't trust her with you."

That was probably the nicest way Page could think of to tell me I was becoming pathetic. An hour ago I was looking at a bottle of Cheerwine in Lynn's fridge because it was the color of Roja's hair.

I looked up, and all I saw were the boxes in this room, the mixing together of Grandma Tess's stuff with Lynn Ashby's.

I laughed. I couldn't not.

"What?" Page asked.

"That day behind the school," I said. "That was about the two of them, wasn't it?"

Page cringed, but was smiling. "Sorry."

Now I couldn't help laughing about it. "What *was* that? You thought my grandmother was trying to get yours to run off with her?"

"That was how my mom made it sound."

"It looks pretty mutual to me."

"Yeah, I guess you didn't deserve that. I'd do it again, though."

"Thanks a lot," I said. "Why?"

"Because I don't think I ever would've talked to you otherwise. I don't think you would've talked to me, either."

I shrugged, my way of saying *Fair point.*

"Barclay." Page's stare caught the envelope again. "What is that?"

I picked it up. I couldn't act like it wasn't there anymore. "Everything. The whole reason Liam wishes I'd fall off the face of the earth."

"What are you talking about?" Page asked.

I tapped the edge against my palm, a nervous habit that showed up every time I handled this envelope. "It's stuff about my family."

"Then show it to Tess," Page said. "She'll know what to do."

"My parents already hate her. And she's with Lynn now, so anything that blows back on my grandmother blows back on yours."

She's with Lynn now. The words on my tongue felt unfamiliar, my mouth getting used to the shape of them. They brought with them the bitter tang of wondering if my grandmother had been lonely in the years between when my grandfather died and when she started her life on the north side of the Ashby orchard.

"How did you get all that?" Page asked.

"How do you think? I took it."

"No," Page said. "I mean why'd you go looking for it in the first place?"

I breathed out. "When I first heard my father and my uncle talking, I just wanted to know what happened. What went on that they didn't want anyone hearing about, you know? But the more I found, the worse it got."

"So what do you want now?"

I looked down at the envelope. Once it had been the color of vanilla wafer cookies, but age had faded it. "I want them not to get away with it."

"With what?" Page asked.

The envelope rested light in my hands. For a minute I made a wish like a little kid would, that the papers in my hands would just fly off like they were wings, taking everything I knew with them.

But it had too much weight to it now. I thought I could keep it away from Page, but it had drawn him into the woods with me.

I owed him this.

I slid my thumb under the flap and ripped it away. I pulled out the stack of papers and set them in Page's hands.

Page flipped through the photocopies of sales records, check stubs, memorandums on letterhead, handwritten notes on plain paper or the backs of envelopes or bar napkins.

"What is all this?" Page asked. Official language cluttered the pages. Anything handwritten had gone grainy from the copier. My faded highlighting and pen marks yellowed and circled certain lines.

I couldn't look at it all for too long. I was still getting used to how my eyes worked now, and if I stared at a printed page the wrong way, the words blurred.

But even without looking, I knew what it said. I knew it as well as Tess knew the stories she used to tell Liam and me.

"It's proof," I said.

"Of what?" Page asked.

"Everything my family built—their business, their money, their name—they built all of it on lies."

"Is that really news to you?" Page asked. "Your mother leaves coats at parties and doesn't bother going back for them. You think that kind of money gets made by telling the truth?"

"I'm not just talking about lies," I said. "I'm talking about fraud."

Page's eyes flashed a harder color, a grayer brown. "What?"

The details still drifted through my dreams. My father and uncle had invented places they knew would never exist. They had made up towns that would never be anything more than names. Towns my father and uncle had talked about as though they were months from being built.

"They sold people land in the middle of nowhere and pretended they had plans to develop it," I said. "And I'm not talking about middle of nowhere like here. I really mean middle of nowhere. No roads go out there, not even dirt or gravel. No wells, no electricity, nothing."

"How?" Page asked, still looking at the papers.

"They talked people into buying land with all these promises about highways and schools and streets with all these new homes," I said. "It's like ghost towns in reverse. Twenty years later, they're still nothing. People sank their savings into these lots, thinking they could move there or sell them at a profit when the roads got built. But no one ever built the roads, or the wells, or brought in power. No one ever intended to."

"But what happened when everyone found out?" Page asked.

"They didn't." I worked at the corner of a photocopy, one of the handwritten notes. "My father and my uncle and their partners pretended that the builds fell through or got delayed. They said they couldn't get the permits for the roads or the wells or the power lines. They said it might take a while, but that it was all a good long-term investment. They made all these promises that everyone's children or grandchildren would see the profits. But all those plots are still worthless. They're still in the middle of nowhere and there's not even a way to get to them. But a lot of those people are still waiting. They still think those towns will get built and they'll make all their money back and more."

"This"—Page stumbled on the word—"*this* is your family's business?"

He didn't try to shear the horror off his words. I saw it clicking in him, the dry truth of all this, barren as those squares of desert.

"I don't know," I said. "But this is how they got started."

"And your father and your uncle didn't want this to get out," Page said. Not a question.

"Neither did Liam."

Page pulled out a memo, one I had memorized. It had told the men selling the land to push harder, to promise more. On its own it wasn't damning. But put together with everything else, the lies came forward.

"And if this does get out," Page said.

"Then they'd actually have to answer to everyone they lied to," I said. "And maybe it's too late to do anything about it, I don't know. But everyone would know."

All these things were etched into me. Towns that would never be, that stood as endless miles of dirt and sage. Places that existed only on maps my father and uncle drew and in the dreams of the families they sold pieces of them to. Streets they'd called names like Lemon Grove Lane and Jasper Circle, so buyers could imagine writing their future addresses on the upper-left-hand corners of envelopes. The shadows of homes that wouldn't be built, swing sets in schools that would never exist, lampposts and lawns that were only real to those who still believed.

My family had turned other people's dreams into currency.

"So what do we do with this?" Page asked.

I lifted my head. The glow from a lamp on my left side turned fuzzy.

"We?" I asked.

"Yeah."

"You want to help me?"

"You're not doing this alone," Page said.

"No," came a voice I couldn't place as Blanca's or Roja's, not at first. "You're not."

I looked to the doorway.

Blanca. She stood at the threshold.

Roja stayed a little behind her, hand on the frame.

"Do you even know what we're talking about?" I asked, half challenge, half wanting to know how long they'd been listening.

"It doesn't matter," Blanca said. "If you need help, we're all helping you."

"Like hell you are," I said. "My family got where they are by lying to people. And I don't even know how they got the land in the first place and how they convinced everyone they had a right to sell it. But I do know we are not people you want to get mixed up with." I made eye contact with Blanca, then Roja. "Neither of you are getting mixed up in this, okay?"

"That's not up to you," Blanca said.

"Excuse me?"

"You can't refuse our help," Blanca said. "I refuse your refusal."

Page pressed his lips together like he was trying not to laugh. Roja's eyes flicked between the three of us.

Blanca looked back at her. "How about you?"

"How about me with what?" Roja asked. "What are we doing?"

I laughed. It sounded slight and worn out, but she was still the girl who made me laugh, even now.

"I guess we're bringing down the Holts." I looked at her, and her eyes settled, staying on me. "You in?"

Her smile caught like a candlewick. "Oh, I'm in."

BLANCA

Page and Barclay were back with their grandmothers now. And I already felt the loss of Page in this house. The sound of her in the shower, the rush of steam lifting the linen curtain as I brought her clothes, her hair dark gold from the water. How she stood under the shower, eyes closed, her head forward so her chin nearly touched the middle curve of her collarbone.

In ninth grade, I heard Natalia Brae telling Anissa Maldanado that that was how to know. If a girl tilted her head back, smoothing her hair away from her face as it got wet, she liked boys. But anyone who stood under the shower with their head forward, the water beating their hair down against their face, those were the ones who liked girls. You knew, Natalia told Anissa, because that was how boys did it.

This was how Page, a boy, did it. Natalia got that much right.

Roja didn't make it to our room. She flopped down on the sofa, saying something into the cushion about how she was too tired to go all the way upstairs.

In those mumbled words, the pieces of last night settled into place.

Yearling liked her. I realized it now, how he couldn't meet her eye for more than a few seconds. How his laugh sounded a little different with her, freer, less controlled. In how he got between her and his own grandmother.

And my sister liked him back. It was there in how she rolled her eyes at him. In how she looked at him when she thought he wasn't paying attention. In how she was on this sofa because she wanted to be where he'd slept.

They wanted each other.

My sister and the blue-eyed boy wanted each other.

The memory of the señora's hands seared into me—the blue flame, the two locks of hair, one twisting into a feather and the other back into a ribbon of blond. The señora's insistence that it was me, only me, who could be spared by the love of a blue-eyed boy.

That was the cruelest thing about the señora's words, the truth it had left us: In my hands, the blue-eyed boy's heart was currency enough to buy my survival. In Roja's, it was worth nothing. And now she was the one who held it.

But I had my own truth, held in my pocket like a polished stone: In our family, no señora's word was law. In our family, the swans' marble-black stare, the cut of their pale wings, held more weight than any flame or spell.

If the swans gave my sister this chance, if I could tether this blue-eyed boy to her fate instead of mine, Roja's body was as good as hers, and my arms were as good as wings.

As my sister slept, I took my father's sharpest scissors and clipped a piece of her hair. Then I cut a lock of my own.

I lit a candle off my mother's pilot light, the closest we had in our house to a blessed and sacred flame.

As the light fell, I went out to the pond.

They weren't there. No flash of white wings. No long, curving necks.

I spoke to the water anyway.

"She can get him," I said to the dark mirror in front of me. "And when she does, you'll take me. Okay?"

All this time, I'd wanted to guard my sister from this game. I didn't want her giving herself to a boy who'd come out of these woods.

But she'd taken to him, our bear-boy, and he wanted her.

I waited for the swans to appear in a flurry of snow-white feathers.

"Do you hear me?" I asked.

The candle's glass heated my hands. The locks of hair in my pocket felt heavier than their weight.

"She's going to do this," I called into the dark. "And you're going to let her go."

I waited.

I knew they could hear me. They just wanted to make me stand out here.

I crouched next to the pond, setting down the candle. I lifted the locks of hair from my pocket and lit them the way the señora had. They caught and fluttered into the air, two unmoored flames. They drifted and spun like leaves. And when they flitted down to the surface of the pond, it was not in a sprinkling of ash. It was not in a single feather and a lock of my hair.

It was two feathers, identical except for their color, one white as frost flowers, one black as the rarest swan. They floated on the pond, the water making reflected copies.

Relief came with my next breath.

These two feathers, made out of flame and locks of our hair, were proof: Either of us could follow the map drawn by the señora's words. They now belonged as much to Roja as to me.

Roja could win the heart of a blue-eyed boy who'd once been a bear. That small ember between them would brighten and bloom.

She would get the blue-eyed boy. She would save herself.

The swans would leave her and take me.

I lifted my face to the pond, imagining los cisnes in the shadows beyond. "Thank you."

A bristling sound like a thousand feathers rose up through the woods.

I startled to my feet, leaves crackling under me. I looked for swans' wings cutting through the dark.

A thin shape emerged from the trees. I looked for wings or a long white throat.

But the shape resolved into Page.

I reached for something normal to say. *What are you doing here?* Or, *Are you okay?* Or, failing everything else, *Hello.*

But all I thought of was Page in the spray of the shower. How I'd imagined the heat loosening the muscles between her shoulder blades. How I thought the steam would bead into drops on her eyelashes. How I pictured water pausing in the curve of her lower back.

I imagined what I had not seen. My hands tracing where the light crossed her skin. The triangle of fine hair between her legs. All of her body at once.

She stopped in front of me, her breath its own sound under the settling leaves. "The way you look at me, do you mean it?"

My own breath stilled in my throat. I tried to ask, *What?* but the sound didn't come.

"The way you look at me," she said again. "Do you mean it?"

There was no accusation in it, no objection. Just that question, laid bare between us.

I nodded.

I waited for the glint in Page's stare or the flicker of motion in her hands. Something to tell me that yes, this was happening, now.

But Page stayed still. And it was only in the quiet falling between us that I realized.

Page was waiting for me to say yes or no.

I nodded again, because I could not steady my breath long enough to form the word *yes*.

Page half closed the distance between us, then hesitated, like she was wondering if my nod was just a carryover from the nod before.

If I couldn't figure out how to say yes with my lips, I had to do it with my hands.

I hooked my fingers through the belt loops on her jeans, lightly enough that I wasn't pulling on her. I wasn't touching her skin or even her shirt. It was borrowed flirtation, something I'd seen girls do at the locker banks at school, their thumbs and forefingers grazing the worn denim, their boyfriends or girlfriends talking to them in voices low enough that I could never make out the words.

It was a gesture small enough that either of us could pretend it hadn't happened. Page could step back, and I would drop my hands. Or I could loosen my hold and turn back to the house.

But Page set her palms on my waist.

The warmth of her hands made me open mine.

My grip spread over Page's hip bones. Then it was the blur of me pulling her and her pushing me until we were up against the smooth trunk of a birch tree, Page's palm on the back of my neck.

Her body covered mine. I could feel the slight contour of her chest beneath the layered shirts.

For everything my body did, Page's had a response.

Newton's third law. The recoil of a shotgun against the hollow of my shoulder.

The heat of Page's back against my hands.

The press of her mouth against mine.

PAGE

Grandma Lynn had this way of reading me fairy tales, like she was telling me secrets I'd need one day. She leaned a little forward, meeting my eye when the knight discovered the trick of lulling the dragon to sleep, or when the shepherd boy found the secret door.

I lowered my head to hide my blush when I thought of the witches and princesses in those stories, of catching my fingers in hair as bright as red wheat or rich as threads of black silk. I thought of those magic-blooded girls taking me by my shirt collar to kiss me, the film of their skirts floating around us like curls of bright smoke.

Grandma Lynn probably knew that. She knew in the same way she knew I would not grow out of wearing pants and collared shirts to church instead of my cousins' passed-down dresses. She knew the same way she knew to call me *young man*, those words like fairy-tale jewels. They were crowns I had found in a mist-veiled palace, while the words *young lady* were a queen's apple or a spindle—things that might turn out to poison me, but that I was expected to take.

Fairy tales were a world I thought I knew. But the one I needed to know most was the one that took me the longest to understand.

It wasn't until Blanca kissed me that I realized why the woods made me into a cygnet. It wasn't because Blanca and Roja's family came from swans.

It was because a story chose me, even when I'd gotten it all wrong.

I thought I knew the story of the ugly duckling, the cygnet who endures taunting and winter cold and being driven out of everywhere before discovering he is a swan.

I thought it was all about the ugly duckling looking into the pond and discovering a magnificent bird.

But it didn't happen that way.

The way it happened was that the ugly duckling was so tired, and cold, and lonely, that he'd been emptied out. He'd run from cats and children and mother ducks. He'd frozen in caves and ponds. So when he saw a flock of swans, wings shimmering like snow, he threw himself at them, deciding he would rather be destroyed by them than keep his distance.

I did not want to be killed. I did not want to throw myself at that which would destroy me.

But in that moment, I wanted Blanca del Cisne, and the frightening certainty of her hands, to annihilate me. I gave myself over to her pulling at my shirt and my jeans as I unhooked the eyelet clasps of her dress. Her hands were quick as wings, and in the space between my thighs they felt as light and numerous as feathers.

That was the effect of her, as great as a flock of swans, and I was the cygnet flying toward her, this girl who was as terrifying as she was spectacular.

The ugly duckling's great surprise was not the moment he saw himself in the pond. That came later. The moment of his greatest shock was when the swans embraced him, took him into their flutter of wings. It was the moment they made themselves his family. It was when they recognized him before he recognized himself.

I had always made a sorry imitation of a girl. Awkward and miserable in dresses and shined-white shoes.

But with the shift of changing into jeans and a plain shirt, with letting go of trying to make myself fit the words *girl* and *young lady*, I came to understand that I was not a girl who was terrible at being a girl. I was a boy who hadn't realized it yet.

Now this girl was in my arms. This girl, letting me hold the weight of her breasts and hips in my hands. This girl had never asked me to name myself, to declare myself duckling or swan. The second I was ready to throw myself across the water, she took me into her. She tasted like the pond, and new frost, and the marigolds she drew from the back garden. White and midnight blue and deepest gold.

She was the girl I wanted, and the girl who knew me. She was the girl who let me choose, because she demanded no choices of me.

This was what I learned, in that second of distance closing between us:

The story of the ugly duckling was never about the cygnet discovering he is lovely. It is not a story about realizing you have become beautiful.

It is about the sudden understanding that you are something other than what you thought you were, and that what you are is more beautiful than what you once thought you had to be.

ROJA

My sister was behind a closed door with Page Ashby.

The señoras had told her how to save herself, and she'd still done this.

Her defiance struck so deep I lost myself in the wonder of it. It was like opening a cupboard and finding a sparrow. It was light gathering like honey in the corner of a closet. It was a starfish appearing in the bathroom sink.

I stayed downstairs, falling into the lie that I'd get up in a minute, I was just shutting my eyes for a second.

When I woke up, the windowpanes weren't morning-pale, or afternoon-bright, or dusk-blue. They were dark as the pond at night. I lifted my face from the sofa, throat scratchy from sleep.

The house had gone quiet, but the air inside still felt thick and shimmering, like the glitter-laced water in a snow globe.

I went outside to get a full breath, taking the glass jar with the candle in it. The rusted handle felt grainy as lichen against my palm.

A familiar silhouette wove through the trees. The moment I knew it was him was the same moment he noticed me watching.

"Can't sleep," Yearling said, answering the question before I could ask.

"And standing out in the dark helps?"

He looked up. "I like watching."

"Watching what?"

He took my waist in his hands. His palms fell light as leaves as he moved me to where he was standing. "When it's this dark you can't really see the trees, so when they move it just looks like some of the stars are disappearing and other ones are coming back."

I looked where he was looking. The candle's light didn't reach the tree branches.

Under this star-salted sky, I was in that snow globe again, but at night. The constellations could have been handfuls of flecked gold or crushed mica.

Yearling dropped his hands from my waist. "What are you doing up?"

I looked over my shoulder, toward a lit bedroom window.

"Got it," he said.

I started to say something, then held back. But it turned to enough of a noise that Yearling asked, "What?"

"Nothing," I said.

"Oh, come on," he said. "You can't sigh like that and then say 'nothing.'"

The same sigh, heavy and worried, came without me meaning it to.

"Do you think she really loves Page?" I asked.

"She better," he said. "I don't want Page getting hurt."

A few days earlier, the act of Blanca and Page behind a bedroom door would have been enough for me. It would have given me the opening I needed. The lowest, most hidden layer of me, like the spongy moss at the bottom of the pond, would have thrilled to the idea of my sister getting out of my way. Whatever blessing and luck the señoras had offered her, this was my chance to take it for myself.

But now guilt pricked at me. It was sharp as thorns dragging against my skin. We had pulled these boys, both of them, so far into our world that I couldn't tell whether the frightening magic of them had come from the woods or from us.

Now my sister, with her bright love for Page Ashby, held so much color I couldn't imagine her as a swan. She was a hummingbird, each of her feathers holding every jewel in the world. She was a quetzal, with plumes as bright as blood and spring grass.

I was a hawk, knife-taloned, with eyes that caught any flicker of movement. But without my father's voice, truing me like a flight call, I drifted. I felt the loss of his counsel and direction like a nutrient deficiency.

While Blanca flared like lamplight, I was a girl going into the woods to eat dirt, searching for some mineral my bones were missing.

"What are you doing here?" I asked Yearling. "Aren't there plenty of trees at Lynn's?"

He fished a handful of small vials from his pocket. He held them in his palms, showing me.

The candle's glow winked off the contents. Each vial held a different color. Sea-glass tints. Teal, turquoise. Vivid green and blue. And warmer colors. Copper. Red. A soft pink that reminded me of rose gold.

"What is this?" I asked.

"It's glass glitter," he said. "My grandmother had it around the house. Take it."

"I can't take something that belongs to Tess."

"She's the one who told me to give it to you. You really think she's going to use it?"

I laughed. Tess Holt didn't even trade in her pants for a dress on Easter Sunday.

"Are Tess and Lynn telling your families you're back?" I asked.

Yearling tilted his head to one side, then the other. "They're doing that thing where they try to get us to, but no. That was the thing about them. They never told us we had to be anything."

Yearling held the vials a little closer to me, each stoppered with a tiny cork. "Take them. I saw them and they made me think of you."

The glitter caught the stars, the glass cut so much finer than anything my family poured into cascarones. I thought of using it for Easter, filling hollowed-out Araucana shells.

Yearling set them in my hands.

The brush of his fingers made my skin feel dusted with glass glitter.

"I should get back," he said. "I'm covering for Page."

"Yearling," I said.

He turned back. "Yeah?"

The words went tight in my throat.

Just tell him. The words came in the same rhythm as my heartbeat.

He deserved to know he was nothing but a prop. Blanca and I would tear him to pieces, because neither of us wanted him as much as we wanted to save ourselves. And Page would get broken in the process for no reason except that he was the one Blanca wanted instead.

Just tell him. The words echoed through me.

Maybe Yearling would hate me if I told him the truth, but at least someone else would know. I could tell him how my cousins had taken my mother and father from their own house. How my sister had lied to me at the first sign of the swans' wings. How the weight of all this fell so fast it was its own meteor, and I was the hollow it left in the earth.

I pressed the handle of the glass jar into his palm and closed his fingers around the wire. "Don't go home in the dark."

"I know the way," he said.

"Still." I thought of him weaving through the woods back toward the orchard. He moved his head in a way that had become familiar to me, a way that let him take in more of everything around him. It was careful but decisive, like a cat gauging distance before a jump.

I still wanted him to carry this small light with him.

He took it. "Good night, Roja."

"Watch out for evil wizards," I said as he faded into the trees.

"Don't worry." He lifted the lantern. "I'm on it."

PAGE

I left her in the morning, so early that the sky still wore its silver. I kissed her, lightly enough not to pull her from sleep. To keep my steps downstairs quiet and soft, I left my shoes off until the back door.

But when I went out into the chilled air, my breath sharpened to a gasp.

It had happened overnight, the woods now as odd and beautiful as a dream. It was frost and white feathers and dashes of black as deep as a sparrow's eyes. It was soft wisps and gleaming edges.

I followed the scent of apple sugar and leaves back to the orchard, back to where my grandmother may or may not have been waiting to ask me where I'd been all night.

But I held with me the thought of how Blanca would wake up, how she would go to her window, her eyes catching the spark of discovering it for herself.

ROJA

I dreamed I wore red, the same predawn red that draws a line between the sky and the mountains. It marked me, so everyone would know me from Blanca.

When I dreamed, the woods were wind-bent and silvered with frost. And I found him under the low-hanging branches, between a small tree of red roses I grew and a tree of white that belonged to my sister. The blooms on the white were slender and neat, like glass figurines. The ones on the red were messy as peonies, splaying open one at a time like the shudder of an anemone.

I ran my hands through the fur on his back and felt him trapped inside the young bear's body. I kissed the crescent moon of white fur on his chest. His fur fell away like cloth, and the wind pulled my dress from me. But I didn't feel the cold of the snow under me. I felt only the sharp brush of ice crystals and the heat of him next to me.

The moon didn't like it. The story didn't turn out this way. Snow-White was supposed to end up with the bear-prince. She was the quiet and sweet one, helping with the housework and reading out loud to her mother. She lit small, tidy fires in winter while snowflakes stuck to the windowpanes. I was the wilder one, catching butterflies in the meadows, pricking my fingers on the thorns of summer roses. I was supposed to wait for the yearling's brother.

But Snow-White wouldn't come. Snow-White had grown bored with the bear-prince. She had lost her heart to a boy who held apples as though they were made of frost and moonlight.

The moon didn't care. It tried to pull at me, but Yearling's heat covered me, shielding me. I was soft enough to be pulled on like water, but he wasn't. The moon couldn't reach through him to get to me.

So the force of the moon twirled the branches from the rose trees, like wool off a skein. The thorn-studded vines tethered us to the snow so we couldn't move. I held my arms against his back to keep the thorns from cutting into him, and the crescent moon on his chest pressed into me. The white roses lay into us like cold glass, and the red sliced against us like the petals had frozen.

But the moon was too late. My hands were already in the hollow of his back. The rose tree vines bore scraps of my red dress.

I woke up with my hand below my collarbone, sure the crescent moon had burned a copy of itself into me. But there was nothing there but my own skin.

BLANCA

I dreamed she was a cygnet again. I stood naked in the woods at magic hour with her down-covered body cupped in my palms.

She shuddered, shaking water from her back. I kissed her just above her beak, and in one flickering second she became a grown swan, the ruffled feathers at the tips of her wings like peony petals.

She flew from my hands. Her wings brushed my shoulders and back, my breasts and hips. They beat against every inch of my skin like she was a whole flock of swans. Some feathers fell soft as petals, others prickled like evergreen needles, and the rest landed like the thinnest blades of obsidian.

This time I turned with her, my arms to wings, my skin to feathers white as magnolias.

And in the morning, the world was something other than how we had left it the night before.

It could have been a world Page had made me, a kingdom this boy had taken from storybooks and brought to life outside my bedroom window.

I stood at the glass, bracing my hands against the sill.

The world outside my window had become a forest of feathers and ice.

The trees wore not only their gold leaves; now fine hoarfrost coated the branches, a covering of frozen needles, delicate and sparkling as raw crystal. Every minute or so, the trees moved enough for the sun to catch them, and they threw out sparks of light. They cast tiny rainbows over the woods.

Among the frost and the yellow slices of the leaves, feathers sprouted like blossoms. The bleached white and rich black of swan's feathers, light as pepper tree leaves. The wispy gray fluff of cygnet's down, stirred by the slightest wind.

And in the spaces between, the soft film of apple blossoms fluttered their cream petals, the buds edged in pink.

The trees were all these things at once, birches and birds and a frost-covered fairy tale. The branches were growing all these things we held inside us.

I ran for the stairs, my lips stinging first to tell Page but then to tell everyone.

Roja. Especially Roja, because in this moment we were children again, sharing everything we had. Our dresses. Lipsticks I borrowed from our mother to play with on Sundays. Books Roja slid from our father's shelves. Our best secrets.

All of us were in the woods, growing from the birch trees.

But when I flew from the bedroom, the thing that stole the breath from my throat wasn't the forest.

It was three of my cousins, standing at the base of the stairs.

PART FOUR

The Swan & Her Sister

BLANCA

The woods damned us. Their beauty, their strange act of sprouting feathers and frost, told our family the things we'd done. They spoke of the pond-water-eyed boy I'd held the night before.

Now I stood in the bedroom I shared with Roja, one foot on top of the other, the way I used to wait for Roja on the stairs.

Two of my second cousins cornered me. I had to close my eyes to keep their words from boring into my temples.

Do you have any idea what you're doing?

Never in all the stories I've ever heard in this family . . .

You two never could follow rules, could you?

One voice took over. Isabel, the younger one. "Do you understand what you've done? I'm surprised the swans aren't tearing this house to scrap wood."

Tears pinched at the corners of my eyes.

"You'll be lucky if they don't take you both," Isabel said. "If you ask me, they should."

"Enough," Sofía said.

My eyes snapped open.

"Out," Sofía told her younger cousin.

Isabel glared, but did as Sofía told.

Sofía shut the door, her downcast gaze thick with disappointment. I felt its weight more than if she'd yelled or thrown a plate at the wall next to my head, like Isabel probably wanted to.

Sofía took a sighing breath. "Don't you want to survive this?"

I held the truth tight in my throat, the bargains I'd made with the swans.

"You have a chance." Sofía lowered her head, as though she was looking deeper into me. "You had a way out."

The words turned over in my head. *If you're a good girl, you can get a blue-eyed boy.* They twirled like the mobile of paper feathers my mother had hung over my first bed.

"Don't expect your hair to do everything for you," Sofía said.

There was no meanness in it, just fact. My hair was yellow but coarse like my mother's. My skin had the undertone of gold and brown instead of peach or pink like the flower-perfumed girls at school.

And my eyes were not blue, but the dark-sugar amber of piloncillo.

What marked me as part of my own family made the world love me a little less.

Closeness to one always meant distance from the other.

"And you can't go against them," Sofía said, with a glance toward the window, her eyes ticking in the pond's direction. "Don't try to push them around. You'll never win." She drew her gaze back to me. "I thought the cuts they left on your sister would've told you that."

The sense of my own body dropped away from me.

She knew.

All my cousins and great-aunts must have known.

I had tried to defy the swans, so they had slashed their feathers across my sister's skin. I loved her, so they had gone after her as though she was a weak point on my body.

Sofía's expression turned sad, her face tilting toward the floor.

She and Isabel were women who knew. Years ago—ten years ago for Isabel, twelve for Sofía—they had lost their own sisters, girls made into pale birds.

Sofía must have known what I'd done the night before. The woods told the story. The apple blossoms were the smallest, softest things to have grown overnight, and their spring pink and petal silk whispered Page's name.

"I can't do anything that hurts her," I said. "Not even to save myself."

"The way you're going, neither one of you will survive this," Sofía said. "Isabel's right, and you know it."

The air between us chilled.

"They'll take you both," Sofía said. "They've done it before. So I don't know what you think you're doing, but whatever it is, this is their warning." She watched the trees, a wary gleam crossing her eyes. "I wouldn't count on them giving you another."

A flicker of motion drew my eye to the window.

Black feathers were pulling off the trees. They drew away like wind was stripping them from the branches, but the air lay still. With every thought of Page, another gust of feathers ripped away and swirled onto the air.

I tried not to think of Page. But the harder I forced down each thought of her, the more they rushed back.

My mouth on Page's bare shoulder blade.

The way her fingers played at the hem of my shirt before reaching under it.

How I kept trying to place what apple she tasted most like.

With each one, more black feathers tore away from the white feathers, the leaves, the apple blossoms, the frost. With each stray memory, more took off into the air, until they were twirling into shapes almost like wings.

My own arrogance prickled over my skin.

I was not smarter than the swans. I had never been smarter.

There was no winning against them.

They won, every time.

These feathers were their last warning, the shape of a girl, my sister, made out of black down and then spinning into a swan's body. They showed her to me in the paint of dark feathers.

My shoulders rounded from the shame of what I'd done, how I'd tried to pass the burden of the señora's words to my little sister. I could pretend it was all for her. But if I stood still for a minute, I flinched under the searing understanding that I had wanted it for me, too. I had wanted her with the blue-eyed boy, not me.

I had wanted a few more breaths held between my lips and Page's.

But it was never mine to decide.

The swans had nodded their agreement once, to leave Roja as she was if I played their game. That was the first and only bargain I knew they'd taken, marked by the bowing of their necks.

But last night, they hadn't appeared. The black and white feathers had not been their reassurance.

They'd been a warning.

Los cisnes wanted me to know they weren't changing the terms again.

They wanted me to remember that I didn't set the rules.

Don't try to push them around. You'll never win.

My second cousin's words sank into me, as sharp as they were true.

The blurred shape of the black feathers unfurled into a wide span, brushing the trees.

"Okay," I said, out loud without meaning to.

How hard I struck the word widened Sofía's eyes.

It wasn't enough for the swans that Roja held the blue-eyed boy's heart.

Los cisnes wanted me to give up the boy who knew apples like another language.

There was no arguing. They had seen in me the softest, weakest part of my heart where I held my sister. They knew I would do anything, give up anything, if it meant my sister keeping her own body.

And now they wanted me to prove it.

ROJA

In another family, the fact that Blanca was getting lectured by two of our second cousins, while I endured the disapproval of just one, might have meant she was in more trouble than I was.

The truth was that, of the second cousins sent to check up on us, only Julieta thought me worth her time. That, or she lost a coin flip.

Our family had seen the trees, feathers sprouting from between the yellow leaves, the wood coated in jewel-frost, and they knew everything.

Blanca and I weren't little girls anymore. We couldn't look at the sudden appearing of hoarfrost and make up stories about hadas sugaring the trees with rock candy. We had learned that so many beautiful things held something worth fearing. The blood-dyed moon during wildfire season. The lace bells of lily of the valley, and how they gave way to the poison of red berries. Trees dressed in the colors of everything we loved and would lose.

Julieta pulled me outside.

"What is this?" I asked. "Are you all placing bets? Is your money on me?"

"Stop it," Julieta said. "I'm trying to help you."

I slipped into a pocket of light spilled from the house, gold as the lettering on my father's oldest books.

"You're losing," Julieta said.

"Of course I am," I said. "She's Blanca."

"No." Julieta's sigh was both weary and impatient. "I mean you're falling in love when you're supposed to get him to fall in love with you."

The words were so blunt, so unsoftened, that I felt something in me catch, a lock clicking shut.

"I am not," I said.

"Then what do you call all this?" She swept her arm toward the feathered and petaled forest.

I crossed my arms against the chilled air. "I can do this."

"You sure about that?" Julieta tilted her chin toward the upstairs window.

I made out the faint silhouettes of Blanca and Sofía.

Sometimes I worried my father's faith in me was nothing against Blanca's soft color and demure beauty. I may have had teeth, but Blanca walked through the world with light held on her tongue. I'd read the story in Tess's book. On the last page, the bear-prince ended up with Snow-White. It was printed and set. It wasn't a fairy tale I could rewrite.

Wisps of black flicked around me, like dark candle flames.

I lowered my eyes, and found black feathers ripping off the birch trees.

The sight of it broke in my body. Each torn-away plume was drawing me closer to the swans. They were waiting to take my skin and hair and craft it into something more like themselves.

I looked back up to the window. As my eyes adjusted to the dim room, I could make out my sister's features.

Her face was hard as the windowpane, chin held slightly up, lips tight.

It was a look of pure resolve I had never seen on her.

Blanca had hands as delicate as cream roses, but they were laced with frightening magic. She could spin anything into something shimmering and luring, like straw into threads of gold. Even the feather-covered branches were on her side.

Every time I was sure Blanca's soul was clear and smooth as a glass marble, she broke into facets. Instead of light gleaming straight through her, she shattered it.

She had raw will I had never imagined. It could strip dark feathers from trees. It could leave nothing but pristine ice and blossoms and white down.

If I wanted to survive this, I had to fight with everything in reach.

A thick coin of heat bloomed between my legs. Blood, the same time each month as my sister. I wondered if Julieta could tell I was bleeding. I wondered sometimes if del Cisne women who'd survived the swans knew everything about us, the girls who hadn't yet. Maybe to them we were young and stupid. Maybe Julieta and all our primas could see through Blanca and me as though our skin and muscles were glass. Maybe they could examine our hearts and spirits, displayed in the museum cases of our bodies.

"Roja?" Julieta said.

I looked at her.

"We're not placing bets," she said. "But if we were, my money would be on you surviving this, not her."

"Really?" I asked, and I hated how small and hopeful the word sounded.

Julieta's smile slackened, weighted by the years since she'd lost her sister. "They all thought the swans would take me, didn't they?"

I almost reached out to her. I wanted to smooth the jagged place in her that had broken the day los cisnes took Adriana. Julieta was the daughter everyone assumed the swans would steal, so much that they could almost see wings sprouting from her back. They all thought Adriana—as sweet and as determined as honeysuckle vines—would stay a girl.

I wanted to ask Julieta how it felt, if she thrilled to the moment of being spared, or if, in the second of winning, she only felt left behind. If she still dreamed at night of her hair becoming feathers, if she walked under the weight of wings that never sprouted.

Julieta straightened. I saw her pulling back the sadness.

"Don't give up, Roja." Her smile was in one moment encouraging, the next wry, coming with a lift of an eyebrow. "You're not a swan yet."

PAGE

I wanted more of her. Blanca, the girl who always laughed like she was a little nervous but who'd stood out in the night rain like there was nothing to be afraid of in the whole world.

I wanted to drink her, like the scent of Pink Pearl apples. I wanted to learn the shape of her collarbone and how it would taste if I set my lips against the back of her hand. I wanted as much of her as she'd give me. I'd keep all of it. I'd lay each detail between peach and sea-foam-green tissue paper like my grandmother stored her old dresses.

These things, and the careful way I had of keeping them, was all Blanca left me.

She did it gently, in her soft voice, her hands worrying the buttons of her dress. *You're perfect, and I want this. I wish I could explain, but I can't.*

I can't, her warning that she would both pull back from me and not tell me why.

I can't be with you right now.

She didn't know that I saw past the thin clouding of the words *right now. Right now* was forever. If a forest made of feathers and frost didn't make *right now* a time worth being with me, there would never be one.

With those words, the air around us turned. It shifted from the kind of fall that grew the best apples, the wind coming right, to the kind of sudden winter that brought the cold too fast, frost silvering the still-fruited branches.

The fairy tales should have taught me. I should have learned from Grandma Lynn's books, the clover-greened, mist-softened stories about Celtic princes and woodland princesses. I was no prince, and it was always the prince whose kiss woke the sleeping girl or who found the enchanted tree. It was the prince who wielded the sword with a blade turned to fire, or that drew the arcs of rainbows, or that held the strength of the sea.

Instead I was an apple farmer's son, the kind of boy who vanished into the background of these stories.

Barclay could have been that prince. And he would have given the chance to me if he could, the possibility of being a prince in my own story. But he didn't have it to give, no more than I could make him someone else.

I wished I had told Blanca the true story of the ugly duckling, to make sure she knew. I wondered if she remembered the part about the ugly duckling throwing himself at the flock of swans.

I wondered if she realized the force of her was more than all those wings.

If she didn't want me, that was one thing. But if she thought she couldn't have me, couldn't take me, I wanted her to understand the magnitude of her own heart, fierce and terrifyingly beautiful as those swans. That was the strength of her. She pretended to be delicate, a girl dainty as fine lace, and I didn't want her to pretend it for so long that one day she believed it.

Now I carried an understanding of what turned in the ugly duckling's heart, how he would have rather surrendered himself to that which might destroy him than never touch it at all.

I would have rather had Blanca wreck me than leave me as I was, my skin echoing with the memory of her hands, my lips prickling with what I had not told her.

But it was her choice, not mine.

ROJA

The moment I knew Blanca had broken her own heart was the moment I knew she'd do anything to win.

My sister came inside, tears jeweling her eyelashes. She held her lips tight, like she might start sobbing if she parted them.

Our second cousins had convinced her to give up the boy she loved. And she had done it.

Part of me reached out to the pain in her, the same part that remembered us pressing leaves between pieces of wax paper and setting miniature pumpkins on our windowsills.

"Blanca," I said, her name soft on my tongue.

She cut me off with "I'm fine" and went upstairs to our room.

The sharpness in her voice brought me back, hard as the swans' call.

The sound of her footsteps left me hollow. Then they faded, the quiet hardening the air.

I breathed into the stillness falling over the house. I still had one weapon left I hadn't used. It lay smooth and hidden as a knife in a boot, a way to learn more about Barclay Holt than my sister knew.

That night, while everyone else slept, I woke. Blanca's soft snores came from her bed.

At that moment, it was the only thing keeping me from hating her, the way she never lay still like some sleeping beauty. Her hair tangled and fluffed. She slept with her mouth open, and on really good nights, I could catch her drooling, the sheen of it on her cheek.

A faint shape crossed the window.

First, I wrote it off as Blanca's sleeping reflection.

But Blanca lay still, while the reflection shivered.

A swan, perched on a branch, quickened my heartbeat to match the flutter of its wings.

It watched through the window, pale head turned, but one eye fixed on me.

In its shining glare, I saw the warning that one day I would have my own wings.

Julieta's words were cold water to me, keeping me awake. *They all thought the swans would take me.*

I stared back, meeting those ink-drop eyes. *I'm not yours yet.*

I went downstairs.

Liam Holt picked up on the second ring.

"What do I need to know about your cousin?" I asked. I almost called him Yearling, but stopped myself. To Liam, he was Barclay. I said it over in my head. *Barclay, not Yearling. Barclay, not Yearling.*

"What are you talking about?" Liam asked.

"I don't know him," I said. And it was almost true. We'd never spoken in the halls at school or when we passed each other on the sidewalk. "If you want me to find him, you need to tell me about him. I can't look for someone I know nothing about."

"You believe me?" Liam asked, a window opening in his voice. "You believe I saw him out there?"

I forced a patient sigh. "I don't know, Liam." The lie spun in front of me. "But if it was Blanca I'd want someone to believe me."

My own words landed back on me, the truth of them stinging.

Either way, I would lose Blanca. I feared the watered-down story we would become to our former classmates and the women who saw our mother buying bread at the market. We would be a fairy tale whispered in spring or a ghost story told in the early dark of October. They would forget that we were not two sisters in a fable but real girls, with real hearts that lay broken in our chests.

"What do you want to know?" Liam asked.

"I don't know," I said. "Just tell me about him."

I kept polite silence through Liam listing off Barclay's favorite color (green, same as their grandfather's), his favorite food (apple pie and cheddar cheese, the same as Tess's), the way he was afraid of raccoons until he was thirteen.

I felt the pinch of what a mistake this had been. How far could I get with the fact that, between November and March, he wore the same thing almost every day? (Long-sleeved shirt, jeans, his father's old jacket that he took from a hall closet and that his father never noticed missing.)

A question I did not want to ask crawled over my skin.

"Liam?"

"Yeah?"

"Are you talking to Blanca, too?" I asked. "About finding him?"

"What?" Liam's shock sounded so true and startled, I believed it. "No."

"Why did you ask me instead of her?"

His laugh was soft, fuzzing over the line. I cringed at how identical it was to Barclay's.

"Tess always used to tell us these stories," Liam said. "You know, before we started thinking of them as girl stories and didn't want to hear them anymore. And Barclay was always a lot more interested in the witches than the princesses. He'd want to hear about the nixie of the mill-pond over the little mermaid every time."

"I don't get it," I said. "What does that have to do with anything?"

"I just always remembered that," he said. "You want something done, you go to the witch, not the princess. Not that you and your sister . . . you know what I mean."

Oh, I knew what he meant.

"It's supposed to be a compliment," he said. "It probably didn't sound that way, but it was."

"I know," I said.

I hadn't read "The Nixie of the Mill-Pond," but I'd flipped past it in Tess's book, the same one that had "Snow-White and Rose-Red." I saw the picture of the woman with pondweed in her hair, luring a young man to his death in the water.

I knew enough about the nixie of the mill-pond to know that she killed, while the little mermaid saved. The little mermaid became sea-foam for love of a prince, while the nixie just stole what she wanted.

Blanca had started this. She had made us enemies, and still, she would be the yielding, beautiful mermaid, and I would be the girl smelling of blood and pond water, with marsh lights for eyes.

I didn't care. If the nixie was the one who survived, she was the one I would become.

An idea caught and flared in me.

I had tried to be Blanca, sweet, softhearted Blanca, when instead I needed to be everything Blanca didn't know how to be.

Yearling had never wanted the mermaid who would give her heart to a thankless prince and her body up to sea-foam.

He'd wanted the mermaid who lured men to the shore because she could.

So this time, when the woods called Yearling back to me, when the feathers and out-of-season blossoms drew him to our door, I crafted my own heart from the frost in the air.

I didn't look at him. When he tried talking to me, I studied my own fingernails, bitten down since the last time I'd seen my father.

Yearling stepped back. "Are you okay?"

I meant to seem bored and flirtatious. I meant to trace my fingers along a knot in a birch trunk, looking distracted. I wanted to give off the languorous effect of a merciless water sprite, patient, just waiting to take boys like him under.

But the words I needed didn't come.

What drifted back, what found me instead, was the story he'd told me. Snow-White and Rose-Red, two sisters told apart by their colors.

In the dark, my sister glowed, but in the dark, I was the dark itself. Blanca, bright and fair Blanca, was the moon and all its stars. I was just her background to shimmer against.

I existed to make her more luminous.

Without the glow off her, no one ever saw me. Without her, there was no me. Snow-White on her own was still a fairy tale, but Rose-Red, alone, was only half a story. I couldn't hold the rage of that all on my own anymore.

It spilled out of me.

"I'm not my sister," I said.

"Okay," Yearling said, taking the word slow. "I never said you were."

"We're not the same." I'd meant to use a voice I borrowed from a storybook, a witch who'd traded her heart to be beautiful and fearless. But my words turned out plain, hard, unadorned.

"I never thought that," he said.

"You did," I said. "Or you wouldn't have made us part of your grandmother's story."

"I didn't mean to make you anything," he said, anger pressing up under his words. "That's not what that story means." He stepped back, gauging the distance between us. "What's going on?"

"I'm not Blanca," I said.

"I know that."

"No, you don't," I said. "I'm not the soft one. If that's what you wanted, you should've gone for her when you had the chance."

Yearling tensed at the sound of my voice, sharp and cold as the hoarfrost silvering the branches. A voice that told him I was not the girl on the floor, afraid of the moon, or the one holding his forearms to help him breathe.

"What are you doing?" Yearling asked.

"You like your grandmother's stories," I said, coming toward him. "How about the ones they tell about us? How we turn brides into birds. My father planting hearts in our backyard. My mother growing poison in our window boxes. You know those? They're all true."

I kept at him, making him back up. He moved away from me slowly, eyes still on me, cautious.

I couldn't look at his brown-edged eye too long. Not because the clouding and blurring was ugly. He thought so—I could tell from how often he let his hair get in front of it—but it wasn't. I couldn't look at it too long because it looked like it hurt, and because the brown of it made me hope for things I could not have.

Brown, the color that made Yearling and me a little bit the same.

Brown, the color my father had taught me to love.

"You're so busy being afraid of your family," I said, backing him against a tree. "You forgot to be afraid of mine."

Your family.

Those were the words he flinched on.

"You win," he said.

He broke our stare, wincing as he looked away.

"I don't know what you wanted here." He set his hands in his pockets and turned back to the woods. "But whatever it is, you win, you can have it."

I laced my fingers together, so neither of my hands would stray into the dark.

My hands prickled, wanting to reach out to every version of this boy I knew. The yearling bear with burr grass caught in his fur. The boy who'd been fearless in the face of the swans that ruled my nightmares. The one with glass glitter filling his palms.

I thought I could lure him by showing him my cruelty, my fearless will. But I was neither the selfless mermaid nor the ruthless nixie. I was a girl who would never exist in a fairy tale, not just because of the brown of my body but because of my heart, neither pure enough to be good nor cruel enough to be evil. I was a girl lost in the deep, narrow space between the two forms girls were allowed to take. I was both too fearful and too selfish. I loved in a way that didn't hold steady like moonlight but flickered like candle flame.

I wasn't enough of anything to win the heart of a blue-eyed boy and the right to keep my own skin.

All I had was the faint, far-off clicking of wing feathers.

YEARLING

My hand hitting a banister. A coffee mug knocked off Lynn Ashby's kitchen table. My shoulder bumping a wall because I didn't gauge the distance right. Every time I got distracted, every time I was too much in a hurry to adjust for how my eyes were different now, it ended with me crashing into something, the sound of broken ceramic, a tipped-over jar of Grandma Tess's straight pins.

Right now it looked like spilled orange juice, missing the glass.

Grandma Tess heard me swear under my breath.

"Parallax," she said, handing me a dishcloth.

"What?" I asked, mopping up the spill.

"You know how when you were a little kid you'd hold your thumb out in front of you and make it jump by blinking one eye closed and then the other? That's parallax. It's how astronomers measure the distance to the stars. They use the earth's own orbiting to do it. The greater the parallax, the closer to Earth."

"Thanks for the science lesson."

"I wasn't done, smart-ass," she said. "It's also part of how our eyes perceive the distance to things in front of us. And now your sense of it isn't the same as it was."

"Yeah, great."

"You'll get used to it."

I shoved the weight of my arm into the counter, soaking up the last of the orange juice.

"That's some elbow grease you got there," Grandma Tess said, sitting back down at the kitchen table. "You in a mood?"

I threw the cloth into the sink.

"You hungry?" she asked.

"Not really."

"You want apple pie and cheddar cheese?"

"No."

"Hey, if you don't like me, Lynn is somewhere out on the orchard," she said. "You got your pick of two old ladies."

I thought of them out there, my grandmother holding a ladder while Lynn twisted apples off the highest branches. I thought of them folding their clothes into the same dresser, forgetting whose mixing bowls were whose, slipping my grandmother's worn paperbacks alongside Lynn Ashby's photo albums.

Something settled into place.

This was why my family hadn't wanted me and Liam around Grandma Tess for more than Sunday church.

They hadn't liked that she was with Lynn.

I felt the space between me and my family widen. My grandmother had spent the year after my grandfather died gritting her teeth, trying to pretend the loss of him hadn't broken her into pieces. She always looked one hard bump away from shattering.

But they still held Lynn Ashby against her.

My grandfather would have wanted it for her. Even from how little I knew him, I knew he loved her enough to want that for her. I had seen the pictures. No one caught those kinds of frames on film, those seconds right after laughing, without loving someone. He had loved her, and he wouldn't have wanted her to be alone.

"Oh, for God's sake"—my grandmother's voice broke into everything I was piecing together—"just go talk to her."

"Lynn?" I asked.

"Roja." Grandma Tess went to work taking apart her oldest gun, sliding open the action to make sure the magazine was empty. "You can't even pour orange juice. Go get your head on straight."

"It's nothing to do with her." I handed her the cleaning oil. "You just said it. I got a bad eye now."

"Not bad. Just not like it was before." She reengaged the action, and then racked it again. "And that girl's got everything to do with all that orange juice, and you know it."

"No." I tilted my head back, breathing in, trying to smooth down the frustration in my voice because I sure as hell didn't want Tess being right, not about this. "I don't. You know what I know? I know I can't read for more than fifteen minutes without feeling like there's a screwdriver in my forehead. I know that if I make the spectacular mistake of looking at anything too hard for too long, I feel it for the next couple of hours. I know that about half the time I reach for things, I miss. That is what I know, okay?"

"And I know you've been getting along okay so far adjusting for what you don't have anymore." Tess stared me down in that way that always caught me and made me quiet. It was a stare that told me she noticed me bumping into things on my left side, how much I had to move my head now to see what I used to see without thinking, the way I registered some things as closer and some things as farther than they really were.

But also that it wasn't all she saw of me.

"You're green enough at it, though, that the minute you lose your focus—" Tess eyed the counter where I'd spilled the carton. "One day you'll do it all without thinking, but right now you still have to think about it. Except you're not thinking. You can't get used to everything all at once, but you can do one thing right now. So go talk to her."

"I don't want to talk to her."

"You're the worst liar in the whole world." She took off the Remington's barrel and ran the rod through. "As bad as your grandfather."

"She wouldn't want to see me anyway."

"I thought you didn't want to see her."

"I don't," I said. "But if I did."

She shoved a brush into the barrel to break up the powder residue. "Get out of here."

I stood against the counter.

"I mean it," she said. "Get out of my kitchen."

"This isn't your kitchen."

"Then get out of Lynn's kitchen." She shook the bottle of cleaning oil at me. "Go on. Out."

I sulked toward the door. Grandma Tess was always right, and always smug about it, and I didn't know which was more irritating. But I still could rage out of there like this was the worst idea she'd ever had, because it probably was.

The woods between the back of the Ashby farm and the del

Cisnes' house still looked covered in a rain of feathers and petals and hoarfrost. The light winked off the ice, casting little splinters of sun over the trees.

In daylight, I carved my route even more carefully than at night. Liam, no doubt, was still looking for me. If my father saw me, if he and my uncle caught me and dragged me back, they'd make me into the kind of Holt I was always supposed to be.

I knew how to be careful. Careful had gotten me records Liam didn't know about. Careful led me on paths that followed creeks and edged the pond. Careful guided me through the woods in a way that kept me far from my family's property, far from the roads, far from the side of the Ashby farm where people came to buy apples.

They weren't taking me. Not yet.

These were the thoughts that went off inside my brain right as I felt the impact on my left temple.

PAGE

I stayed on the far side of the orchard.

My grandmother's house sat on the corner diagonal from my mother and father's. They'd been built that way to keep a better eye on the land, watching for crows or the water in the ditches rising too high.

It was something that made me feel both strange and lucky, how I was sleeping in my grandmother's house and my family had no idea. The orchard spread wide enough to let me hide.

But if I went deeper in, if I slipped into the dappled shadows, sometimes I could see my mother or my father without them seeing me.

I watched my father inspecting a tree, checking the leaves for blight, testing the weight of the fruit in his hands.

The inside of me clenched with the memory of him and my mother and me in the kitchen each fall. After the trees were free from the weight of their fruit, after we'd sent the Frequin Rouge and Muscadet de Dieppe off to the cider house up the road, we made pies and jarred sauce and apple butter for all the Ashby cousins who'd come in for picking season. My father would never use the metal turn-handle peeler my mother mounted on the kitchen counter. He peeled each apple with a few flicks of his wrists, leaving a single, spiraling peel.

"They miss you, you know," Grandma Lynn said.

I'd had the sense of her there, the slight perfume of lemons on her clothes. But I hadn't registered her next to me until she spoke.

"It was too hard for them," I said.

"It was pretty hard on you, too. It's okay to say that."

I watched my mother come out to meet my father, setting a hand on his shoulder. Them standing next to each other always made the red of my father's hair look brighter and the gray-blond of my mother's paler.

For so long, all I'd had was the brittle worry that they didn't know what to do with me. I was something so unknown to them that they just stayed still. They feared saying the wrong thing to me so much that they didn't say anything.

But there was more. It waited in some quiet, forgotten place, a back pocket of my heart.

My mother teaching me all the apple varieties, by color and taste, by the smell of the blossoms, by the weight of the fruit.

My father showing me how to graft a tree, guiding my small hands as I made my first back-cut on a scion branch.

The two of them letting me pick out my own clothes from the time I first went to school. They let me get jeans and shirts exactly like Barclay's. They let me wear the same kind of plaid button-ups my older cousins wore when they came for the harvest. If we were going to church on Christmas Eve, they told me to put on good pants and a collared shirt.

They had always done that, even if later they would feel as

though they did not know me. Even if realizing I was something other than a tomboy froze them still.

"Page," my grandmother said. "I know all parents probably seem the same age to you, but they are young." She watched my father twist a perfect apple off its branch and hand it to my mother. "They had you so young. They started out scared and they still are."

Even from this distance, the apple looked round and perfect as red blown glass. My mother took it with a smile as sad and worn out as my father's. They both looked duller than the last time I'd seen them, like a key collecting a coat of tarnish.

"You know, just because they don't understand you doesn't mean they don't want to," my grandmother said. "And just because they don't understand now doesn't mean they never will."

ROJA

The shine on the trees struck me first as rain. Even from the window, the trunks gleamed.

But something in the way they caught the falling light pulled me closer to the glass.

The water on the trees dulled the gold instead of reflecting it. It darkened the sun's light instead of refracting it.

That strangeness drew me outside.

The closer I got to the birch trees, the more my steps slowed. The resolving color of the trunks choked the breath out of me.

It wasn't rain.

I knew the contours of these trees, the strips of bark peeling away from the trunk to show the ash-dark layer underneath.

But under those peels of lighter bark the wood wasn't gray-brown.

It shone wet, and bright.

I knew better than to touch it. I already knew what it was. And still my hand reached out, and came back trembling. Red stained the pads of my fingers, the same sheen as pomegranate seeds.

Blood was drifting up from under the birchbark.

I shuddered as though the trees were my own body, my blood under the wood instead of resin, my hair the same as their leaves. The knots in their trunks like the hard points of scars.

Blood seeped into my fingerprints. The fear in my throat wavered too much to become a scream.

Birch wood. Meadow of birch trees. Thanks to the inscriptions in Tess's family Bible, and how trusting she was of me looking through her books, I knew what Barclay's name meant.

And I knew that, right now, Tess was the first person to call.

I dialed Lynn Ashby's house.

Tess picked up.

"Which one of you am I talking to?" she asked.

"It's Roja," I said. "Can I talk to Barclay?"

"He's not with you?"

My lips froze parted, the air in the living room growing hot on my tongue.

I hung up, my hand leaving red streaks on everything I touched.

Grabbing the shotgun felt laughable. What could I do, fire at the air until it told me where he was? With every needle of light, the trees reminded me how small I was against their venom and magic. The woods stole boys and gave them back only when they wanted to. The leaves shadowed the swans on their thrones of mirrored water.

A wooden-barreled Winchester wouldn't be any more help than my mother's tamal steamer.

But it was all I could think of, so I brought it with me, trying to remember the path Yearling had taken between our house and the Ashby orchard.

YEARLING

When I woke up everything was red. The trees. The air. All of it wore a red wash, dark as cranberries. It stained the sky and clouds. And underneath it was the searing brightness of the overcast sky, with its glare like wet silver.

I tried to get up, but pain held my forehead. It shot from my temple through the left side.

Every time I moved, he got me again. And with each blow to my head or my stomach I felt like something was both getting into me and breaking at the same time, the shards skittering out to every part of me.

At first, I tried to find the rhythm of our old fights. I tried to wrench out of Liam's grip, hit him back hard enough to stun him still.

I couldn't.

Then I wished for the woods and all its shadows to take me again.

They didn't.

He grabbed me like he wanted to know if I was some ghost of myself or if I was my own real body. He beat me down into the shadows like he could will me out of being.

When he took me by my shirt collar, it brought us close enough for me to see the scars even the best doctors had left behind. A thin slash below his nose. Another on his jawline.

In those small marks, I found the story of what had happened. What I had done. I could tell, even if no one else looking at him ever could. Every mark left behind was a reason to let my cousin work out his rage on me now.

So I let him.

I let him because of what I had done to him that day. I let him because he was bigger than me, and I wasn't fast anymore.

I tried to keep my eyes open, so he'd have to look at me. But my brain felt too heavy, spinning down, trying to find the moment everything had shifted, the one thing that had made Liam who he was now.

By the time it stopped, the blame didn't matter. Liam was who he was. So was I. And, slowly, we had become less cousins and more things for each other to hit.

He stood over me, his voice sounding both distant and like it was coming from inside my own head.

You're lying, I know you have everything. Right before he got me on the left side.

What did you think you were doing? Then, a second later, him driving me into the ground.

You sure as hell better tell me the truth this time. And then a blow against my shirt.

My ribs felt like the crumbling wood of a going-out fire. Brittle as embers.

I had been wrong. I had hidden from Liam because I thought he wanted to pick up a fight we'd left half finished. Or, I thought he wanted to kill me because of the things I knew. And maybe both of these were true. But as he threw his fists into me, as the pain dragged me down, I understood.

The rage fueling his hands wasn't over how I'd left him with a busted jaw and a broken nose. It wasn't even about the papers I'd saved, proof of what my father and uncle and their partners wanted no one to know.

The force behind my cousin's knuckles was about not only what I had tried to take from him, but from both of us.

I had broken open our family's secrets like an oak nut. I had worn at the shell every time I got into a file cabinet or a desk drawer. And with every crack, I had proven myself worthless as a Holt. Worse than that. A traitor.

How Liam stayed on me now, how he wouldn't let me go, maybe even this was mine. Maybe I'd made him into this the day I hid papers in the back of an old dresser. I had lied to my cousin, and with every lie, he became more someone I had to lie to.

I tried to grab him, to make him look at me. But even this close, my hands missed his shoulders, misjudging the distance and depth. The mistake seemed to fuel him, his fists coming heavier.

My vision pulled in and darkened, like the world was folding up and closing in on itself. I looked for the hard light between trees, but there was nothing except my cousin and this rage I had left in him, a firework I'd lit and then run away from.

"Liam," I said, the blood in my mouth thickening the name. I was still under here, under how everything hurt, the wash of red over the world.

But saying his name just made it worse. His next strike was harder, like he was trying to stop me from saying it again.

The hard, echoing sound of a shotgun broke the air.

How loud it was felt like another blow, rattling my brain. It came slow through the red haze, so that when Liam dropped me I wondered if the noise had been my body hitting the ground.

"My father taught me to shoot." I couldn't see Roja, but I had learned her voice as well as I'd learned her laugh and the smell of her hair.

I opened my mouth to tell her to leave me here. It didn't matter anymore. Page had all my proof, and would figure out what to do with it. Roja could let me go. Everything worth saving I'd handed to Page in a paper envelope.

But I couldn't lift my voice out of its wet whisper.

"I learned on the crows eating our back garden," Roja said, speaking to the space above me, to Liam. "They were a lot smaller and a lot faster than you. So if you feel like testing me, go ahead."

It startled him off. His steps trembled the ground.

Roja dropped the Winchester and put her hands on me, but I was no more solid than the birch leaves. I was made out of paper and lost blood.

"Don't." I heard the word, the breaking in my voice, and realized I'd spoken it.

It was the only word I had in me. *Don't.*

She set my arm over her shoulder, gripped my hand, wrapped her other arm around my waist. Her hold both softened the pain in my body and turned it into something flickering and alive.

"Get up with me, okay?" she said.

"I can't see them," I said. The only way I could think of to tell her not to bother was to tell her I wasn't even good for finding the stars anymore.

"Get up," she said, harder now.

"Parallax," I said, almost hearing Tess's voice over mine. "I can't even tell how far away they are anymore."

It didn't make sense. I knew it didn't. But I was in that space where everything I was about to say made sense until the moment I said it.

"Get up." Now Roja wasn't asking. Her hands were all force and insistence. She pulled me to standing. She held me up, making me walk with her.

I tried to pull myself out of the feeling that there were pieces of me left on the forest floor, on the backs of my cousin's knuckles, in the aspen-scented air that took me once but would not take me back.

I had gotten lost so many places. I was a boy who could neither reclaim my bear-body nor live in this one. What there was of me felt too heavy to carry but too insignificant to have its own gravity. Roja might look away for a second, and turn back to find I'd vanished from under her hands.

ROJA

I had done this. I'd given weight to Liam's certainty that he'd seen his cousin in the woods, and he'd gone after him. I had been the one to believe him, the witch who knew the woods better than anyone.

I left Tess Holt's Winchester. I didn't have enough hands to get both her gun and her grandson home at the same time. So I buried it under the leaves, and I held on to Yearling hard enough to make him go with me, his blood patterning my shirt.

He was out by the time I got him back to my mother and father's house. His body reacted when I moved him, his muscle memory helping me. But I talked to him, said his name—both of them—and he said nothing back.

"What happened?" Blanca asked when I pulled him through the door. A gasp thinned her words.

I was out of breath from holding him up, so I took a second too long to answer.

"I'm calling Tess," Blanca said.

"No," I said, the word sharp enough to halt her.

Tess couldn't see him like this. She'd have him in the car to a doctor before Blanca hung up the phone. And it would get back to the Holts, and to Liam.

The thought of when I'd have to tell Tess bore into me. I'd failed her and Olive and Page and everyone who cared about him. Yearling had gotten me through a night when my own body was wringing the will out of me, and I couldn't even keep him safe.

Worse than not keeping him safe. If I hadn't called him, Liam wouldn't have gone after him. I had pulled Yearling so deep into this it had almost gotten him killed.

The guilt was fingernails pressing into the back of my neck. Tonight I would dream of my primas clawing at my hair, setting my hands against the red-stained birch trunks, telling me this was what happened when wicked girls tried to survive.

I set Yearling down on the sofa where he'd slept. "Call Page."

"What?" Blanca asked. "Why?"

I took Yearling's arm off my shoulder, easing it down so it didn't fall.

"Call Page." I said the words slower, heavier this time.

Blanca's eyes flashed toward the kitchen, as though Sofía and Isabel or our mother might be in there watching her. "Roja."

"I need him to meet you in the woods so I know you're not alone," I said.

"Why am I going into the woods?" Blanca asked.

"Go get Tess's gun," I said. "I had to leave it there. It's about a quarter of a mile away from the pond. Near the alder trees. You can find them, right?"

"Yes, but—"

"Good." I cut her off. "Now do it. Call Page, get him to meet you. Ask him to bring birdshot if Tess has it."

"What?" The word wavered in Blanca's throat. "You want to load it?"

"I don't care what we have to do." I checked Yearling. This would take more than peroxide, and I had to know if he had wounds I couldn't see. "Liam's not getting near him again."

Blanca swallowed hard enough to show in her neck. "His cousin did that?"

I ignored the question. "Call Page. Go meet him. Then bring him back here." I brushed Yearling's hair out of his face, looking at a cut on his temple. His hair caught on his skin, dried blood sticking it to his forehead.

When he woke up enough to know what was going on, he wouldn't trust me. I had broken whatever had begun growing between us, like shattering a forest of frost into glass glitter.

"You want Page here?" Blanca asked. "Why?"

I tried to take in her words, let them spread through me so that no one point of my body felt them most. It was what I'd done with Yearling's weight, with the salt-smell of his sweat and blood, and what I did now with the pressing tone in Blanca's voice.

But then I registered the flickering of blood that told me I was bleeding past my pad, probably staining my underwear. It was so small compared to everything else, but it took the last space I had in me. That familiar annoyance was the thing that made me snap at my sister, "Stop asking questions, okay?"

My voice came so sharp that Blanca straightened.

"Just go," I said. "Now."

She did, and for once I was the sister who knew what to do. I was the one leading us through the pale blur of swans' feathers, and the blood seeping up from under birchbark, and everything else in our world too strange and sharp for us to hold.

PAGE

Blanca stopped me. She felt how badly I wanted to go after Liam before I did.

She put a hand on my shoulder and said, "Don't."

With that one word, she stilled me. Being near her, being so close I could smell how the scent of her shampoo stayed on her hair, was the point of an icicle traced down my back.

So instead I told lies.

I told my grandmother and Barclay's that Blanca and Roja didn't want to be alone. I told them Liam's friends had shown up in the back garden again.

We couldn't lie forever. We couldn't go more than a day or two without our grandmothers wanting to see us, to make sure we hadn't gotten lost again. Even with our best efforts Barclay would still be in bad enough shape to rattle Tess.

But for now, we lied. For now, helping bring Barclay back to life was the only thing holding me up.

Barclay slept, and the three of us tried to pretend we weren't all watching to make sure he was still breathing. We stood around, hands fidgeting because we hadn't settled on when we would call Tess, or a doctor, or both.

Roja worked with a clean efficiency I hated—her unmoving expression, her sureness, her lack of feeling at this broken boy in front of her. But at the same time, I swallowed gratitude over it. There was no space for anyone to cry or scream, and I sure as hell didn't have the space for her to.

She knew enough not to wrap his rib cage in all-cotton elastic. I knew that from Grandma Lynn catching me binding down my chest with it, warning me that I could bruise a bone or even crack a rib. She got me compression shirts the next week, ones I wore on days when I wanted strangers who didn't know me to call me *him* more than *her.*

Roja stripped off his bloodied clothes so fast it left us all less embarrassed about seeing him naked. Once she checked him below the waist, she put another pair of her grandfather's jeans on him, and for a flinching second I wondered if Barclay and I had angered the del Cisnes' dead by wearing their clothes.

She kept his left side toward the wall, his right side toward us, so none of us would accidentally startle him, and I silently admitted that Roja was more careful than I had ever thought. She got him sitting up, even in his sleep, in case his nose was broken, so he wouldn't choke on the blood going down his throat. "Come on," she said as though he was all the way awake. She cleaned where he was cut, iced where he was bruised, changed the butterfly bandage on his temple, even against his half-asleep protests. She woke him up to give him whatever painkillers she could find, ones in bottles and ones from her grandmother's recipe books.

Whenever he half woke up, he said Tess's name like a question, like he thought she might be in the next room. Or Roja's name like he was trying to find her in the dark. Or Liam's, in the withered voice of fearing his cousin's shadow had fallen over him.

It was only when he woke up all the way that he said mine.

He was sitting up now, his eyes holding the last trace of a startled look, like he'd woken up unsure of where he was.

I sat next to him, forearms on my thighs, like the nights we spent out by the cranberry bog with hard cider we weren't supposed to have.

"I'm sorry," he said, his voice so hoarse he sounded sick. "I wanted it to be good for you."

"What?" I asked.

"Everything." He only shook his head a little, but it showed every bruise on his face, purple as a Blue Pearmain apple. "The world."

He understood. I cringed thinking of the moment he'd realized it—had Liam's fists mixed up everything he'd ever thought?—but now I knew he understood.

There was no making the world take me as I was. All I could do was make the people who did my family.

"You can't go back home, Page," he said. "Please, don't go back home."

I saw my fingers reaching for him before I knew I was doing it. "Barclay."

"They'll turn you into someone you don't want to be."

I set my hand on his back, as lightly as I could. And I said the words I'd been afraid to say out loud since the day we became boys again.

"That's your family." I made the words come as soft as I could. "Not mine."

For so long, I thought I had to put distance between me and my parents. But the truth of the Holts was as far from the truth of my family as the cranberry bog was from the sky.

I didn't blame Barclay. He'd been working from what he knew. But he'd been wrong.

My mother and father had been scared. It had led to mistakes. It had made them cautious and hesitant when I'd only wanted us to be the family we'd always been. Grandma Lynn told them to just love me, and it made them even more nervous, because then they worried they weren't even doing love right.

But I wasn't giving up on them.

I'd always thought Barclay was the one who'd teach me what to hold on to and what to throw out. He'd been the sharp red needle of magnetic north.

But sometimes he spun and wavered. He lost his way, and instead of admitting it, he decided things just so he'd feel like he'd gotten his bearing again. I knew things he didn't. He needed me as much as I needed him.

"I'm sorry," he said. The hitched sound of held-back sobbing splintered through his voice. "I'm so sorry." He ran the heels of his hands over his eyes. "You don't want to be around me, Page, trust me."

I set my palm flat against his back, giving it just enough weight to remind him I was there. "You can't decide that for me."

He shook his head again, then stopped, like it hurt. "You don't know what I did."

"I know you were trying to do the right thing."

"No, I mean with Liam. You don't know what I did to him."

The faint gloss of tears on his bruised temple almost made me call Tess right then, because I did not know how to do this. I saw his shame coating his skin like blood, drying and cracking.

I put my other hand on his upper arm, turning him toward me as slowly as I could. "But I do know you."

I stayed with him until he fell asleep again. He slept deeper and breathed more slowly than he would've, thanks to what Blanca made him drink.

I heard the click of metal and wood.

Roja was sitting at the kitchen table, opening the box I'd brought over. She stared into the center of the unlit kitchen, only the flame blue of the pilot light revealing the shape of things.

"Thank you," I said, the words catching in my throat.

Gratitude for this girl did not come easily. I might have been friends with Roja del Cisne if she hadn't had my best friend's heart. But it was hard to settle around anyone who held something that valuable without seeming to realize it. It was like a visitor coming into my family's house, picking up an antique glass ornament. Shifting it from one hand to another while I looked for the right moment and the right words to mention how much it was worth to us, and how suddenly it might break.

Roja didn't look up.

"For what you did," I said, in case she didn't hear me.

She took a birdshot round out of the box.

The cut to her eyes made me tense. The gauge she was loading might not kill Liam, but it'd mess him up enough that there'd be doctors and a hell of a lot of questions.

No one with that look belonged within a hundred feet of a Winchester. Grandma Lynn always said if you're too worked up to fill an ice cube tray without spilling, you're not steady enough to hold a gun. Rage or fear or clouded-over thinking turned something dangerous into something not just dangerous but unpredictable.

"Liam's not getting near him again," I said. "I won't let that happen."

"I know. But if he does"—Roja jammed it into the magazine hard enough that I thought the old gun might break into scrap metal and wood—"we'll be ready."

ROJA

I hoped everyone wanted scrambled eggs in the morning. I'd cleared out the shells, the blue-green and brown now empty and drying.

Yearling wandered into the dark kitchen, the front of him catching the faint glow off the stove. His steps were slow and careful, like he was getting used to his body.

The things I wanted to say weighted my tongue. Telling him I was sorry. Confessing everything about the awful game he'd gotten dragged into. Admitting that I felt for him some glimmer of what Blanca felt for Page, and it left me panicked and cruel.

But all these things got pulled so hard between the truth that lived in me, unspoken, and what I had to do to survive, that they didn't hold together.

All I landed on was "Look who's up."

He gave me a faint smile. He looked like he was trying not to wince from the effort.

I went over to the counter. "You hungry? Can I interest you in a"—I lifted the glass bowl on the table and counted yolks—"nine-egg omelet?"

"Where is everyone?" he asked.

"Asleep." I picked up a hollowed-out egg. The sheen of water was gone from the inside, the shell dry. "I told Blanca to make Page take my side of the room."

"What are you doing?" He sounded like he was still shrugging off sleep.

"Making cascarones."

"What?"

"They're something we make every Easter."

"It's October." He looked toward the window like he was checking to make sure he was right, searching the world outside for winter ice, or spring blossoms. He'd forgotten that, right now, the woods wore both. "Isn't it?"

"You gave me these." I neatened the row of vials on the table, each glinting with its own shade of glass glitter. "So I thought I'd try now."

"What's a . . . ?" he asked.

"Cascarón?" I handed him a blue shell to hold, and then poured moss-green glitter into it. "It's a hollowed-out egg filled with confetti or glitter or perfume powder. We break them over each other's heads for good luck."

"I hope you're not planning on doing that to me. I think I'm a lost cause. Not worth the egg."

"No one's a lost cause." I covered the opening with a square of teal tissue paper.

"Careful when you and Blanca go breaking those on each other," he said. "You don't want glass glitter in your eye, trust me."

"Oh, we know how to be careful," I said. "These've been around for a long time. My great-great-great-grandmothers filled them with minerals. Galena. Mica. Hematite. Malachite. You don't want any of those in your eye, either."

His laugh was weak. But it was there, a sound I wanted as much as the soft brush of my father pulling books from the shelves, or my mother whispering in the kitchen, not realizing she was reading Abuela's recipes out loud.

"What's funny?" I asked.

"Nothing," he said. "I just realized you know a lot more about my family than I know about yours. Tell me something else."

"Well"—I shook copper glass glitter into a blue-green shell—"this isn't just about my family, but back where my family came from, there are temples that are thousands of years old, and there's glitter paint on the walls."

"Thousand-year-old glitter paint?" he asked. "How stupid do I look?"

"I'm serious." I almost bumped his shoulder with mine, like I might have once, but I stopped myself, remembering how broken Liam had left him. "The colors they find most of the time are red, green, and gray. They're probably made of the same minerals my family used to fill cascarones with."

I poured more glitter—a vial of dark rose, another of deep turquoise—into the empty shells.

"Thank you," Yearling said.

"Anytime. Next time I'll tell you about how my great-grandfather tamed a quetzal to help him pick up women. No idea if it's true, but it makes a good story."

"No," Yearling said. "I meant for today."

The words felt like something too hot in my hands, a ceramic cup heating through as I held it.

I set the cascarón on the counter.

His fingers brushed mine.

He pulled away. "Sorry," he said, a sharp breath under the word. "I didn't . . . I didn't see your hand there."

It was the inverse of what I'd seen him do before, how he'd reach for a pen or a spoon and be a little bit off, and slide his hand over to find it.

My fingers met his again, slowly enough to let him draw back if he wanted to.

He stayed.

I traced the crescent moon on his chest, following the curve of the outline. It wasn't smooth; it felt rough, uneven like a scar.

Yearling took shallow breaths to steady his voice. "Please don't do this because you feel sorry for me."

I narrowed the space between us, and with my next words I gave away more than any nixie or witch or ruthless mermaid ever would. "I'm not doing anything I haven't thought about before."

He slid one hand on the small of my back, his fingers pulling at my shirt until his palm was against my bare skin. He pushed the heel of his hand into the hollow of my spine. I had to fall into him to keep my balance. He cupped the back of my neck in his other hand.

Right then, we held the air of every season in the space between our mouths. The middle of spring, when the perfume of apple blossoms is so sweet it draws ribbons of ants up the trees. Deep in summer, wildflowers leaving yellow pollen on our skin and in our hair. Fall, with its warm and ash smell of leaves becoming mulch.

Early winter, with the scent of clean snow and the brush of pine needles.

We stayed there, our breath held between our lips, and I realized he was asking for permission. I nodded, my forehead still against his.

He held me up against the kitchen counter like it was a birch tree and we were outside, the stars flickering on and off with the leaves.

He kissed me, hard, and in that moment, we were October. We were the taste of rain and of cranberries becoming their deepest red. We were everything turning bright and brilliant before it falls away.

I felt the mirroring of my own wonder, how we both wanted to know what the other one felt like. Even with him bruised and me careful, he was warm and alive under my hands.

I put my mouth to his ear every time I wanted to say something, still afraid the moon might hear us. But we kept the moon behind the lace film of the curtain linings. There were no rose trees in the woods to reach their thorns through the windows. Not tonight.

YEARLING

In that second, I would have taken any name she called me. *Barclay. Yearling. Holt.*

Wind shook the trees outside the windows, and the branches cast leaf patterns over the counters. I could hear it. I could feel it, like the sound and shadows had teeth. Everything hurt.

I didn't care.

I kissed her, and she kissed me back. Hard, fearless, like nighttime made her free to do whatever she wanted with me.

The way she almost bit me as she kissed me back left the feeling of her teeth hot on my tongue. The rose oil she wore on her lips came off on mine.

The feeling of her mouth left a charge on my skin. It lit me up from inside. It stayed with me as I slept.

This girl, with her hair like rosewood and her skin like the inner peels of birchbark, she wasn't the kind of girl who showed up in fairy tales with a name like Snow-White. In my dreams, she took the name Rose-Red, as easily as if it were an apple she'd twisted off a tree. She was fearless as she found me in my bear-body, unhesitating as she took me into the house and beat the snow out of my fur. Her hands were sure holding the hazel branch, like in the story, but with one flick of her fingers it silvered into a birch wand, wood from the same tree that gave me my name.

She didn't know when to stop. I was supposed to tell her. The story said I should. But I didn't stop her. I didn't want her to stop.

My coat fell away like the snow. The only fur left became my hair. She let the hazel branch fall from her fingers, and ran her hands over my raw skin like she was trying to learn my new body.

She held her hand against the lighter spot below my collarbone and kissed my forehead, lightly, like she might kiss her brother if she had one. Then she kissed me on the mouth and moved her hand down my chest. Not like I was her brother.

It hurt, her hands on a body I hadn't gotten used to having. But I didn't stop her. I didn't want her to stop.

ROJA

The rage I had for Liam whirled and bloomed. It made my heart and blood feel hot as a nebula, a spinning star held in my body. It spread through me so fast it was a sound in my brain, louder than the drone of wings.

But I had to pretend. To keep Yearling's cousin from coming after him, I had to convince Liam I had been on his side this whole time.

I found him filling his car up at the station just outside town.

"Could you be any stupider?" I asked.

He slid his wallet back into his pocket. "What, no shotgun this time?"

"I know what you want," I said. "And it has nothing to do with making Barclay part of your family again."

"Fine," he said. "Prove it."

"I don't need to." I pressed the edge out of my voice. "And I don't really care. You were right the first time. I like the idea of you owing me."

"You really expect me to believe that now?"

"I saved you from yourself. You could've killed him. And how would that help you when you need to know what he knows? I can find that out."

A considering look worked its way across Liam's face. I both reveled in a lie well told and sickened at the words I'd made myself say.

"And now he trusts you," Liam said, his voice buoyed by realizing.

"Guess you're not as stupid as you look." I leaned against his car to make myself look more careless than I was. "Now get out of my way and let me do what you really want me to do. I'll find out what he has and what he knows. But you can't pull anything like that again, okay?"

He flicked a leaf off his side mirror. "Fine."

"Good." I pushed off his car. "Now stay back this time. I will get you what you want but not if you mess this up. I can't fix all your mistakes."

I turned my back on him and the pump.

This was what I did best now. I lied. I did it to use Yearling. Now I could do it to save him.

"I'm not as stupid as you think I am," Liam said.

I should have kept walking. I knew it even then. But I kept remembering Yearling on the forest floor, his blood on the yellow leaves.

Liam was an enemy I had to know as well as I could.

I turned around.

"I know you're playing me, Roja," Liam said.

I held my throat tight. There was no better way to convince someone he was right than to argue with him. My father taught me that before my first day of school.

So I kept quiet.

"But that's okay," Liam said. "Because you're also playing yourself."

I let a slow breath out between my lips, letting it take the words I shouldn't say.

"You care about him," Liam said.

Now I opened my mouth to say something back.

"Don't bother." He lifted a hand. "I saw it. You probably think that matters to me. It doesn't. I'm still choosing to trust you. Want to know why?"

When the nozzle clicked, the gas tank full, I still hadn't said anything.

"Because you care about your family more than you care about him," Liam said. "You want me to owe *them* something, not you. You know who you owe your loyalty to. That's the difference between you and Barclay. And that's the reason you'll do all this, even if right now you don't think you will."

I felt myself rising to his words. The things I wanted to say collected in my mouth, like the first bubbles in a pot of boiling water. I tried to keep the lid on tight.

But a few slid out.

"My family is not your family," I said.

"That." Liam set the nozzle back on the pump. "That right there is how I know I'm right. You can't stand me saying anything you don't like about them. And that's good. I respect that."

"We're not friends, Liam," I said. "I don't care if you respect me or not."

"Fine. But I do care what you think of me." He shut the gas cap. "Think about it. How nature works. Brothers destroy brothers. Gulls peck each other to death. Wild dogs from the same litter kill each other. Fire salamanders eat their own siblings while they're still in their mothers' bodies, before they're even born."

I set my back teeth together.

"Don't like that one?" Liam asked. "You want a prettier example? How about the mourning cloak butterfly? One of the most beautiful you'll ever see. Black wings with gold edges and bright blue markings. You want to know something about them? The larvae that hatch first eat the eggs of the ones that are slower to hatch." He opened the driver's side door. "The strong devour the weak, even when the weak are your own. It's how any family gets stronger."

I looked up without lifting my head.

If anyone had mapped my family against the Holts, Blanca would have been Yearling, and I would have been Liam. Blanca was the one who read me fairy tales when we were little, set on finding out which was my favorite, while I was the one who'd taught Olive Lindley's new kitten to go after anything she could get her claws into. Blanca was the one who made me our grandmother's remedio every month, and I was the one who spread the swans' poison to birch trees and bear-boys.

"What, you don't like that kind of science?" Liam got in the car. "You believe in a god who made the world in seven days. Who made all the birds on one day and the cute little animals on another, right?"

I hadn't understood quite why Yearling would hide in our old weatherworn home when he could have been among great stone houses and hilled lawns.

But in Liam's laugh, in the moment of it turning mocking, it registered.

I wouldn't have wanted it, either.

"Six," I said.

"Sorry?" Liam asked.

"God," I said. "The world. It was six days, not seven."

BLANCA

The minute Roja came in the door, I threw my hand across her face, hard enough that she reeled back.

I hadn't meant to do it this way. I'd meant to talk to her. But all I saw in her was what I'd done to Page. In some moments, I thought I'd dreamed it, breaking the heart of the boy I loved. In a minute, I'd wake up, startle with the worry and horror of it, then sink into the drowsy relief that none of it had happened before remembering that it had.

I had done it for Roja. And all Roja had done back was betray all of us.

Roja put her hand to her lip. The tips of her fingers came away blood-spotted.

She looked up at me, red on her lower lip and on one front tooth.

"What was that for?" she asked.

"You saw what Liam did to him," I said. "And you're friends with him now?"

"What?" Confusion bloomed on her face. Then it contracted and settled. "No. I was lying to him."

"That's not what it sounded like," I said. "He saw you."

"Of course he did." Roja licked the blood off her lip. "I wanted him to."

"No, not Liam." How slowly she understood broke apart the force of my anger. But that left jagged edges, a new kind of wrath, compact and sharp. "Barclay. He went looking for you and he saw you."

Her lips parted, showing the thin red stain along her lower lip. "What?"

"You better thank God he told me and not Page because I think Page might've killed you."

"No." Roja went for the back door. "No."

"Don't bother," I called after her. "He doesn't want to talk to you."

She whirled back. "Yeah, that seems to be going around."

The bitter cut to her voice threw me. "What?"

"I know."

She gave each of those two words such weight.

Her eyes flared into me, her head tipped down so her glare sharpened.

I lost the gravity of my own body. The sense of it came with the sudden worry that the rest of me would fly away from my heart. I would be star-stuff thrown off a nebula.

"I know what they told you," she said, "and I know you didn't say a word to me."

In that second, everything since the swans arrived shifted, like a change in light.

And I saw how all this must have looked to her.

The señora telling me a secret she did not tell Roja.

Me going after Yearling as though getting him would save me.

The swans bringing their beaks and sharpest wings down on my sister.

She knew everything.

Except that I had done all this to save her.

I registered a familiar sting and warmth between my legs. But I had caught on Roja's last words, so I was slow to recognize it, that first small rush of blood. I always started a couple of days after Roja. Her cramps had long been my warning to carry a pad in the back pocket of my jeans.

The back door slammed. The sound both broke me and opened me.

Roja knew just enough to think I had left her to the swans. She thought I'd forgotten us lying awake during storms, counting on our fingers the seconds between lightning and thunder. She thought I'd thrown away every Christmas Eve we'd stayed up together, making our parents atole in two colors. She thought I'd cast aside those midnights of blue corn and white, of cloves and cinnamon and vanilla.

I lost every version of her all at once. The little girl brushing her hands through the grass, looking for garden snakes. The sister who stole sprays of our mother's perfume. The Roja of earlier this fall, running her palms over a yearling bear's fur in a way as guileless as when she was small.

I lost every Roja that had ever been mine.

YEARLING

She called my name through the trees. First *Yearling*, the name I'd asked her to call me so I could forget my own. Then *Barclay*, the name I could no longer think of without my last name attached to it.

Roja caught up with me, the reddened centers of her cheeks matching how she tried to get her breath. "It's not true."

"Yeah, go ahead, lie to me," I said. "Tell me you weren't talking to my cousin like you're friends. Tell me I didn't see that."

A slit of red on her lower lip stopped me. A fine cut slashed it.

The rage in me rose. Even if I wanted to put whole forests between me and Roja, I wasn't letting Liam do to her any of what he'd done to me.

"Was that him?" I asked.

"No." Roja laughed. "My sister." She sounded disbelieving, but almost proud.

So that was what it took to get Blanca angry. She had always seemed so distant and quiet, like she kept her feelings hidden under floorboards.

"What were you even doing with me?" I asked.

Roja's lips parted. I could see her holding air between them, measuring her words.

"You know what, I don't want to know," I said. "I don't want anything to do with any of this. You, your family. Just leave me out of it, okay?"

Her posture stiffened. "You think you get to judge any family?"

"Is that supposed to hurt me?" I asked. "Come on. I know what I am. I get it. Page, Tess, Lynn, they all got through to me." I took one slow step toward her, not quite knowing I was doing it until the undergrowth stirred. "Who's getting through to you?"

"Did you think it'd be you?" This time her laugh was bitter. "Did you think you'd save the bad del Cisne girl? You only wanted me because I'm worse than you. Because I make you feel good about yourself."

"No," I said.

The word landed with enough force that it cut her off. Saying it that hard made my jaw and forehead and ribs hurt, everywhere Liam had gotten me.

I wouldn't let her do this, strip everything away until it was small enough to fit the story she wanted to believe.

But the force of her certainty, it wasn't something I could fight back against. It could've laid the trees bare of their leaves. It could've made the sky blaze a searing blue or frozen it over into gray. That was the force of her. If she wanted to make us into something else, she could do it. The story she told about us was the one that became true.

Her shoulders moved a little with her breathing. Leaves fell through our stare, but didn't break it.

"None of that's true and you know it," I said.

"But the story," she said.

My anger fell as I tried to figure out what she was talking about. "What story?"

"About the sisters and the bear-prince," she said. "Who was the one who ended up with him? Snow-White. It's always Snow-White."

What did that have to do with anything? It was a few pages out of a book so long I'd never read all of it.

"It's just a story," I said.

"It's never just a story," she said.

"Yeah?" I asked. "Well, you'd know, wouldn't you? You wrote this whole story for both of us. So thank you." I backed away from her, spreading my hands to let her know she'd won. "At least now I know how it ends."

ROJA

The heat of Blanca's hand stayed on the side of my face. I could feel my pulse in my split lip, the cut from my own tooth.

It reminded me of what I already knew.

Blanca was the siren who lived between water and shore, the one who seemed so gentle until she lured the curious to the sea. She was the pond nymph, the ends of her hair floating on the surface, beckoning with outstretched fingers to anyone she might pull under.

We were the same. I was just less skilled at drawing what I wanted toward the salt-covered rocks or the pond's edge. I wasn't like her, a girl as glowing and soft as feathers or blush blossoms or gold leaves. I was winter, with its trees stripped to brown and white. Winter, in its veil of blue and gray. Winter, with its stars so sharp that if I lifted my hands to the sky, I could cut my fingers.

The flick of throbbing on my lower lip became the beating rhythm of all I'd lost. I had lost my sister. I had lost Yearling. And however little Page had ever been my friend, I would lose him, too.

That was the problem with lying to everyone. When I told the truth, no one believed it.

I didn't blame them.

I wouldn't have, either.

BLANCA

We sat by the pond, both of us on a low branch. The wind fluffed the edge of my skirt, brushing it against Page's jeans.

Now Page knew everything. For the first time, I had spoken it all out loud. Los cisnes. What of the rumors was true. What was the invention of so many retellings.

What I had to do to save Roja, even more now.

Page had stopped saying *Please don't do this.* I had begged her to stop saying it, each time ripping a little deeper into me.

She hadn't said anything for a few minutes.

"Is there any other way?" Page asked now.

"I can't let them take her," I said. "No matter what she's done, she's still my sister."

Page watched the water like it was a distant ocean.

To me, Page was a handful of sea glass. What I knew of her I had collected one piece at a time. And now I kept her inside me like I was a locked jewelry box.

"Do you think you could ever be with me like that?" I asked, imagining Page blooming from a fluffy gray cygnet into a grown swan. "Not all the time. I wouldn't want that for you. Just, sometimes."

Page shook her head at the water. "It wasn't like that. I didn't get to choose what I was. I just let the woods take me when they wanted to." She looked up at me, pieces of her hair falling in her face. "I can't turn myself into a swan for you."

"I wouldn't want you to," I said. "Not forever."

"But I would, if I knew how."

Her voice shivered through me, light and echoing as the touch of her fingertips.

The words, even if they solved nothing, rushed through me like a swallow of hot water. Page Ashby wanted me, and that was something I could take with me when I became wings. Even if all I could have of her was this pond, the same gray-brown as her eyes, and the sky that saw everything we'd lost.

PAGE

They filled the cranberry bog on the Lindley farm, twelve to eighteen inches drawn off the river and reservoir that they'd put back when they were done. They borrowed it twice a year, harvest and winter, the blanket of water insulating the vines from the frosts.

I watched the blue rising in the ditches until I couldn't see the tips of the woody vines anymore. They looked like faded photographs of themselves now. The vines moved softly under the surface, like rubies in a kelp forest.

I wanted to dream of that, nothing but leaves and points of red underwater. I wanted to dream of anything but the story I thought of as I fell asleep.

Of all the fairy tales in all my grandmother's books, this was the one I wanted to dream least.

It came anyway.

I floated on the edge of a marsh pond. Seven swans descended onto the water from the cold sky, as though their wings were made from snow, their necks from icicles.

I saw her among them, a younger one with a neck that looked almost gilded.

I saw the fowler before the swans did. I tried to call out to her, to all of them. But I wasn't really there. I was as faint as marsh light, a green glow over the water. I had no voice to warn her.

The fowler shot the gilt-neck swan. The other six flew and flapped around her, trying to protect her, guard her with their wings. But the fowler brandished an iron knife, and the other six scattered off, leaving her.

The fowler found her alive, hissing and writhing. There was nothing I could do about any of it. I was only that far light, watching as she became a girl.

The fowler was not her father, or anyone who looked like her, or anyone I had ever seen. He was nothing but her own blood, come to life, coming to take her back. He was as much mist as flesh.

Three nights turned over in the same dream. Down grew from her skin. Her arms spread into wings. Her neck stretched and thinned, and her eyes darkened.

She beat her wings against the fowler's skin, her feathers sharp as obsidian. Her own feathers were the only things that saved her.

This time, he couldn't reach his iron knife. The other six swans joined her until he was dead. I hovered over the pond, a green light for them to see by, the glow caught in the blood on the ends of their wings.

YEARLING

I wanted out.

Out of my own body, out of everything I knew and didn't know what to do with, out of the life I had walked away from weeks ago.

The world shifted and blurred at the left edge, worse than how it usually did. The weight of what I couldn't see on my left side pressed up against me, like everything there wasn't just dimmed but was closing in on itself, folding up and disappearing. I couldn't breathe in deep enough to shake that off. I couldn't get enough air to remind myself that the world was still what it was, even if I'd been relearning how to see it and move through it. It was still wide but with a million hard edges to look out for. And now I was better than I'd ever been at noticing all those corners and sharp places, but worse at gauging exactly where they were.

I kept flinching over my shoulder, starting with the sense that Liam or anyone else in my family had found me again. But no one was there, and I got the feeling that the trees and the air itself were watching me. They knew I had no one left. No one I could trust and who I could trust myself not to hurt.

The few right things I'd tried to do had gotten me here, back in the woods, both me and the world worse off than when they first took me.

So I waited for the woods to take me again. I breathed in rhythm with the wind. I imagined my skin turning to birchbark. I thought of my veins becoming roots and my tongue turning to the red blaze of a maple leaf.

Each skitter of rabbit's feet or a far-off deer made me jump. I snapped back to where I was, far enough from the del Cisnes' house that its light didn't touch me. And each time, I had to begin again, sinking down into the feeling of losing myself.

But I stayed me.

I tried to hear my voice vanishing under a hawk's call. I tried to let every thought in my head fade beneath the skimming of water over stones. The woods could turn me into anything they wanted. I left myself so open to it I lost any sureness of my own body. They could make me a fox, or a few flashes in a lightning storm. They could make me the Irish moss or reindeer lichen coating a tree's base, I didn't care.

But they wouldn't do it. My body stayed, my life and my name tethered to it.

When the woods first took me, I felt the sighing of the air in the branches above me. I felt them giving me a place to fall.

Now I felt their refusal, like pressing my hands against a stone wall, hoping it would give, knowing it wouldn't.

Whatever the woods once thought worth saving, it had gotten

torn out of me. The loss had its own weight. The absence had enough gravity to wear me down.

All that was left was that wall that wouldn't give. But I still wanted to drive my hands into it. Pitch the weight of my fists at it. Throw my knuckles against it until they bled. I wanted my blood on the stone to prove I had tried to get through.

I raged against how this place would not take me, even though I knew why. I just didn't like why.

"You think I didn't try that?" Page's voice fell behind me.

I turned around, looking over my right shoulder so that when I found him, he'd be clear. Him. Not a Page made of the contrast thrown between shadow and light.

Page put his hands in his pockets, the look on his face less sad than resigned. "They're not letting us hide anymore."

PAGE

Please don't tell her, Blanca had insisted. *She doesn't know.*

I didn't believe it.

Blanca and Roja were as braided together as different-color thread woven into cloth. They breathed in the same way when something startled them, an almost-whistling sound. They both had laughs louder than anyone would guess by looking at them. And in the short time I lived in the del Cisne house, Roja watched her sister so closely, as though where Blanca stood was the center point of a map.

If Blanca had meant to give herself up, Roja must have known it. I had caught the off-kilter sense Barclay gave off when he was hiding something, and he wasn't even my blood. I hadn't even grown up with him.

The way all of this had twisted inside Blanca, how it had wounded her, Roja must have seen it. Roja would have noticed the weight of the secret Blanca carried, even if she didn't know the shape of the secret itself.

"Is this just what you do?" I asked Roja when I found her. "Do you just like hurting people?"

Roja's glare was so hard it brought a sound with it, like the buzzing of fig beetles. "You don't know anything about me, Page."

Even with the air humming like a june bug's drone, even with her anger as bright as the iridescent green of their bodies, I wasn't backing down from this.

"I know Blanca did all of this for you," I said. "She's ready to sell her soul to a flock of swans to save you, and you don't even care."

The anger on her face softened. "What are you talking about?"

"Everything she's been doing has been for some bargain she made with those swans. Everything she's put herself through has been for you." I didn't stop. I was losing the girl I loved, and this was my chance to make sure it meant something. "You're turning your back on her. You're leaving things like this between both of you. Is that what you want? For things to be this way when you lose her?"

Roja pulled back like the ground in front of her was caving. She wavered and stared at the leaves like they were spinning into a whirlpool.

"I—" Her try at words came clipped and half breathed. "She . . ."

All that humming and green wound down into a single bright point.

"You really didn't know," I said, "did you?"

ROJA

My sister loved me. Even now, when it felt like there were oceans and islands and whole years between the beds in our room, she loved me.

And that only twisted the rage I had for her. It wove it into something else instead of dispelling it. The hate I held for her, kept against my chest like a locket under a shirt, condensed around how much she'd kept from me.

Blanca was willing to become the swan so I wouldn't have to. She meant to give herself to los cisnes.

All this made the rage in me rise and bloom. It was worse, her giving herself up without ever warning me, than to let the swans take me.

My sister was in the house, paused in the hall next to our father's study, as though she'd forgotten where she was going. In that stillness, she was the girl who used to crawl into my bed when the power went out, because even though she was older she was the one more afraid of the dark.

I meant to tell her all these things at once. But only one word came.

"Why?" I asked, the question more breathed than spoken.

She turned around, and the broken look on her face, the horror held in her eyes, told me she knew what I was asking.

She knew how much I knew.

"I wanted to tell you," she said, wavering on the first syllables.

"Why didn't you?" I asked, my voice coming back to me. "We always told each other everything."

"But I couldn't tell you this." She strained to bring her voice up to my same volume. "I wanted to protect you."

"And how did that go?" I asked. "Is this what you wanted? Each of us doing this alone?"

"Do you know what keeping this was like?" She lifted her hand toward her chest, her fingers hovering near her sternum. "Do you have any idea how many times I wanted to tell you everything?"

"Then why didn't you?"

"I couldn't."

"Because you didn't trust me."

"Because I didn't want you to think you were marked, Roja." In those words, her voice rose into a yell.

I stepped back without meaning to, a floorboard creaking under me.

It was nothing I hadn't thought my whole life, that I was the one the swans would take. But to hear it in my sister's voice, to know she knew it, too, left a mirrored ache in my own body.

"Our whole lives," Blanca said, "I had to convince you that you had a chance. And the only way I could do that is to promise you we'd fight back. I spent my life trying to tell you this wasn't over. I couldn't let you down."

"Lying to me was letting me down."

"You were ready to give up as soon as the swans came. I thought me telling you would just break you apart."

"I did break apart. *We* broke apart. You broke us when you decided to keep me in the dark."

"What would it have done to you if you thought the señoras were on my side?"

"Everyone is on your side. You pretend they're not. You pretend we're the same. But people look at us differently. Boys. Teachers. Our own cousins. Even people who look more like me look at you like you're better."

Blanca shut her eyes. "All I wanted was to save you from this."

"All you did was make me think you abandoned me," I said. "You should've told me. You should've trusted me enough to tell me."

"I didn't want you to have to carry this."

"And I was just supposed to know that? You stopped talking to me. It stopped being about us facing this together and started being about you taking care of everything by yourself."

"I thought if you knew, you'd think you had no chance."

If I'd ever had a chance, it was by what my father made me.

I understood it now with the halting feeling of stopping short before falling into water.

Our father had taught me to fight hard enough that I could never be kept inside a snow-fair body and a pair of white wings. Our mother had taught Blanca to be so lovely, so much like a swan already, that the swans could not bear to alter her.

My mother had taught Blanca to be one with grace enough that the swans might let her be.

My father had taught me to be the willful daughter, so los cisnes would see my fierce heart and leave it in my girl-body.

We were trapped in this. Blanca and me. Mamá and Papá. Even Page and Yearling. We were as caught in the possibility of wings as if we were all becoming swans.

Blanca and I stood here, in an emptied house, with our own hollowed-out hearts.

"I—" I fought for each word, choking it out. "I am so tired." My try to keep the crying out of my voice only put cracks in the words. "I am so tired of fighting you."

"You never had to."

"Of course I did." My voice thickened. "Look at you. Look at me."

She shook her head, studying the floor. "It's not like that."

"You don't get to decide that." I was yelling now. "Everyone else did. The world did. You're blond and I'm—" I gestured toward my own body, unable to say the words *red* and *brown*.

Red. It was my name. It was my bloodstained hair. It was the petals Blanca set on her tongue, even when there weren't enough roses in the world to save me.

And brown. Brown had been my favorite color for so long, shared with my mother and father. But I couldn't say it now, not in the face of this girl whose hair was the deepest yellow and whose skin was the fairest gold.

Brown was now a color I picked up like a lost stone, reexamining it.

Once, *brown* was trees in October. It was the flyleaves of my father's books. It was copper cosmos flowers. It was the earth that grew everything. But now it turned both sharper and duller, a twist of metal, a tarnished version of my sister's gold.

"The colors I am and the colors you are," I said, "everyone looks at us and they think they know everything about us."

Maybe Blanca would never be mistaken for the pastel-wearing

girls at school; her eyes were too brown, her skin touched with a little too much gold. But the straw-yellow of her hair made people trust her. It made them like her. It made them think she was worthy of a little more consideration.

I wasn't just fighting her to survive the swans.

I had been fighting her my whole life to be seen.

"You made us enemies," I said.

"No," Blanca said. "I didn't. You decided that."

"You did it the second you started lying to me."

Now my breathing was halting, stuttering. It broke against the back of my throat, like the noises I made when my cramps came each month.

But this was my heart, clenching in my chest until it wrung tears out of me.

Blanca was as much a part of me as my own teeth and blood. We were trees with intertwined roots, so tangled together that if we tried to rip apart from each other we would only destroy ourselves.

"I'm sorry," Blanca said. The set to her teeth when she said it cut into me, like she was biting my shoulder. "I thought I was doing the right thing."

I felt her sureness, her conviction, leaving her body.

Blanca and I had lived so far under the swans' spell that we had never seen it from the outside. It was a house we'd tried to understand when we had lived our whole lives in a single bedroom.

We had each done the thing we were certain we had to do.

We had both been wrong.

"Just stop, okay?" I backed toward the door. "You've done enough."

I felt no guilt over lying.

She'd lied trying to save me.

I could lie now to save her.

YEARLING

I was up on a ladder, scraping damp leaves from Lynn Ashby's gutters with a garden spade, when Roja showed up.

She came up on my right side. I couldn't even pretend I didn't see her.

"Whatever this is," I said without looking at her, "I don't think I want to hear it."

I kept my words hard. I wanted to line them up like rocks, build a seawall against everything Roja del Cisne had become to me. She was the second of finding the stars between tree boughs. She was the cut and shine of glass glitter. She was the feeling of coming back to life after my cousin had beaten me down so much I thought I was turning to crushed leaves.

"Me and Liam," she said. "It wasn't what you thought it was."

"Then what was it?" I asked. She knew by now that my cousin was as much a Holt as my father and my uncle. All those towns, all those lies on paper maps.

Roja's sigh was something I could almost feel, like the cold breath off the metal ladder. "It's a long story."

"Do you want to tell it?" I asked.

"Not really."

"Good." I cleared a stretch of gutter. "Because I don't really feel like hearing it."

She stood at the base of the ladder. "What are you doing?"

"The leaves can't just stay up here. When the rain comes, the water won't drain."

"I don't mean what are you doing up there."

I dragged the spade through, hitting the edge of the gutter without meaning to.

"Talk to Tess," she said. "She might know what to do with everything you found out."

"Just let it go, okay?"

"You're not alone in this. We're all with you."

The sight of Roja leaning against my cousin's car struck up against everything else I knew about her.

"Are you?" I asked.

"Fine," she said. "You don't believe me? Believe Blanca. Believe Page. Believe Lynn and your own grandmother. They are all on your side. You can do something about all of this. Why aren't you?"

"Because guys like Liam always win, Roja!"

I hadn't meant to yell it. But now I heard my own voice ringing off the metal downpipe.

My temple throbbed, pain stinging along the line of a cut that was still healing.

The thought of carrying around my body, this body I had lived my whole life in, wore on me. It wasn't just knowing I had to keep being Barclay Holt. It was all the little things added up, the spilled orange juice and the broken plates and things I'd trip over because I didn't see them on my left side. It was how Grandma Tess told me that, even when I adjusted to having one good eye and one that missed things, there'd still be times I caught myself, times I'd always have to pay closer attention than everyone else.

If you get riled up, she told me, *if you're tired, if you're sick, if you're drunk—not that you're going to be drinking before you're legal, right? Right?*

She said all of it would come harder, slower, with more work. I asked her how long before I wouldn't have to think about it anymore and she said something about patience, which was Tess Holt for *forever.*

"Why are you even here?" I studied the roofing instead of looking at Roja. "What do you want?"

"I need a favor," she said.

Now I did look at her. "Oh, you have got to be kidding me."

"Trust me, you'll like this one. It involves you never having to see me again."

I came down from the ladder, saying a prayer of thanks for muscle memory because right now I didn't trust my ability to judge the depth to the rungs. "What, are you leaving town?"

"Something like that."

I brushed my hands off on my jeans. "What's going on?"

"I need you to tell me how you did it."

"Did what?"

"Be a bear."

"I was a lot of other things first." Even through the ache of healing bruises, I could still remember the feeling of losing myself to water in a creek bed, or the roots of underbrush, or a left-behind blackbird.

"And how did you do that?" she asked. "How'd you become something else?"

"Why do you want to know?" I asked. What had happened was mine. It was my body and my losing it. Hiding was the one thing I'd done right, one single thing I could hold against everything else I'd screwed up.

I didn't want her picking it apart.

"Do you want me out of your hair or not?" she asked. "Please. Just tell me how."

"I can't teach you how to do it," I said. "It wasn't something I did. I couldn't even do it again. It just happened. I felt it happening and I let it happen."

"How did you let it happen?" she asked.

The back of my neck pinched with the memory of Liam holding my shirt collar.

"You don't know how bad things had to get," I said.

"You don't know how bad they are now," she said, her voice rasping into a whisper.

That was when I found it, the glint of something else. The flick of light off her eyes was familiar not because I'd seen it in her before.

I'd felt it, weeks earlier.

That first spark of something desperate flared and brightened. It wasn't how her hair looked, like she'd been pulling her hands through it. Or how her shirt had gotten wrinkled from her fingers grabbing it. Or her lipstick drying and fading on her mouth. These things were just Roja, like how the back hems of her jeans dragged on the ground, the mud and rain soaking halfway up to her knees.

It was the widening of her eyes. How her stare never flinched away from me. How the brown of them seemed both bluer and redder, like the way the colors of the stars shifted depending on the time of year.

The possibility of becoming something else, of letting the woods turn her into something that belonged more to them than to herself, that was the only thing she could get her hands around. She wouldn't have been here otherwise.

"It may not work," I said. "If the woods don't want you, they won't take you."

"I know that," she said. "And it's not the woods deciding this time, anyway."

"Even if it does work, you won't like it," I said.

"I know," she said.

"It hurts."

"I know."

"And you know what you're doing?" I asked.

I didn't know why I asked it. It wasn't up to me to look out for her. Even if I'd wanted to, there was so much I didn't know about this family that called swans their relatives, and this girl who told lies as easily as she said her own name.

"I know what I'm doing," she said.

It was the way she said all the words back—*I know what I'm doing*, not just *Yes*, or *I do*—that made me sure.

I stepped back into that day, how my body and my heart felt both splintered into pieces and reclaimed into something else. It was pain and relief, fight and giving in all at the same time.

"It felt like"—I shut my eyes, slipping back into the memory—"when there's nothing left at the center of you, when it feels like the only things holding you together are things you don't even want to remember, and there was just this second of something skimming past me. You ever been in a river and had a fish brush by you? It was kind of like that." I fell back into the feeling of it, close enough to remember, but with the distance of knowing the woods would never take me again. "It started that small and it just got bigger. Like when you find a part of the water that's colder than the rest of it, and you choose whether to swim away from it or go into it. It was like that. Like a current I could fight or go with."

It was a current that had broken me apart. I had been a comet burned up, a meteor vaporized into dust. I had been scrapped and made into something else.

I opened my eyes, watching those last minutes of Roja as she was. Her hair that looked black at night and dark red during the day. Her mouth set, and her eyes in that stare that could sear the woods into a wildfire.

Shock and wonder moved over her face, like she was willing herself into freezing water. She was holding back how much it hurt, and in that will, I knew she understood how much this would cost her, how much it had cost me.

She followed what I told her like a map. I could feel her tracing the thread of my words. I felt her effort, like she was fighting up through water.

The edges of her blurred and glowed, like she was made of light, not flesh.

She tipped her head back, breathing in as though she welcomed it.

In the next second, her hair looked less like hair and more like black feathers, her arms less like arms and more like wings.

ROJA

I always wondered how it might happen. I wondered if the humming of wings would pronounce one of us a girl and one of us a swan, and the wind would twirl the swan daughter's body into feathers right then.

But I wasn't waiting for the swans to decide.

I followed what Yearling told me, like picking out the shape of a constellation.

To Yearling, Blanca and I were probably sisters in a half-remembered story, Snow-White and Rose-Red.

We had been like that once, sisters in a fairy tale. We had been as different from each other as sweet-tempered Snow was from never-quiet Rose, but we had been close and entwined as two growing-together trees.

But there was another story interlaced with that story. One filled with swans and nightmares and sisters too skittish to tell each other the truth. That was the one Yearling didn't know. That was the one I had to find a way back from.

I looked to the clouds, where I thought I could see the far-off shadowing of swans' wings.

"I'm ready," I whispered into the sky, to all the swans I could see and couldn't, every one who might have once been our family.

I said it again, so quietly the voice sounded outside of me, an echo. I whispered it with as much defiance as willingness.

In the last moment of being myself, I let go of this boy who'd taught me how. I let go of the moment he came back, smelling like the fur of the bear he'd been and the sweat of the boy he'd just become again. And I wondered if maybe this was the way bloodied and broken-down boys hid from the world. I wondered about the weeks Yearling and Page made their homes in the bodies of foxes or stags. I wondered if Yearling lived in the dark as an odd-eyed bird, shivering on a stripped-bare branch, and I had never noticed.

And in wondering, I became lost. The possibility of becoming a swan took me the way the woods had taken them.

I slipped into that sense Yearling had told me about, that ribbon of cold current.

I took with me the questions I would never get to ask Blanca.

Can I save you the way you wanted to save me?

Do I have the reckless love in me to do what you would have done?

Can I be the sister to you that you've been to me this whole time?

My body answered.

The pain of my skin turning to feathers was victory and vindication.

The swans always claimed a daughter.

And it would have one. But this time I wouldn't wait for them to choose.

I gave in to it, and the relief of no longer fighting was so sharp it was its own pain.

The ache splintered through me. My body bloomed into feathers and wings. And I lifted my face to the sky.

PART FIVE

Those of Us with Wings

ROJA

I didn't forget. Anything I wanted to take with me, I held inside my feathered body.

My mother reading newspapers even though nobody else did, even though the ink grayed the tips of her fingers.

My father letting me hold the fountain pen he'd spent a year saving for, and then another few months for the ink, because a pewter-barreled pen deserved the deepest green-gold.

A boy putting glass glitter in my hands in a way that made me believe it was as enchanted as polvo de hadas.

Luring my sister into the pond with me, promising her that the fish she hated brushing her shins were actually tiny mermaids, finned women as small as fairies.

My sister.

My sister.

My sister.

Because I could not say these words, my heart said them over and over.

I parted my lips only to remember that they were a swan's beak.

I spoke, and heard the sharp pitch of a birdcall. My thin, feathered neck stung as I remembered I had neither my own mouth nor my own voice.

But I found a chilled freedom in how the wind held me. With each flick of my muscles, I lost the memory of ever having arms. I felt the shape and power of my own wings, how the air skirted past them, flowing through my feathers. With each draft of wind, I forgot how it felt to walk. Flying became my first language. I rode the sky like it was water, the leading edge of my wings cutting through the gray. My speed turned still air into wind.

My new lungs felt so much smaller, but they took in enough air to keep me soaring. Each flush of breath lit me up. My breaths came quickly, like I was drinking the whole sky.

The tips of my wings flashed at the corners of my vision, black, when I had always thought I would be forced into a white-down body. Black, the color of my hair if my mother and the señoras had ever managed to strip away the red.

My swan-body felt heated, like each feather met my skin in a spark. My heart felt so heavy in this new body that I thought it would rip through, a raw jewel in a bag of weak netting. But it held. My hollow bones and my shell of dark feathers kept it.

I could live this way. I could hold my jewel-heavy heart in my swan's body and I could still fly.

I just needed Blanca to see me. If she found me at the pond, if she recognized me in the black swan waiting for her on the water, she'd know she was free.

A song of approaching calls opened through the sky. The swans were coming. They would take me. I lifted my wings, ready to join their flock.

But as they neared me, their call sharpened. It charged the air around them. It was a shift as strong as the moment between one season and the next.

A long time ago, swans had given my great-great-great-grandmother two daughters, in exchange for how, someday, they would take one back. And one from the next two daughters, and the next two, and the next.

But this time, I had stolen the choice of which they would take.

I should have known the swans hadn't finished with me.

BLANCA

I had dreamed it every night since the swans came. I dreamed of the moment los cisnes would weave my girl-body into a bird's form, like the fairy tales of straw spun to gold.

But now all those dreams fell away, and in front of me, the truth of what was happening took on a glare as hard as daylight.

My body stayed. Instead of watching pale feathers grow from my arms and fingers, the corner of my vision flickered with wings that weren't mine.

Roja. Her hair had become the longest feathers. Her body had grown a coat of down, shining and dark. She gleamed like a spill of ink, a swan with black plumes instead of white.

She flitted to the pond, her low flight through the trees carrying her to the water.

The inside of me broke watching her, this girl who was both my sister and my mirror, now lost to wings.

I had underestimated my little sister, both in what truth she could bear and what will she had in her.

Papá. How would I tell my father that his Roja was no longer a girl but a swan? To Papá, she had been the one with teeth and with a will as sharp as broken glass, and I had lost her.

I followed my sister's path through the trees, making her out against the dark water.

Sheets of white drifted down over the pond. The swans, with their wide, magnificent wings, landed on the water. They surrounded my sister, their feathers forming a white ring.

I watched for them to welcome her. I waited for them to lift her into the sky so she could fly with them.

Within the flurry of their wings, their necks lashed out at her. Their feathers both sheltered and confined her. Their beaks prodded her, bills nipping at her.

I ran to the edge of the pond.

"Stop it!" I yelled at them.

But I was not one of them, so they did not hear me.

Roja beat her wings to fight them off.

These pale birds did not like her. She was the deep-ocean black of the rarest swans. They both hated the sheen of her feathers and envied it. They understood her as apart from them not only in color but for having once been a girl.

She was both different from these white swans and more beautiful, so they trapped her within their wall of wings.

Even in a swan's voice, I recognized my sister's cry, her frightened call.

I waded into the water, splashing to startle the swans. "Leave her alone."

But they turned their feathered backs to me.

I rushed to the house, grabbed Tess's Winchester, and ran back to the pond.

"Blanca." I heard my own name in Page's voice, the stock of the shotgun already in the hollow of my shoulder, my feet already anchored to absorb the force.

Roja was trying to rise off the water, but their white wings beat her down.

I aimed the barrel at the proudest swan, the most vicious. She hovered low in the water, nipping at Roja's dark-feathered belly so she could not fly. If I wounded this swan, the rest would fall back.

It wasn't until my shoulder took the recoil that I remembered what Page had taught me.

How shotguns kicked up when they fired.

How I had to aim lower than I thought I had to.

And how, if I didn't, the birdshot Roja had set inside the chamber would strike higher than I meant it.

At the first low click, the other birds reeled back, leaving my sister unshielded.

Roja drew down, comprehending the same danger they did, a shared swan-instinct built over generations of surviving hunters.

But the spray off the round opened.

The edge of its burst caught her.

Roja made no noise as she took the beads. She only flailed under the pain and impact.

My next breath came as a sharp gasp.

Page appeared, as suddenly as if the gray sky had made her. She grabbed the gun from my hands, but I was already dropping it. I filled with the understanding of how I had torn into my own sister's new swan-body.

In trying to save my sister from these spiteful, perfect swans, I had wounded her.

The truth of it pinched. It clawed at my throat. But I did not cry. I was too emptied.

The shot's echo faded. Page's raw breathing filled the space.

With a bird's cry, shrill and sharp, Roja lifted off the pond, her wounds keeping her path low and heavy.

The white swans rose up on the water, their wings taking their weight from the surface. They stretched their necks the way Roja had flown.

They took flight, riding the wind toward the other side of the sky. Every promise I had ever made my sister, my wild hope that we could keep each other, she now carried it all on her wings. She left me here to watch the sky at night, looking for a single black swan. She left me to touch my fingers to the windowpanes, reaching for the raw heart of me that would always live in her.

PAGE

If it hadn't been for the way Blanca looked at the black swan, I might not have known. But she watched like her heart was held within those dark feathers, and I understood.

I felt Blanca's longing to speak the language of the other swans, to tell them to leave her sister alone. In the clenching and unclenching of her hands, I felt the rage that made her want to wring all their necks.

In the sheen on her eyes, I saw her fear that the swans would pursue her sister for as long as she survived her wounds. In the slight way she inclined forward, I saw her wanting to be one of them, like she was waiting for her own arms to become wings.

My grandmother had told me once that swans could migrate four thousand miles.

Four thousand miles. Many times farther than I'd ever been from my family's apple trees.

Four thousand miles. But if I didn't do this, if I held Blanca back when I could have helped her, I would lose her to a distance neither of us could measure. The far-off longing in her eyes would stay, and I would never get her back.

"You want to follow her, don't you?" I asked before I'd even decided to.

Blanca turned to me, her face full of more fear and hope than I thought could exist in one girl at the same time.

No matter what body held it, Blanca's heart would always be trued to her sister.

I had to let her go.

My fingers brushed Blanca's. Her touch sparked through me, reminding me of how badly I had wanted to follow Barclay. She wanted something so close to what I'd wanted that I could feel it.

I had wanted the woods to take me so I could go after the closest thing I had to a brother.

She wanted a new body—feathered, winged—that would let her fly after the sister she was losing.

"You have to want this more than you want yourself," I told her.

I knew the words I would say only as I said them. I had to make her understand that Roja turning had left a door barely open, and Blanca had the smallest chance to follow her through.

It was how I had gone after Barclay.

"You know her," I said. "And you know how to go after her."

Even in the sickening anticipation of losing Blanca, my sureness took root. It grew sapling branches and tendrils.

I held Blanca's hand, our fingers barely interlacing.

She kissed me, her mouth on mine certain and calm. That was how I knew she'd heard the words I didn't know how to say.

The door is open. Just go through it.

I didn't say this, because it wasn't that easy, and I didn't want to make it sound that easy. Following Barclay had torn away part of me that I still hadn't found. When I slept, I dreamed of wandering the woods looking for it.

But I had gone after him, because standing by, doing nothing, would have taken more of me. It would have left me hollow and crumbling.

Blanca and I were the same. Doing nothing for the people we loved would have diminished us to nothing.

She pulled her lips away from mine. She let go of my hand so slowly that I felt the first brush of her hands becoming feathers.

BLANCA

When we were growing up, I used to swear Roja and I could feel the things that lived in each other's bodies. Sometimes a faint clenching between my hip bones warned me when her cramps were coming. Sometimes she woke up with pressure in her forehead and knew I had a fever before I did.

Now I felt that again, my wings not only mine but hers, the span of us like one great bird. The wind's updraft combed through my pale down and I swore I could feel it in her dark feathers.

I felt the tiny knives of pain in her body. And if this was what I felt, that pinch and heat, I shuddered at how deep it must have gone in her. I winced, and instead of my girl-shoulder flinching, my feathers flashed at the edges of my wings.

I flew a little in front of Roja, wanting to cut through the sky so her wounded body could fly on softer air. But the rasp of her breathing was so sharp I felt her fighting for it. My own lungs pinched for hers.

My swan's call was unfamiliar to me. I didn't know if she'd hear what I meant. *We will survive this. I will find somewhere the swans can't reach us.*

The other swans flashed white through the air. I tried to cut faster through the sky, clearing the current for both of us. I felt how small my new heart was, running fast, and seeming so tight it was like a wet stone in my new body.

But the swans didn't come after us. They flew toward the far horizon, into a corner of sky so silver it made the whole day look like morning.

For once, they left us alone.

As they flew away, I felt them drawing the breath out of me and Roja, like they were dragging our spirits from our bodies. The dread and fear of our whole lives drained out of us. I felt the worry of so many mothers and sisters stripped out of our swan-bodies.

We were two sisters who had both given ourselves up to be swans. We were a generation of del Cisne daughters who had abandoned our own bodies. We had given ourselves to what we feared.

That understanding was both bright and cold. It was a spark flaring, and water filling dry hands. Even in losing ourselves, we had stolen power away from los cisnes. There had to be something for us in that, even if it was only the sharp edges of our nightmares being worn smooth.

Instead, I felt a spreading heat, shared across my body and my sister's. It bloomed and darkened, like the swans were hollowing us out. The sense of it both filled and emptied me, like they were reaching into us and taking the hearts out of our swan-bodies. I braced for it tearing out of me, a fist of deepest red ripped out of white feathers. A hot knife of fear flashed in me, worrying it would happen to my sister. They would take our hearts even as we flew, the centers of us becoming flashes of red against the silvered sky.

But our swan-bodies did not open. Red did not bloom on my

chest and stain my feathers. There was only the dragging pain of los cisnes taking something from us we could not see, and the shudder of wondering what.

The white flock grew smaller.

Roja dipped lower, fighting her wounds, trying to stay up.

Her dark feathers flashed red, deep and vivid as her hair had been. I would have thought I'd imagined it if I hadn't, in that same moment, felt the weight of my girl-heart coming back.

No. It was the only word in me as I judged the distance beneath us. *No.* I gauged the fall to the ground, and then the hard mirror of the flooded cranberry bog. *No.*

The swans were not only taking the curse from our family.

They were stealing even our swan-bodies from us.

They were letting us go, turning us back to girls, at the worst time.

No. The word echoed as I felt my wings becoming arms, as I saw the brown and red of my sister appearing where a black swan had been.

Panic made my feathers feel brittle as dry branches. I wanted our wings to stay wings, so we could keep flying, but I wanted my hands and fingers back so I could grab Roja out of the air. I wanted to halt her still, my broken little sister who could not survive this fall. I wanted to pin her in the sky like the moon, so the distance to the ground or the water wouldn't kill her.

And the swans knew it. I saw nothing but the distant flecks of their backs, like blown snowflakes. But the chill of their wrath was so thick in the air it felt like frost. It was sharp as needles of ice. It had the gravity of hail and sleet, slowing our wings in the last moments Roja and I had them.

Under that cold, dragging weight, I understood.

We had violated the ways in which the swans had always taken del Cisne daughters. Our will had withered their reign like salt against snow. And for that, they would take my sister from me. It was an act of vengeance as graceful as the swans themselves.

We could have our bodies back. But only in the moment it would destroy us.

Even as I clawed at the air, I cursed every inch of their frost-white forms, their slender necks, the gracious spread of their wings.

I reached out toward Roja. But my arms did not span the distance my wings had.

So we fell.

ROJA

Each wound bit into me, each point so hot and deep I felt them meeting in the center of me. The air streaked through my wings, dragging on my feathers. I flew as far as I could, keeping up with the perfect swan my sister had become. I followed the crisp sound of her wings.

But then we had no wings. I heard nothing but the distant turning over of clouds, and the cranberry bog beneath us. I heard the bog below lapping at its own banks, the wet brush of vines.

The wind traced my bare skin. My down and plumes became my bloodstained hair. In the red-studded mirror of the water, our reflections rushed toward us, showing us the girls we were again.

The pain in my body made me remember everything that hurt about being Roja del Cisne. Driving my fists into the ground as a little girl, because there was so much rage in me I didn't know where to put it. The flash of my sister's hand across my face. The dragging ache that made the inside of me feel like a glass pear.

And that brought with it things that did not hurt. It brought the feeling of a boy's hand on the space between my hips. That same boy's mouth on mine.

It gave me back the brush of fingers as my sister braided my hair. The warmth of my mother's sleeping remedio in my throat, the soft bite of passion flower and magnolia. My father setting a book's weight in my hands, the chilled metal of his best pen when he let me use it.

We broke the water. The bog soaked my hair, weighing it down. It dragged me to the bottom, a layer of water covering me. My fingertips drifted over the sandy soil, the low, trailing vines stirring the water.

Pain blurred everything I saw. The berries made the bog look like a jewel box, and I was nothing but a bead lost off a necklace. I looked for my sister, but couldn't find her through the vines.

The enchantment of the dark water, and the drifting green, and deep red of the berries filled me.

Maybe, in the end, los cisnes won. Maybe this fall would take me from my sister, the wounds deepening in my body. But the swans had to give us back our girl-bodies to do it, the hands and hair and teeth that made us Blanca and Roja.

YEARLING

The black swan Roja had become flew low. The tips of her dark feathers brushed the trees. The clouds silvered her wings. It was only when she started falling that I saw the white swan she was flying after.

As she fell, her wind-thrown wings became her arms. Her swan's body became the shape I knew, her back and her hips. Her hair reappeared, fast as a brushstroke of deep red paint. The fingers of one hand reached toward the sky like some of her was still there.

The yellow sweep of Blanca's hair showed up so fast it looked like the arc of a wing. The way she fell seemed less like falling and more like following Roja.

They fell from the sky over the cranberry bog. I knew it for sure when I got there. The force of them had stirred the surface.

Page was already there, wading in. Blanca had already come up out of the water and was looking for Roja. She raked her hands through the vines, trying to stand but stumbling to her knees every time.

I went in after Roja, this girl who was glass glitter and blue eggshells, hazel and birch wands, secrets she kept for me and from me. I didn't think of how I was losing her. I didn't want that to make my hands slower or less sure.

Everything under the water was so blurred and dim my eyes couldn't hold on to it. Light and shadow broke through, the light piercing, my eyes straining to see the details of the darker places. I couldn't tell the red of the cranberries from the red of Roja's hair. I couldn't tell the fine, glinting silt of the bog from the brown of her skin.

It was my hands that found her first, the warmth of her under my palms clearer than anything I could see refracted through the water.

When I found her, when I took her in my arms, she felt as difficult to hold as water. Her fall had left her too broken to grab on to me. But I got her out.

She opened her mouth, sputtering water and tiny leaves. Red berries had come off their vines and stuck in her hair, the bog darkening it to redless black.

Page was holding Blanca up, so hard that I thought if Page let go, the flooded bog would dissolve her. Blanca looked like she wanted to scream into the sky, and I kept bracing for the sound, but it never came.

Roja's eyes shut. The chill of the water left the brown of her skin paler.

A weak sound came from the back of her throat. Her wet eyelashes shivered like she was trying to look at me.

A cluster of red points stood out bright against her body.

Cranberries, I thought, wet and crushed on her skin, like the ones caught in her hair. But then they opened and spread.

BLANCA

There was a story I never told Roja. When we were small, I whispered tales of cursed dresses and enchanted trees in the minutes before she fell asleep. But I never gave her this one.

I heard it one day when my mother took Roja to the señoras. I couldn't remember why. A fever, maybe, or a nightmare that visited as often as a stray cat.

The tall señora took Roja into the back room, my mother following after.

The short señora kept to the front of the store, filling the jars and folding the sheets and lighting so many candles the walls looked made of fire.

She must have felt sorry for me having to wait alone, or she worried that I might touch things. She gave me dried roselles to hold in the side of my cheek, and she told me a story she called "El Príncipe Oso."

It was a story not so different from the one Tess Holt would tell us later. Sisters. A bear-prince. But in this story of el príncipe oso, the youngest sister used her will and her teeth on the whole world. She offered to marry the bear-prince in exchange for the life of her woodcutter father.

And when the bear-prince demanded she not look at him in daylight, fearing the enchantment that held him, she ignored him. She bound and gagged him to break the spell that made him a bear instead of a man. And when the spell stole him from her again, when it dragged him to a castle on a road she could not find, she demanded the help of the moon and the sun themselves.

That was the thing neither Roja nor the señoras understood. Sometimes what a story needed was not a girl who would do what the prince told her, who would content herself with meeting him only in the dark, who would not question why she must not open her eyes. Sometimes a story needed the girl who would find him among the crumbling stones where he hid, pretending all of it was a castle. It needed the girl who took the prince's orders and crushed them between her back teeth, who bound his wrists if that was what it took to set him free.

Because in the end, it was Yearling who was lost. Page may have been the one following him around like she was his younger brother, but Page was the one drawing her own map to the world. It was Yearling who was breaking. I could never have held him together. And I didn't want to. The señoras thought I was suited to the task, that I had soft hands and shy smiles enough for me to hold up a blue-eyed boy.

But he'd needed Roja. He'd needed a girl with teeth. He needed her like I needed Page, the boy who'd reminded me my hands were for doing things. They were not just for opening my palms to whatever the world wanted me to hold.

If I'd told Roja the story of el príncipe oso, speaking it into the dark between our beds, she might not have believed me. She might have thought I made it up myself. Even when I insisted it came from the short señora, the one who taught us to hold yellow rock salt in our pockets for good luck, she might not have believed it.

But at least I would've said it. I would've told my little sister that the biggest lie of all is the story you think you already know. Then it would've been up to her whether she heard.

I wished it now, as Page kept me from sinking into the cranberry bog. I wished it as Yearling pulled Roja out, his eyes on the air in front of him because he could not look at the wounded girl in his arms.

I wished it even as Page and I took her weight into our hands, worried that seeing her like this had broken Yearling down too much for him to hold her.

PAGE

I knew so little about Roja del Cisne. But I knew enough.

Blanca had been willing to give herself up to the swans, and Roja had enough love and spite in her to do it first.

Now Roja lay still on the ground in front of us. Her wet hair shielded her face. The wounds she'd taken as a swan spread and opened as she became a girl again.

I caught Blanca's fear only in the way she held her lips together. Barclay's breathing came hard and frayed.

I wasn't letting either of them lose her if I didn't have to.

There was a moment—growing up, understanding who I would become—when I realized that sometimes there is no putting things back. There is no making them what they were. I learned that while folding away dresses I had never worn and would never wear, in opening my hands and letting go of the Page I would never be, the life I would never have and did not want.

Maybe Roja del Cisne would never be whole in the way she had been this morning. Maybe there would always be part of her that wore the wounds of today. But maybe she could go on, still, as a Roja none of us had imagined.

I set my hands on her damp stomach, lightly enough not to hurt her, but with enough intent that I hoped she could feel my wish, how much I wanted to fill her in with anything I had to give. The trembling in Blanca's hands reminded me of the faint line between her body and Roja's, how anything that hurt her sister wounded her.

I was a boy Roja barely knew. My hands alone wouldn't take her far.

Blanca was saying *I'm sorry, I'm sorry* over and over, the words wet and rattling and so soft I could barely hear them.

I took Blanca's hands, slowly enough to quiet her, and I put them on Roja.

Blanca let me. I saw the shudder in her body, the shiver of feathers she'd grown and then lost. I felt it as though I were still a cygnet, that prickling beneath my skin.

I reached for Barclay's hands.

He resisted, catching my gaze like he was searching for what in me had slipped out of place, why I was doing this.

I didn't let his hands go. I set them on Roja's skin.

This was the thing I knew, the thing I'd been trying to tell Barclay for so long: even if there is no retracing your path, no unbreaking what has been broken, the heart of you, the heart of everything, can still knit back together.

There were ways to carve away from your heart everything that did not truly belong, and still come back to life.

BLANCA

Our whole lives, Roja and I had felt the possibility of feathers under our skin. We waited, wondering if plumes were a breath from sprouting out of our backs.

Now, whatever feathers I had left in me, whatever the swans had not taken with them, I did not need. Whatever hard veins and down brushed beneath my skin belonged to them.

But I wasn't giving them back.

As Roja's water-chilled skin cooled my hands, I let her have them.

YEARLING

The harder it got to find the rhythm of her breathing, the more I wished that my blood was water or glass glitter, something I could pour out and give her. I knew what it felt like to get broken open, and now I wished I could do it myself, offer Roja anything left inside me.

I almost didn't feel Page's hands on the backs of mine. His palms stilled me until everything was quiet. The soft rush of the water in the cranberry bog. Roja's heartbeat under my fingers, the breath I held so tight it stung the back of my throat.

With all those sounds gone, I understood.

Roja didn't need anything I could break out of my own rib cage. She needed something I had asked her to forget.

She needed me to give her my name.

ROJA

I felt them do it, mending my broken skin with all they had in them. Feathers, light and soft like the ones that had covered Blanca's back. The blushed blossoms of apple trees, the same mark Page had left on the woods. Birch leaves, from the tree Barclay Holt had been named for.

I was neither all the girl I had been, nor the swan I had become.

I was Roja again, but where I had been torn open, feathers appeared. Leaves grew over where I was bleeding. The tiny petals of blossoms closed the smallest spaces.

Where Blanca and Yearling and Page set their hands, where their palms covered my wounded places, they marked me. I became a girl who was part swan, part birch, part apple tree.

To keep me, they each gave me a little of themselves.

They claimed me as theirs, all three of them.

So I stayed.

BLANCA

I walked onto the Holt estate from the far side of the property, where it backed against the woods. No one stopped me. The sweep of my hair was a shield, a blond flash that let me go unnoticed where my sister would have been watched, remarked on. My hair slowed anyone from noticing that my skin was not the peach-pink of most fair-haired girls.

Anyone who noticed me probably thought I was one of Liam's girlfriends. Especially when I found Liam behind his father's house.

"I know what you're looking for," I said.

He turned, my voice the first thing to tell him I was there.

I stepped into the shadow of the house. "I don't know how many copies he made or what he did with them. That's your work, not mine." The wind pulled at my skirt, and I thought maybe I could smell feathers on the air. "But I will bring him and whatever he still has to you. So you'll have him, and you'll know what he has."

Liam's eyes flashed a blue so bright it seemed like it didn't belong under the gray sky. It looked like a painted-in part of a two-toned photograph. "Why would you do that?"

"I know I'm nothing to you. I know my whole family is nothing to you." I crossed my arms against the chill of the air and my own nerves. "But you will never forget that you owe me for this. I won't let you."

"And why would I believe you?" he asked.

"If I don't bring you Barclay and those papers," I said, "may the swans who fly over us kill me themselves."

He looked to the sky. He couldn't help it.

I drew a slow breath in, afraid for a moment they might not come.

But then the flitting white arced across the clouds. Six swans cut their wings through the air, necks stretched out toward the horizon.

Liam's look of wonder, tinged with fear, was as good as a yes.

I took a step back on the brick path. Everything here looked so formal, the mowed grass and cut hedges. It seemed more sculpted than grown. I couldn't understand both this and my mother's fluffy herb beds existing in the same word, *garden*.

"And just so you know," I said, "Barclay's not at our house, and he's not at Tess's, or the Ashby farm. Don't go looking for him. You won't find him."

Even Liam couldn't knock on every door in town, and the Lindleys weren't telling.

With a twist of a smile, Liam almost looked impressed.

The swans passed over us, the beating of their wings an assurance that I was the right del Cisne girl to strike deals with.

"I'm the only one who can get you what you want," I said. "You just have to be okay with that."

ROJA

My second cousins found the swans first. Beatriz and Julieta spotted them in a pond closer to their houses than ours.

I recognized these birds who'd dipped their white necks to me and snapped at my dark feathers. I knew them, how they'd stripped the curse from our blood at the moment it would make us fall out of the sky. And I couldn't keep the vengeance out of my heart as my mother and I drove them off the surface.

We carried nothing to hurt or kill them. We came only with our rushing steps and our swan-women's calls.

My father carried the name del Cisne. He had watched one sister stay while the swans claimed the other. But in that moment, my mother flapped her hands as though they were wings, the cry from her throat so shrill it sounded like a swan's trumpet. Her vicious will startled the swans off the water.

I ran at them. My wounds still stung, knit back together with new feathers and birch leaves and blossoms. But I threw my body forward.

We drove them off in the direction Blanca needed them, so they would appear in the sky as though she had summoned them. My mother and I made Blanca into the kind of witch everyone feared we were.

My mother watched the sky as the last swan rose above the trees. "Did I do the right thing?"

"Of course," I said. "Blanca won't be half as convincing if they don't show up."

"No," my mother said. "I meant taking you out of school. Should I have left you there, with those boys putting brooms in your locker?"

The idea lit up, like a window I did not know was stained glass until the sun came through.

"You took us out of school because of what was happening to me?" I asked.

The brown of my mother's cheeks warmed.

My mother had never been blond. She had never had skin fair enough that, in winter, it shed enough color for her sometimes to be mistaken for one of the gringas. Her hair was a brown so deep it was almost the black of raven's wings.

But this was the first time I wondered if my mother had grown up a girl less like Blanca and more like me. Maybe not a del Cisne. But caught in what everyone thought they knew about her.

My mother never answered me. But that stained-glass feeling stayed, brightening.

"Come on," she said. "It's time you learned to cook."

My mother had so seldom invited me into her kitchen. When she did, it was on Christmas Eve or Sábado Santo, to give me and my father small tasks she and Blanca didn't have time to do themselves.

She had never before talked of teaching me to cook, to make things instead of just chopping walnuts or shelling pomegranates. As we walked back to the house, I was a whole bright church, with stained-glass windows for walls.

YEARLING

She came for me, like I knew she would, the girl who loved my best friend.

Blanca had never planned on breaking her word to my cousin. And I went with her, the del Cisne girl everyone considered compliant and docile.

Blanca called Liam to the center of town, where I wore the bruises and gashes he'd left on me like they were a family crest.

Liam came, eyes flaring open but not yet afraid. I didn't flinch from him even as he took inventory of what his own fists had done.

I let everyone see me. I drew power from their gasps instead of letting them strip it from me.

Liam hadn't counted on me letting myself be seen. He'd bet on me hiding. I guess I didn't blame him. It was what I'd done up to now.

Blanca handed Liam an envelope that held grainy copies of everything I'd collected. Now Grandma Tess and Lynn Ashby had extras, thanks to Page. So did Blanca and Roja's father, thanks to Blanca. And once the mail came on Monday, so would the families who'd sunk the most money into towns that did not exist. That was thanks to Roja and her mother.

Blanca gave Liam enough to know how much damage I'd done. But there was no containing it now.

She kept every promise she'd made Liam. She even brought me to him.

Cars slowed, wanting to get a look at me. If Liam wanted to grab me by the collar in full view of everyone, he could have at it.

He didn't.

I wasn't Liam's to keep anymore. He couldn't do what he wanted with me just because I was smaller or younger or scared. Holt may have been his last name, and our fathers'. But it was also Tess's, and it was mine.

Liam tried staring me down but couldn't.

"I can't even look at you," he said so far under his breath I barely caught it.

I didn't know if he meant what I'd done, or if something about me now unnerved him, if he didn't know whether to look me in both my eyes or just my right.

Maybe it should've hurt. But I'd lost the part of me that buckled under Liam's stare. It was the same part of me that would've once cared what he thought of my left eye, whether he thought it made me weak or less Holt-like.

But I'd lost track of that part of me somewhere in the woods between my father's house and the del Cisnes', so I didn't care anymore. And it was the first time I realized how fighting back could look—sometimes, from the outside—like giving up.

I stood there, a pinned specimen for everyone to look at. Just for a minute, though. Then I put my hands in my pockets and walked down the road, where Blanca waited with the boy she loved and the sister she'd gotten back.

The sight of Page brought a new tide of whispers, a round of echoed questions that all started with *Is that* . . .

But Page and I turned our backs on those stares, the words shielded behind cupped hands.

We were more than two vanished boys reappearing.

We were more than what they made us.

BLANCA

Maybe Papá would never love me the way he loved Roja. Maybe he wasn't meant to. Even though Roja and I were more alike than we'd ever admitted, we were not the same.

But when I passed his study, he looked up from his desk, and I caught a glint of pride in his face.

I thought Papá would hate me for wounding the daughter he had always loved a little more than he loved me. I thought it even as I saw him and my mother thawing to each other.

In the warm wake of the curse leaving us, they no longer pitted their daughters and their own hearts against each other. I thought I might be imagining it until I saw my mother handing my father coffee grounds for his roses, his hands accepting the jar as though it held water from a blessed fountain.

My father went back to his work, studying an open ledger.

For years, he had looked at me like I was no more remarkable than a milk pitcher.

But I had been the one to understand something before anyone else did. Before my mother and father. Before Roja. Before my cousins, and maybe even before the señoras.

I knew it now. I knew it with the same thrill of waking up and realizing I still had my girl-body: getting a blue-eyed boy had never meant getting him to love me. It meant getting him to trust me. And that blue-eyed boy turned out not to be Barclay Holt, but his cousin, who I betrayed even while doing exactly what I promised him I would.

Good girls had their own ways of hitting back.

I crossed the threshold, the way I'd seen Roja do since we were small, always as easily as though this were her own room. I waited for Papá to stop me.

He didn't.

I pulled a book down from his shelf, a heavy, clothbound one the color of dried bay leaves. Roja had done it so many times, Papá welcoming the questions the pages stirred up in her.

The heft of the book was new in my hands. I held the cover to my nose, breathing in the smell of ink and dust, the deep vanilla of worn pages. I waited for Papá to notice that I was not Roja.

But he didn't stop me.

I held the spine in both hands, the cover against my wrists and forearms. I walked it toward the door, waiting for him to object. I went slowly, in case it took him a minute to register what I was doing.

"That's a good one," he said.

I hadn't realized he'd looked up enough to see which one I'd taken.

I turned from the threshold.

He met my eyes, his desk lamp showing one side of his face. "Let me know what you think."

ROJA

Blanca and I watched them drive the water reels through the cranberry bog, beaters knocking the berries from the vines. Our father told us that, because of a little air pocket in each cranberry, they floated to the surface, covering the bog in dots of deep red and blond-white.

Olive Lindley told me that, even as they took in the harvest, next year's crop was already growing on the vine. Sixteen months of growing, so they were always nurturing two seasons at the same time. She said it like that was the best thing in the world, two seasons of fruit becoming at once, two harvests living on the same trailing vines.

Now the water's slate blue surrounded the fruit's red. Yearling was one of the boys wading in for the wet harvest, sweeping the loose cranberries into the center of the bog.

He'd live with Tess and Lynn now. His family had enough on their hands that they weren't going to fight his grandmother keeping him. Yearling hadn't been there to see this part, but according to Page, the entire conversation consisted of Tess asking, "How about it, Lynn? You up for raising a seventeen-year-old?" and Page's grandmother didn't flinch.

Yearling showed up that night, out of his waders but still smelling of pond water, the tart acid of cranberries, the wet green of the vines.

I met him outside, the trees slicing the moonlight into pale ribbons. I wondered if he was looking up through the branches again, taking the measure of the stars by how the leaves made them vanish and reappear.

"Couldn't sleep," he said.

"Ten hours corralling berries and you can't sleep?" I asked.

"Here." In the space between us, he held a glass jar, the kind reused after holding applesauce or blackberry jam.

White and red roses crowded the brim. At first I thought they were a mix, some white, some red. But each one was both, red petals and white intertwining. They mixed at the center, and stained each other at the edges. Cranberry red touched the white outer petals, and the fanning red ones looked frost-tipped.

These red and white petals, slotting together like shuffled cards, mirrored my own body. Under my clothes, I was as much made out of different pieces as these roses. Feathers. Blossoms. Birch leaves.

Yearling tugged at his collar, straightening it out. I'd never seen him nervous like that. The brown in his left eye shone a little brighter than the blue, like deep maple ink.

I had never been the kind of girl a boy would bring flowers. I had known it so deeply that I wondered if a señora had said it over me when I was born, the words spilling onto my forehead like water for a christening.

But Blanca had already refused the things everyone else had decided. She was the fair-haired sister who would not keep to the story as it had been told. Instead, Snow-White fell in love with a boy who brought her apples, a knife in the back pocket of his jeans.

I accepted the jar from Yearling's hands. I breathed in their scent, like winter and wine.

I said, "Thank you."

PAGE

Blanca and I leaned against my grandmother's fence, eating cuttings from the snow apple I found deep in the orchard. The blushed red of the skin showed the frost-pale fruit underneath. It broke against our tongues, tart as lemons and early strawberries.

"Are you ready?" Blanca asked.

"No," I said, and we shared a soft laugh. "Not even a little."

"Lynn'll be there," she said. "And so will I, as long as you want me there."

Maybe if my mother and father saw me as I was now, they wouldn't get caught in their worrying. They would stop wondering how to be around me. If they let it, it could be like their eyes adjusting at night, the stars sharpening overhead as they walked the orchard.

They loved me. And they wanted me even when they could not make sense of me. So maybe if I was sure, it would make them less tentative.

I wanted to see my father, to know if his smile still made me think of us looking for four-leaf clovers every spring. I wanted to hear my mother's laugh, the sound as silver as her hair.

They loved me. And if they didn't know how, they'd learn.

It was time to stop wishing I could be a cygnet who might one day grow into a swan. It was time to stop wishing the trees would take me back into their shadows until there was no me left.

I had to choose this life that was mine.

I was Page. I was an Ashby.

Anything else I needed to know I would figure out as I went.

I pushed myself off the fence. I crossed the orchard, Blanca walking the leaf-lined rows with me. My hands went hot and damp even in the fall air. When I felt Blanca's touch cooling my palm, I couldn't remember taking her hand, or if she'd taken mine.

The front steps rose in front of me, ones I'd counted out every day growing up.

Ones I hadn't walked in weeks.

Now I counted them again, my shoes making the familiar hollow sounds against the wood.

I lifted my hand to the door, and I knocked.

BLANCA

The first frost was coming. Yearling said he could tell by how the trees caught the sun, the wet light thinning and sharpening. Page said she could smell it on the air, a clean smell like starched fabric and the pond in spring.

We came out to welcome it, the four of us sneaking from our houses after midnight. Roja and I took cascarones from where they rested in a hall cupboard, three in each of the abandoned nests I'd collected from the forest floor.

It was me who lured Roja out.

At first she hesitated. I read in her half-asleep face her worry that if we left this house at night, we might come back at dawn to find it different. For once, there was enough room for both our hearts, and our mother's and father's. Roja must have feared that if we turned our backs, it would all collapse in on itself.

But winter was so close I could taste the ice on my tongue. The birch leaves and the feathers and apple blossoms were falling away from the trees, even as they clung to Roja's body. So I took her hands and drew her out of bed, like we were still small and I wanted to show her the first snow of the season.

Our mother always told us not to tell lies, even to ourselves, because they became truer every time you said them.

But we had told ourselves lies, and they had become the truth. We had started to believe that Roja was the sister whose heart was a handful of hard red jewels, and I was the one as insubstantial as the hollow center of a cranberry. The lie of who we were had killed who we might have been. It had buried us. It stripped us down into girls uncomplicated enough to be understood.

Now we pulled ourselves free from the lies we had taken into our own bodies. We crushed them to stardust and let the wind steal them. We held on to our hope that the truth was water, so there was nowhere it could not get in. Or that it was light, spilling into all the unseen places.

The air that night felt so clean and hard we could crack the eggshells on it. We crushed our fingers into the cascarones, and the wind drew out bright ribbons of glass glitter. The air turned to glinting mists of deep copper and blue and red. The night winked green and gold. We saw the stars through clouds of rose and violet.

We painted the woods that night. We gave it the colors we were and the colors we borrowed.

We were opening our hands. We were giving up the stories we thought we already knew.

We were becoming.

AUTHOR'S NOTE

The idea of reimagining Snow-White and Rose-Red as Latina sisters has been following me for years. It started with a wish to write my own communities into a fairy tale I had loved growing up. I wanted to envision the bear-prince in the language of Latinx folklore. I wanted to write a story as much about family as about falling in love. But when I thought of my reimagined fairy tale, something wasn't quite coming together. I was missing some twist of magic, some essential spark.

I found it when I was reminded of words I'd heard as a child: "If you're a good girl, you can get a blue-eyed boy." As a child, I think I had some innate sense of the racial and gender politics those words held, but it wasn't until I started thinking about this story that I understood how to talk about them. Remembering those words brought me back to my two reimagined sisters, one considered a good girl, one considered anything but. And imagining these sisters drew me toward similar themes in stories like *Swan Lake*—the white swan, the archetype of purity and virtue, and the black swan who, by contrast, is portrayed as seductive and deceptive.

So often, Latina women are called to rip ourselves apart, to reduce ourselves to versions who can be easily understood. So often, it pits us against each other. And the only way we survive is to find our way back to each other and ourselves, to resist the idea that we must be one version of ourselves or another.

Though no two experiences of marginalization are the same, sometimes parallels reveal themselves. Page Ashby is sometimes asked to identify as *she* or *he*, when the truth of Page's identity is far more nuanced. This book uses alternating pronouns to reflect how Page expresses that identity; both *she* and *he* feel true to Page depending on the context, as does the word *boy*, while *girl* does not. My husband, who identifies as transgender and non-binary, has taught me that gender identity and expression are varied and complex, but that the first step to supporting our transgender siblings is always the same: respect how they identify.

This book is a work of fiction. Blanca and Roja aren't me any more than the del Cisnes are my family. But, in some ways, I had to tear my heart in half to write this book, because even though neither sister is me, I have been both of them. I have been the light-skinned Latina who, if she's careful—if she wears the right clothes, puts on the right makeup, strips certain intonations out of her voice—can sometimes pass for not-Latina. And I have also been the girl whose presence is considered provocation. I have been the good girl, fitting the shape of the small space the world leaves for me. And I have been the daughter who throws herself at locked doors even when she's sure they will never open.

For me, the point where fairy tales and magical realism intersect is this: We find what is beautiful in what is broken. We find what is heartening in what is terrifying. We find the stars in the woods' deepest shadows. Snow-White and Rose-Red are not just sisters growing up in their mother's garden, but young women pushing back against what the world has decided for them. The bear-prince is a boy who is adjusting to losing vision in one eye, and who is slowly understanding that everyone's heart is a little broken. The boy who becomes the bear-prince's brother is a boy whose gender identity is seldom represented in storybooks.

My hope for you, reader, for all of us, is two sides of the same wish: that the world gives us each the space to write our own story, and that we leave room for each other's stories. They are where our hearts survive.

ACKNOWLEDGMENTS

For a story that braids together two fairy tales and the themes of a well-loved ballet, I should start with gratitude to the men who wrote them. And I will, because without their breathtaking work, this story would not exist. But with much respect to the Brothers Grimm, to Hans Christian Andersen, to Tchaikovsky, there were many others without whom this book would never have been. Those who, either directly or indirectly, made this fairy tale of two Latina girls possible. Here, I'll name a few.

My agent, Taylor Martindale Kean, whose wisdom, wit, advice, and caring spirit I'm constantly grateful for. Stefanie von Borstel, Adriana Dominguez, and the entire Full Circle Literary family; I feel so lucky to work with you.

My editor, Kat Brzozowski, who I have long wanted to write a sister book for. I'm so thankful for you and for your help guiding Blanca and Roja through these woods.

Jean Feiwel, for making me part of the wonderful home for stories that is Feiwel and Friends.

My publicist, Brittany Pearlman, for being someone I always know I'm in good hands with and for showing me pictures of cute animals when I'm nervous before events.

Rich Deas, for the incredible art direction MacKids authors are so lucky to have on our books, and Danielle Mazzella di Bosco, for giving the story of these two sisters such a beautiful cover.

Everyone at Feiwel and Friends and Macmillan Children's Publishing Group: Jon Yaged, Kim Waymer, Allison Verost, Liz Szabla, Angus Killick, Molly Brouillette, Melinda Ackell, Teresa Ferraiolo, Kathryn Little, Julia Gardiner, Lauren Scobell, Ashley Woodfolk, Alexei Esikoff, Mariel Dawson, Romanie Rout, Brenna Franzitta, Mindy Rosenkrantz, Emily Settle, Amanda Barillas; Katie Halata, Lucy Del Priore, Melissa Croce, and Amanda German of Macmillan Library; and the many more who turn stories into books and bring them to shelves.

Taryn Fagerness and the Taryn Fagerness Agency, for helping my stories travel the world.

Dhonielle Clayton and Sona Charaipotra, for encouraging me to try writing this story. I'm grateful for your books and your friendship.

Dax Murray, for making Page's identity and Page and Blanca's love story clearer and truer on the page. Katherine Locke, for introducing Dax and me, and for all you do for queer YA.

Elsa Sjunneson-Henry, for brilliantly refining how Yearling navigates the world. Kayla Whaley, for connecting Elsa and me, and for being someone I'm so glad to be writer friends with.

Lindsay and Clayton McCarl, for patiently explaining birdshot, recoil, and more.

Las Chicas Malas, whose creative spirit I got to be around as I outlined this book: Lily Anderson, whose insights refined this story and whose genius I'm thrilled to have on my bookshelves. Tehlor Kay Mejia, who spent many hours helping me figure out these terrifying swans and who made me laugh at times I was sure I couldn't. Candice Montgomery, there are scenes I probably wouldn't have had the courage to keep in here if we weren't friends.

Claire Legrand, for believing in Blanca y Roja when they were still becoming.

My mother and father, who both taught me that our fierce hearts and caring spirits are worth protecting, because they hold the best parts of us.

My husband, for being the one who first listens to the odd stories I want to tell, and for graciously and patiently answering questions about his identity as a genderqueer trans guy.

Readers, for giving stories space in your hearts. Thank you.

Thank you for reading this Feiwel and Friends book.

The friends who made BLANCA & ROJA possible are:

JEAN FEIWEL PUBLISHER

LIZ SZABLA ASSOCIATE PUBLISHER

RICH DEAS SENIOR CREATIVE DIRECTOR

HOLLY WEST EDITOR

ANNA ROBERTO EDITOR

KAT BRZOZOWSKI EDITOR

VAL OTAROD ASSOCIATE EDITOR

ALEXEI ESIKOFF SENIOR MANAGING EDITOR

KIM WAYMER SENIOR PRODUCTION MANAGER

ANNA POON ASSISTANT EDITOR

EMILY SETTLE ASSISTANT EDITOR

MELINDA ACKELL COPY CHIEF

Follow us on Facebook or visit us online at mackids.com.

Our books are friends for life.